Till Death Do Us Part

DIANE GRAVELLE GIROUX

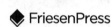 FriesenPress

Suite 300 - 990 Fort St
Victoria, BC, V8V 3K2
Canada

www.friesenpress.com

ISBN
978-1-03-911602-3 (Hardcover)
978-1-03-911601-6 (Paperback)
978-1-03-911603-0 (eBook)

1. FICTION, CONTEMPORARY WOMEN

Distributed to the trade by The Ingram Book Company

Dedication

I want to thank God, St. Therese and St. Jude for giving me strength and guidance.

I want to dedicate this book to my loving husband Rene for believing in me when I didn't and to my four wonderful children; Michel, Stephane, Celine and Danielle and my grand-children Ellyn, Edison and Thomas. I love you all so much.

I also want to dedicate this book to my father who passed away from cancer at an early age and to my mother who I hold dear to my heart.

My family is my everything.

Chapter 1

Till death do us part, Renee believed in those words with all of her heart and soul. Paul had proposed to her on New Year's Eve after dancing the night away at his family's social club. You would never see Renee's family at this type of club, as it was for elite families only. You see, Paul's parents and friends considered Renee and her family to be from the "other side of the track," and they did not allow the riffraff to join their social club.

Paul's family did not really approve of Renee from the beginning; they believed he was seeing someone beneath his social *status*. His parents pleaded with him not to be so hasty and to look elsewhere for a bride to be. Paul held his ground, defying his parent's wishes, and he and Renee became husband and wife that summer.

They loved each other and had planned every detail of what they wanted their life together to be. They talked about buying their first home with a white picket fence and having a few kids: he wanted a girl that looked like her and she wanted a boy that looked like him. What they had together was the real deal.

Who would have believed that a month after celebrating their fairy tale wedding, Renee would be planning Paul's funeral.

The first chapter of their life together had started with a perfect wedding, followed by a fabulous honeymoon in Paris. When they came back from their honeymoon, they moved into their new home on Blueberry Hill Road, with that white picket fence they both wanted. Their dream ended quickly. Renee had always believed that the death of the hero came at the end of the story, certainly not at the beginning.

A few weeks after being home, Paul had to go out of town on a business trip. He had business dealings in New York that he could not postpone any longer. If only he could have postponed this meeting or had sent someone else to take his place, he would still be here with her. Paul had business to take care of in New York on September 11, and in one of the Twin Towers.

This horrible day will be remembered by all Americans as one of the worst terrorist attacks ever to take place on American soil. It was all over the news—everywhere you turned you saw or heard about the planes crashing into the Twin Towers of the World Trade Center in New York City. The entire country was in shock and frightened for the people in those buildings. The country was in full alert, as they did not know if or when other attacks would take place.

The people who heard the crash or saw the event take place were in shock. The entire city was running for safety not knowing what was happening and where to take cover. Paul was one of the many who had died that day. He was in one of those Twin Towers when the plane crashed into the building, killing him and so many others.

Renee had been sitting in the lunch room of her school when the vice principal came running in and flicked the television on to watch the live footage of the terrorist attack in New York. At that moment, Renee started crying hysterically. The staff tried to calm her down, not understanding her hysteria, but Renee could not breath. She needed some air, so she ran outside, still sobbing and jumping up and down like a crazy person. Kayla, the teacher's assistant, came running outside to try and comfort her.

Through sobs, Renee said, "Kayla, Paul is in New York on business . . . and he . . . he might be in that burning building on the television! I need to know . . . if . . . Paul is okay!"

Was Paul dead? Or by some miracle was he alive and breathing? Renee wanted answers to her questions. The bell rang, recess was over, and Renee was in no shape to teach her class. Kayla offered to take over her class so that she could go home.

Renee needed to get in contact with Paul's co-worker and best friend, Peter Lockwood, to find out if he had heard something of Paul's whereabouts. Kayla made Renee promise to phone her with any news and that she would stop in to see her after the school day was over. Renee needed to call a cab since she was too shaky and teary eyed to drive herself home. Frank, the janitor, a real sweetheart of a guy, volunteered to see that she got home safely.

***

When Renee arrived home, Frank offered to stay with her for a while, but she thanked him and sent him back to school. As Renee entered the house, she felt this empty feeling come over her—a feeling that she was all alone now in this house that she and Paul called home. She began to look at photos of their wedding day. It had been a magical day for the both of them.

Paul and Renee had a huge wedding, not that it made any difference to them, but Paul's parents, Ted and Nancy Hamilton, wanted something elaborate for their only child. Nancy wanted a social event like no other. Paul wanted so much to appease his parents, so he got Renee to go along with their wishes.

Renee had always dreamed of having a beautiful garden wedding, with just their closest friends and family. The wedding that Paul's parents gave them was a wedding most girls dream about, but for Renee it was too grandiose for her taste. The entire guest list was made up of the Hamiltons' country club friends, the rich and the famous as Renee called them. Renee personally invited her family and a few close friends. By the time it was over, the wedding had not turned out to be Renee and Paul's special day but instead the social event of the year that Paul's parents wanted. For that, Renee would never forgive them. They took over the one day that was supposed to be theirs.

Renee held their wedding invitation that they had framed, which read, "*You are cordially invited to the marriage of Renee, the daughter of James and Christine Clark, and Paul, son of Ted and Nancy Hamilton, at Fairways at Woburn Country Club.*"

While Renee held the invitation, she asked herself, "How could this be? It wasn't supposed to end like this. We got married in front of God and promised to love one another, be there for one another, forever and ever."

Renee pressed the framed wedding announcement and their wedding picture against her chest, over her heart, and began to cry uncontrollably. Aside from her sobs, the house was so quiet. It was like being in a mausoleum;

everything was so still and she felt so alone. Renee had a feeling at that moment that Paul was never coming home again.

Something caught her eye. The red light was flashing on the answering machine. When she pressed the button on the machine, it said, "You have twenty new messages."

Renee hoped that one of the messages was from Paul, telling her not to worry, that he was fine and coming home on the next flight. Sadly, every call was a family member who wanted to know if everything was okay and if she had seen the broadcast on the television. They all wanted to know if Paul was in one of the buildings at the time of the disaster, and they wanted her to contact them as soon as she could. But, at that moment, Renee could not deal with them. One message interested her, though, the one from Peter, Paul's coworker and best friend. He wanted her to call him as soon as she received his message.

Just then the phone rang and Renee jumped to get it, hoping it was Paul, but it was the school informing her that Peter Lockwood had called the school, looking for her. They had asked if she had heard anything from Paul, and she had told them that she had not. Peter wanted to talk to her, so she held her breath and called him straight away. He was crying at the other end, telling her how sorry he was and that Paul was not picking up his cell. He reassured her that he would not leave work until he heard news of Paul.

Peter had been trying to contact some of his acquaintances in the Big Apple to try and see if they could help him find out any news of Paul's whereabouts. However, it was impossible to get through to anyone, as the phones were all busy. Peter guessed people from all over the United States and abroad were calling to check on their loved ones living in New York, making sure they were all accounted for, praying that they were alive and well.

Renee told Peter that she would stay by the phone to await any news on Paul's well-being. To her, all this waiting without any word from Paul meant the outcome was not looking good. He would have called her if he could; he knew that she would be worried sick about his safety. Renee needed to know that Paul was all right, that he was alive, and that he was coming home to her.

Several hours later, Peter arrived at Renee's door with terrible news. It seemed that Paul's meeting took place on one of the floors that got hit. Search and rescue informed Peter that no one on those floors survived.

At that moment, Renee's heart dropped—she was in shock. She fainted at the news. She would never see her Prince Charming, the love of her life, her soul mate, and husband of one month ever again.

Peter carried Renee to the sofa and got her a cold cloth and some water. He then phoned Renee's parents with the horrifying news. They drove over to Renee's house right away, to be with her during this terrible time. Peter stayed with Renee until her parents arrived, and before leaving, he apologized again.

"Let me know if there is anything you need," Peter asked before he left.

Renee did not answer him. Her mother, Christine, thanked him and walked him to the door. Renee's father, James, asked to speak to Peter privately outside. James then took hold of Peter's hand and said, "Peter, my wife and I are grateful to you for being here for Renee. She will need all of our support and help in the weeks to come."

Peter replied, "You can count on me to help her out with anything that needs to be done. You know, Paul and I were like brothers. Whatever Renee needs: help with the funeral arrangements, look over paperwork, or just a shoulder to cry on. Just call, and I'll clear my schedule and be right over." Peter said his goodbyes and then left.

James returned into the house where his family were grieving.

***

The next few days were very hard on all of them, but mostly on Renee. James had known that after the shock wore off and the truth sank in that Renee's world would fall apart. He knew his daughter needed their support now more than ever. Renee did not want to believe that her husband was never coming back to her, that he had left her all alone, and that she now was a widow.

Renee's way of coping was to shut down and stay in her room, crying. Her parents were thankful when she finally fell asleep; she needed all the rest she could get for the days to come. Morning finally came around, Renee's parents tried to get her to come down for breakfast, but she refused; she was not ready to leave the comfort of her room. Renee's parents wanted Renee to get up and eat a little to keep up her strength so that she could help them out with the funeral arrangements, but Renee did not want to contribute to the planning of her husband's funeral.

James decided to call Boston's best funeral parlor to ask about making funeral arrangements for their son-in-law, Paul Hamilton, but he was advised that all the arrangements had already been taken care of by the parents of the deceased. The funeral director informed him that all would take place the day after tomorrow at ten a.m. The service would take place at the family's church, and there would be no showing since there was nobody in the casket to view. Paul's body was never found or expected to be found because of the fire, and he had likely been buried under the collapsed building. James thanked the man for his help, and the funeral director respectably conveyed his deepest sympathies to the family for their loss.

James was thankful that all the funeral arrangements were taken care of because it was something he was not looking forward to doing. He found it odd that Paul's parents did not come and see how their daughter-in-law was holding up. He knew they had lost a son, their only child, but Renee had lost her husband and she was part of their family now too. James thought that even though they had their differences, this ordeal should bind them closer together. They should be supporting each other during this terrible time. He did not understand why they did not ask for Renee's input on the funeral arrangements, but he knew that Renee would not have been much help to them anyway.

Renee's father was just about to call Paul's parents when he saw that there were many messages on the answering machine that had not been answered, so he decided to listen to them and return messages if needed. A few were from Paul's parents wanting to know if Renee had heard anything at all from their son, as they were worried sick. Paul's parents sounded upset that Renee was not returning their phone calls. They had to call Peter to get the horrifying news of their son's death. You could hear how upset and hurt Paul's father was on the answering machine, and rightly so, as their son had just died and Renee did not seem to have the decency to call when she was advised of his death. They, on the other hand, had the decency of leaving her a message stating that the funeral arrangements were all taken care of. They also mentioned where and when the funeral services would take place. They told her that there would be a little get together after the service at their home for all Paul's friends and family.

James was upset that the Hamiltons did not ask about how Renee was doing or about her well-being; it sounded like they just did not care. He understood that they were grieving the loss of their son. They were going through their own hell. Together, Renee's parents phoned all of their family and friends to let them know about Paul's death and when the funeral would take place.

Renee stayed in her room with the curtains closed. She did not come out of her room for anything, not even to eat. Every day since his death, Renee would awake to what seemed like a dream but, in reality, was a nightmare.

***

The day arrived for Paul's funeral. Renee's mom, Christine, got her daughter showered and dressed in a black simple dress for the funeral. Renee did not want to go, but her parents put their foot down and insisted she go. The service seemed to go on forever. Renee could not cry anymore; she was out of tears. Paul's parents were devastated about losing Paul a second time: the first time to Renee and now to God. Renee was having trouble believing in God now—Why were her husband and all those innocent people taken away during the terrorist attack on September 11?

Renee was right: Paul's parents blamed her for Paul's death, as she was the one who had let Paul go on his business trip to New York. Renee would have preferred Paul stay close to home, but Paul wanted to pull his weight at the firm, so he took on some of the out-of-town clients, which meant traveling. In all honesty, Paul's family had lots of money, so he did not need to work to survive. But Renee and Paul had decided that they would make it on their own, that they would live on their own earnings. She did not want to live on Paul's family's money. So in a way, she was responsible for her husband's death.

During the service, she could not get up to speak. She just could not get up in front of all those people, knowing it was all her fault, that she was the one who killed Paul. Even though she believed in her heart and soul that Paul was gone forever and that it was of her own doing, she was also mad as hell that he wasn't coming back to her. He had promised her a life full of happiness, dreams coming true and that story book ending where they lived happily ever after.

Renee's father decided to get up to the podium and say a few words on his daughter's behalf. He talked about the first time Renee introduced Paul to both of them and how well they had gotten along together. He talked about all the things they had in common: they loved to fish and watch the games on television. They even got in a few live sporting games together. Renee's father started crying while telling the story of how Paul and his daughter had met and how happy they had been together, how they had started their life together as man and wife, and how short lived it all was. James said his goodbyes to Paul, but before leaving the podium, he looked at Paul's casket and stated lovingly, "Paul, you will always be part of our family, the son I never had."

At that point, Renee lost it and started shouting hysterically, "Stop it, just stop it, Dad. Paul promised me that he would be here for me forever and that we would grow old together. What kind of man doesn't keep his promises to his wife? How could he leave me here all alone?" Renee collapsed across the top of the coffin and shouted, "Why?! Why?! Why?!" She started crying again, and this time, the waterworks were gushing. Renee could see Paul's parents through blurry, tear-filled eyes. She knew that they loathed her. She could see they were ashamed of her outburst and wanted nothing to do with her. Renee's parents took her aside to console her, knowing the grief was too much for their daughter to bear and that she was not in her right mind. They apologized to all and walked Renee out of the chapel.

After being consoled and reprimanded as if she was a child, Renee dried her eyes. Her parents told her that they should make an appearance at the Hamiltons', where they were hosting a little get-together for Paul's family and friends.

Renee didn't want to go, but her parents pleaded with her to do it for Paul. She knew Paul would expect her to be strong, so for his sake, she would make an appearance and try to make amends with his parents. She was not the only one affected by Paul's death. Paul had family and friends who loved him and who were also mourning his death. She knew her parents were right, so she made an appearance and went through the motions of a grieving widow.

Everyone present was thoughtful and sympathetic. People who congratulated Renee at her wedding were now giving her their sympathy.

In the end, Renee just wanted everyone to leave her alone. She wanted to run away and hide. She did not want to be there. All she wanted was to be in the safety of Paul's arms. When the house finally emptied of all their family, friends, and neighbors, it was time for Renee and her parents to leave. Her parents thanked the Hamiltons for arranging the beautiful church service and for hosting the delicious lunch, then told them they were leaving.

Renee looked at Paul's parents and saw that they were deeply grieving too. She felt sad for them and felt like she needed to say or do something to help them through this terrible time. Renee asked her parents to wait for her in the car; she needed a few minutes alone with Ted and Nancy.

James and Christine thanked the Hamiltons again and left their daughter to say her goodbyes.

Renee asked Paul's parents to please take a seat so she could talk to them for a moment.

She then said, "As Paul's parents, I would like you to know that Paul loved you so much. I know that he hoped that with time, you would care for me as a daughter. All he ever wanted was for you to accept me as part of your family. I, myself, would love to be part of your family if you would have me."

Paul's parents just stared at her in awe. Then Nancy could not keep quiet any longer; she had to tell Renee how she truly felt. "There is no way in hell that we would want a gold digger like you to be part of our family. If it weren't for you, Paul would still be alive. We blame his death on you. We would rather never see or hear from you again. You are as dead to us as our son is. You should be able to survive on Paul's life insurance and his trust fund. I believe that you never loved my son. We know that the marriage was just a way for you to get hold of our money. You thought you would get all our money when we passed away, but you will never get the mother lode. Paul did not want to get a prenuptial agreement written up as we had asked him to, but now that he is no longer with us, your cash for life is nonexistent. Now, get out! Get out of our home and know that you are not welcomed here."

Renee could not believe what Nancy had just said to her. In shock, she got up and ran out the door; she didn't want to cry in front of them. Renee then ran to the car and asked her father to drive her home. James wanted to know why she was so upset.

Renee replied angrily, "Just get me home, Dad. I don't want to rehash the terrible and haunting things the Hamiltons had to say. Just know that the only good thing to come out of all this is that I never have to see or deal with those arrogant blue-blood Hamiltons ever again." Renee cried on her mother's lap the entire ride home.

When they arrived home, she thanked her parents for being there for her, but she told them she wanted to be alone for a while. They hugged her, then left, telling her that if she needed them, no matter the hour, they would come right back. She blew them a kiss and entered her house.

The house was so still; Renee never felt so alone. She picked up Paul's photo, and as she looked at it, she asked him aloud, "Paul, why did you have to leave me? You promised me you would never leave me and that we would start a family together. You said that we had that once-in-a-lifetime love that would last forever. How do I go on living my life without you?" She placed the photo back on the shelf where it belonged.

After a tiring day, Renee walked upstairs to the master bedroom and grabbed Paul's pillow. She took in his scent and cried herself to sleep.

***

As morning light beamed through the window, Renee opened her eyes, hoping that it was all a bad dream. But looking beside her, she was all alone in this queen size bed. He was really gone. The nightmare was real. Paul was gone from her forever.

The doorbell rang, but she didn't want to see anyone. She hoped that the person would just leave her alone, but they were persistent. The ringing doorbell began to drive her crazy, so she got out of bed and put on her slippers, robe, and dragged herself to the door. The person at the door was not leaving. It was. her mother-in-law.

Nancy had boxes in her arms. Renee was annoyed. She had thought her mother-in-law had never wanted to see her again. When she opened the door, she asked, "Nancy, what are you doing here? What's with the boxes?"

Nancy replied, "Oh, Renee, I just thought I would come and pack up Paul's things."

Renee was confused. This lady had thrown her out of her home yesterday and here she was on her doorstep, wanting to come in and pack Paul's things. Renee was not feeling well, and she wanted nothing to do with this craziness this morning. "Nancy, this can wait. I'm not sure if I want to get rid of his stuff, so please go back home." Renee suddenly felt nauseated and immediately ran to the bathroom to throw up. She came out of the washroom, wiping her mouth with a wet cloth, looking pale and very tired. Nancy suggested that she should go and rest while she packed her son's belongings.

Renee's patience was wearing thin, so she pleaded with Nancy, "I don't want to pack Paul's things right now, and when I'm ready, I will do the packing. Nancy, I'm not feeling quite myself today and need to go back to bed, so if you wouldn't mind showing yourself out. If I am not mistaken, you said to me yesterday that you never wanted to see me ever again, but here you are in my home, wanting to take away all I have left of my husband. As you were so inhospitable toward me after the funeral, I will repay you with the same lack of kindness. Get out! You are not welcome here EVER. Now, you know the way out." Renee went back upstairs to rest; she did not feel very well at all. In fact, Renee felt quite ill after speaking to her mother-in-law that way. She wished things could be so different; she knew her husband would be ashamed of their behavior. Renee started sobbing, thinking of how much she missed him, and then shortly after, fell asleep. This was becoming another exhausting day for her.

As Renee slept upstairs, Nancy, who had never left the house, started packing her son's belongings. She worked quietly so as not to wake Renee. She wanted to take all of her son's belongings—his trophies, pictures, books, everything that belonged to him. Nancy left nothing of her son's in that house. She wanted Renee to have nothing at all that belonged to Paul. Looking back into the dark house, she realized with all of her son's belongings gone, it looked like Paul had never lived there at all. Nancy felt pleased with herself. She hoped to God she would never have to step foot in Renee's house or see or deal with that wrenched girl again.

Chapter 2

When Renee woke up it was dark, she slept the day away, she decided she would go downstairs for a bite to eat to settle her stomach. She still felt queasy and dizzy. She did not notice at first that all of her husband's belongings were gone. She walked right to the kitchen and had a glass of milk and a few cookies. When Renee started walking back to her room with her snack, she realized she had been robbed. All of Paul's belongings were gone. She then realized who the thief was.

"Nancy! That conniving witch, she took all of Paul's belongings!"

Renee felt ill again. She placed her milk and cookies on the coffee table and ran to the washroom to vomit. She was sick to her stomach; all of this drama was very stressful on her. Finishing up in the washroom, she decided to take action and called 911.

Renee explained to the first responder that she had been robbed. The police arrived momentarily after she called. She explained that while she was upstairs sleeping, someone had entered her home and taken all of her husband's belongings. She gave them a list of a few things she could remember that were missing. She then mentioned to the officers that her mother-in-law came by earlier to visit her and perhaps she forgot to lock the door when leaving. She had been the only one to visit her today, so perhaps she had seen something or someone suspicious in the neighborhood.

They dust for fingerprints and took down her statement and Nancy Hamilton's address. They told Renee not to worry, that they would take care of this matter for her, and advised her to lock up after they left. They also told her to try and calm herself down, as there was nothing she could do right now. They suggested she get in touch with her insurance in the morning, and they left the crime scene.

Renee did not tell the officers she knew who the bugler was; they would find out soon enough. She took her cookies and milk back to the kitchen; she could not eat anything with her upset stomach. Feeling ill, she went to the washroom, took two Gravol tablets for her nausea and upset stomach, and then she crawled back into bed.

***

After leaving Renee's, the police went directly to see Nancy Hamilton to question her about the robbery. Sergeant McDonald and his partner arrived at the Hamiltons' estate and rang the doorbell. When Mr. Hamilton answered the door, he was shocked to see the police.

"What's the problem officers?"

Sergeant McDonald spoke first, "Mr. Hamilton, I presume? I am Sergeant McDonald and this is my partner, Sergeant Collins. We are sorry to have to disturb you, but we would like a word with Mrs. Hamilton. Would she be around?"

"Certainly, she is taking a nap. What is this about, if I may ask?" Ted Hamilton asked.

"Well, your daughter-in-law's home was burglarized earlier today, and she mentioned that your wife had visited her this morning. So, we were wondering if perhaps your wife saw someone or something peculiar around Renee's neighborhood before or after her visit today?" Sergeant McDonald asked.

Ted asked worriedly, "Is Renee all right? Was she hurt?"

"No, she's fine. The perpetrator just took a few things hanging around the living room and the den, it seems. Now, if you can get your wife, we just have a few questions to ask her. Then we will be on our way," the sergeant said.

Ted turned and walked upstairs to get his wife.

Nancy came downstairs, directly followed by her husband. Ted had told his wife that there were two officers at the door wanting to question her about a robbery that took place at Renee's home that morning.

Nancy came down directly and asked the men waiting, "Yes, officers, you wanted to ask me about my visit with Renee this morning?"

"Yes! As we mentioned to your husband an intruder came into your daughter-in-law's home and took some of her husband's belongings. We wanted to know if you had seen anything out of the ordinary while you were there?" Sergeant McDonald asked.

While his partner was talking, Sergeant Collins noticed a few boxes on the floor next to the entrance door containing trophies and pictures. He asked her, "Mrs. Hamilton, the items in these boxes wouldn't by chance be the missing items that we are looking for, are they?" He decided to take a better look in the boxes and found that the missing items were not missing any longer. The sergeant then asked, "Mrs. Hamilton, while you were at your daughter-in-law's home today, did you take these items from her home without her knowledge?"

In a panic, Nancy answered, "You see, Sergeant, my son died a few days ago and I went over to his home today and took his belongings. I did not steal anything that was not ours to begin with."

The officer asked her again, "Mrs. Hamilton, did your daughter-in-law say you could come into her home and take these items?"

Nancy tried to explain to the officer again, "Officer, these memorabilia belong with me, with us. Renee would have never given us our son's things. So, Yes! I took them without her acknowledgement. I hate her. She does not deserve to have my son's things, and I will not hand them over to her either. That's all we have left of our son. Can't you understand?"

The sergeant did not like what he had to do to this distraught mother, but she did commit a criminal act. He then walked toward her and said, "Mrs. Hamilton, I'm sorry but we have to arrest you. Taking things that do not belong to you in someone else's home is a crime. So, I will have to read you your rights now. You have the right to remain silent. Anything you say can and will be used against you in a court of law. You have the right to an attorney. If you cannot afford an attorney, one will be provided for you. Do you understand the rights I have just read to you? With these rights in mind, do you wish to speak to me?"

Mr. Hamilton then spoke up, "This is preposterous. You just can't take my wife away like this. She's not a criminal. We have our rights too, you know."

Sergeant Collins cuffed her and asked Mrs. Hamilton if she understood her rights while taking her to their car.

Mr. Hamilton lashed out angrily saying, "Sergeant, is this really necessary? It's not like she killed the bitch. What will our neighbors think?"

As Nancy was put into the cop car, Sergeant Collins turned and looked at Ted and said, "Mr. Hamilton, you can follow us to the precinct and you should call your lawyer. I will be taking the stolen items back with me. Again, I'm sorry about all of this."

Ted, upset, answered, "No! I know this is not your fault. It's that conniving bitch of a daughter-in-law who is to blame for this disgrace to our good name and my son's memory. She has no sense in that brain of hers, no heart. We have just lost our son, our baby boy, and she wants to hurt us even more. She's upset about the money; it's all about the money. She never cared for our son, you know. She is a money-grabbing bitch. Mark my words, if she wants war, she better be prepared for Pearl Harbor because the war has just begun."

Sergeant Collins replied, "Sir, I don't think you should be venting like this in front of me. We will be going now."

Ted told the sergeant to convey a message to his wife. "Tell my wife not to worry. I'll get in touch with our lawyer, and we will meet her there."

The sergeant shook his head and replied, "I'll do that, sir."

When arriving at the station, by chance, a reporter from a local newspaper in Boston was walking out of the police station. As the police were taking Mrs. Hamilton out of the police car, she quickly hung her head down so as not to get noticed, but the reporter recognized her and started asking her all sorts of questions about why she had been arrested. *Great,* she thought to herself, *my picture is going to be plastered on the front page of the newspaper.*

The police took Nancy to a lockup and called Renee Hamilton to tell her they had found her stolen belongings and that the burglar was in custody at the station.

Knowing damn well who it was, Renee still asked the sergeant who they had arrested for the crime.

The sergeant informed her, "Mrs. Hamilton, it was your mother-in-law."

Renee made sure she sounded shocked at the news. "I can't believe it. Why would she do that?"

The sergeant answered, "I don't know, Mrs. Hamilton, but do you still want to press charges now that you know who the intruder is? You know, this is really a family situation, and I know right now you are all under a lot of stress. Perhaps you should just let this go and talk this over amongst yourselves?"

"No, I don't think so. She had the audacity to steal from me, and she knows how hard my husband's death has been on me. How can she be so callous, heartless? We are family and this is how they treat me? No, she can rot in jail—that's what she deserves. Thanks again, Sergeant, for all your help, but when it comes to my mother-in-law, I think I will let the charges stick," Renee replied.

Nancy waited for her husband and their lawyer, who was a family friend, to come and post bail so she could return home. As she waited, she had her fingerprints and mugshot taken. The police were processing her as if she was a regular felon. She could not believe she was being treated like a common thief; how degrading for a person of her stature, a woman of high society.

By the time Ted and their lawyer arrived, it was too late to post bail, so she would have to spend the night incarcerated. Nancy yelled, "This is not acceptable. I demand to be left out of here so I can go home."

As Ted said good night to his wife, he promised that he and their lawyer would be back at the break of dawn to get her out of prison. Nancy kissed him goodbye, with tears running down her face.

Ted wiped her tears and said, "Be strong, my dear. We are the Hamiltons; we will get through this ordeal." Ted and his lawyer left, as, that night, they could do nothing to help Nancy out.

Chapter 3

In addition to being sick a few times during the late hours, Renee tossed and turned all night. She could not stop thinking about how Paul would be so ashamed of her for putting his mother in jail. She realized that she was behaving no better than her in-laws and that was not who she was. She reached for the telephone and called her father. She told her father of what had taken place the day before and that she was so ashamed of her behavior. She told her father that she would contact Sergeant McDonald and tell him that after thinking about it, she would like to drop all charges against her mother-in-law. She also asked her father if he would convey her apologies to Mr. and Mrs. Hamilton for her conduct. Her father could not believe all that had happened in such a short time; he could not believe all this animosity between his daughter and the Hamiltons.

As James, Renee's father, was running out of the house to go to the Hamiltons, he picked up his newspaper from the front step and was shocked to see Nancy Hamilton's picture on the front page.

The headline read: *"Nancy Hamilton arrested for burglarizing her own daughter-in-law's home."* The article stated that she was arrested by two officers, Sergeant Henry McDonald and Sergeant Lewis Collins, at her home late yesterday afternoon. She had spent the night in the city jail, waiting to be let out on bail. This was the first time this rich blue blood had to slum it for an evening, as she was used to five star accommodations. The rest of the story continued in that same manner. James could not believe how they were belittling Nancy and making fun of her because she was wealthy.

He drove directly to the police station and spoke to Sergeant McDonald. "Renee has changed her mind about charging her mother-in-law. My daughter is just angry that anyone would come into her home and take things without even asking her permission. My daughter is mourning her husband's death, so she is still very upset. The situation just got out of control and it sort of snowballed."

Sergeant McDonald understood and was happy to see the situation get resolved amicably. The sergeant released the items that were taken to Renee's dad, and he helped him carry the boxes to his car. James apologized again for all the trouble this situation caused the police force, and then he drove off to return Paul's belongings to his daughter.

Mr. Hamilton and their lawyer arrived. The sergeant advised them that Mr. James Clark just left not two minutes ago and advised them to drop all charges and that the daughter was sorry for all the inconveniences.

"That's great, but the damage to our name and our social standing in this community is ruined,"Mr. Hamilton said.

Mrs. Hamilton came out from where she had spent the worst night of her life. She was so happy to see her husband that she ran and gave him a great big hug. "Dear all I want to do is go home, take a hot shower, change my clothes, and just try and get over this terrible ordeal."

Coming out of the jailhouse, the Hamiltons had reporters all over them. Their lawyer advised the news crews that all charges were dropped, that it was all a misunderstanding, and that his client was free to go home. The news crews tried to get more on this story, but all that was said was, "No comment."

On their ride home, Ted told his wife that Renee had changed her mind about charging her for stealing.

"We must go back. They forgot to give us Paul's belongings. I need Paul's belongings," Nancy replied.

Ted explained to his wife that James Clark picked up the boxes and was returning Paul's things to his daughter. Nancy started to cry and her husband tried to console her.

As they entered their home, he told her to take a hot bath and go rest for a while. She did as she was told. She was still very angry by the way she had been treated and was heartbroken to have lost Paul's memorabilia. Ted went to the kitchen and asked their cook to send up a tray with chamomile tea and croissants to Mrs. Hamilton's bedroom.

The cook started preparing a tray to take to her. Mr. Hamilton then entered his den and started reading the newspaper once again and could not believe all the slanderous things they had said about his family, mostly his wife. He was appalled and angry at the nonsense written in the paper. One thing for sure, he knew he had to keep the paper away from his wife. Seeing the picture of herself entering the jailhouse with two officers on the front page would literally kill her—she would never leave the house for shame.

After her long hot shower, Nancy sat down to enjoy a hot cup of tea that the cook brought up for her, along with some freshly baked croissants and a little marmalade. She asked the cook if she could also bring the newspaper up, as she would like to read it before taking a nap.

The cook could not find the newspaper anywhere. She asked the other staff if anyone had seen this morning's paper, and the chauffeur said he had put it on the entrance table this morning as usual. Everyone helped look for the paper, but it could not be found. The chauffeur said he had bought one for himself this morning but had not read it yet. The cook asked if he wouldn't mind lending it to Mrs. Hamilton for a while. He went out to the car to fetch the paper for her. The cook thanked him and promptly took the paper up to Mrs. Hamilton, as the cook knew she did not like to be kept waiting. The staff knew that Mrs. Hamilton was a very hard lady to work for; she got angry easily if things were not as she wanted. These past few days, she had been a tyrant, granted it was understandable after losing her son. She had been getting angry at every little thing they did or did not do correctly.

As Mrs. Hamilton began to read the daily news, she screamed frantically, scarring all the staff and mostly her husband. She then began to yell for her husband. He ran upstairs to see what all the fuss was about and that's when he saw the newspaper flapping around in her hand.

"Ted, did you see today's paper? I'm on the front page, being dragged into prison for all to see. It's that bitch's fault. She started this entire nightmare. How can I ever leave the house ever again? We will have to move away from all of our friends and neighbors, where no one has ever heard of us."

Ted, trying to console his wife, told her, "Calm down, dear. It's not as bad as all that. I already got the paper to write a retraction saying it was all a misunderstanding and that it was only a family squabble that got out of hand. So, don't worry about it. In a few days, it will be all forgotten."

To show her gratitude, she put her arms around her husband's neck and kissed him on the lips. They both decided to take an afternoon nap, holding and caressing each other, both falling fast asleep in each other's arms. They had gone through a lot in the past week, Nancy especially. Not only had she felt the stress of losing a son, but she had been treated like a common criminal, been fingerprinted, had her mugshot taken, spent the night in prison, and had her picture plastered on the front page of one of Boston's daily newspapers. They both faced the possibility of losing face with family, friends, and neighbors.

Chapter 4

James arrived at this daughter's home and rang the doorbell, but no one answered. He then started banging at the door, but still no answer. He was beginning to get both upset and frightened, so he took out his cell phone and called her—but still no answer. James knew his daughter was at home and she stayed in her room most days. He remembered that she kept a spare key under the flowerpot in the backyard. He went to the back of the house and found the key exactly where he had remembered it to be. As he let himself into his daughter's house, he found it to be very quiet. He called out for her, but no sound was made and he became frightened at what he may find.

He checked on the main floor. She was nowhere to be found, so he marched upstairs, diligently calling out her name, but still no response. As he entered the master bedroom, he found the bed unmade but no sign of his daughter. He took a big breath, relieved that he did not find her hurt or dead. He kept on searching in the other rooms but found nothing, and she still did not respond when he called her name. James decided to look in the basement, though only the washer and dryer were down there, but it was the only place left to look.

The lights were on in the basement. He descended the steps quickly. There she was lying on the floor unconscious. She looked pale and frail. He shook her lightly, then more forcefully, but she gave no real movement. He decided to call 911.

James said to the 911 dispatcher, "Hello! I am with my daughter, and she is not responding to me. She is unconscious. I don't have a clue what's wrong with her, but, please, I need your help. I'm at 43 Blueberry Hill Road. HURRY!"

The dispatcher tried to assure him that an ambulance was on its way.

After he hung up, James looked up and started speaking to the ceiling, "Paul, it's Dad. If you see Renee heading your way, please send her back. I know you miss her and she misses you like crazy, but it's not her time. We still need her, so if you see her, please kiss her goodbye and tell her it's not her time yet. Tell her she still has so much living to do. Can you do this for me, son? I'd appreciate it and know that we love you and miss you so much."

Tears flowed down his cheeks. He kept on rubbing his daughter's forehead, and then he thanked God he could hear the ambulance sirens. He placed Renee's head on the floor and ran to open the door for the emergency crew. As he directed the two paramedics to his daughter, they asked him a few questions about their patient. James advised them that these past few days, she had been feeling faint, nauseated, tired, and distraught by the death of her husband.

"This is your daughter? What is your daughter's name?"

"Yes! Renee Hamilton is my daughter and I am her father, James Clark."

The paramedic then asked him, "Do you think she was distraught enough to—" He did not have enough time to finish his sentence before James said, "There is no way in hell that she would try and take her own life."

"Okay, sir, but we need to ask you this: Did you check to see if there were any empty pill bottles around the house?"

James again shook his head and said, "No, she wouldn't do that. I didn't see any empty pill bottles, but I was not really searching for them."

The two paramedics transferred their patient onto a stretcher where they strapped her in and carried her out to the ambulance. The paramedic asked James, "Mr. Clark, could you look around in search of empty pill bottles and perhaps bring her some toiletries that she may need?"

James said he would. Then the paramedic said, "We are taking your daughter to Winchester Hospital. You can meet us there. I'm sure the nursing staff will have questions for you."

"Okay! Okay! I'll be right there," James replied. He was trembling as he saw the ambulance leave. James then went back inside to look for empty pill bottles, but he could not find any. He then called his wife.

He sounded so panicked on the phone, his wife could not understand all that he was saying, so James said loudly, "Christine dear, can you just please meet me at Winchester Hospital where Renee is being admitted, and I'll explain everything to you there."

Christine wanted questions answered but replied, "All right, dear, but what about my baby girl?"

James, now frustrated, said, "Christine, I'm going to throw a few things in a bag for Renee and I'll meet you at the hospital."

They both arrived at the hospital at about the same time and went directly to the emergency desk. James advised the nurse of who they were and if she had any news of their daughter, Renee Hamilton. The person at the front desk advised them, "Mr. and Mrs. Clark, we admitted Renee Hamilton."

" Is Renee going to be alright?" Christine asked the nurse.

"The doctor is with her right now, but we will let you know as soon as we know anything" the nurse advised her.

James described his morning to his wife and told her he had never been more afraid in his life. When he saw his daughter on the floor, he thought for sure she was dead. He never felt more useless in his entire life, not knowing what to do or how to help her. His wife started crying again; she was so frightened for her daughter. They waited for news of their daughter's well-being, but as the minutes passed, it seemed like they had been waiting there forever.

The door from the emergency room opened, and the nurse asked for the Clark family. They got up, anxiously awaiting to hear news of their daughter.

The attending physician, Dr. Ross, spoke to them telling them, "Your daughter is fine. She's just very: tired, dehydrated, and weak, so we are admitting her. She will stay here until she regains her strength and is well hydrated. The poor girl is just exhausted. I think a little TLC is just what this doctor prescribes for your daughter."

Renee's parents were thankful and relieved to hear the news. To thank him, James gave him a firm handshake and Christine hugged the stuffing out of him.

Seeing how worried Renee's parents were, Dr. Ross took them aside and told them, "Now that Renee is in the hospital, she will be well taken care of, I assure you."

They were so pleased and thanked him again. James wanted to ask the doctor one more question in private before he left them. Christine excused herself and went into her daughter's room where she was resting so peacefully. She sat by her side and kept watch over her frail and sleeping daughter.

In the privacy of a closed door, James told the doctor of the turmoil and hardship his daughter was having with the recent loss of her husband. He wanted to know if, while she was here under his care, it was at all possible to get her some professional help. The doctor took out her chart and jotted down a few things and told him, "I think that I can arrange for a psychiatrist to come in and evaluate her and get some sort of bereavement counseling started for her as well."

James was pleased and thanked the doctor once again. He then left the doctor and went looking for his wife and child. He was advised by one of the nurses that they had transferred his daughter to Room 300. He thanked her and rushed to the elevators to find that the elevator was on the top floor. As he did not want to wait for the elevator to descend, he decided to take the stairs, two at a time, anxious to be with his family.

Chapter 5

Renee was still asleep when her parents left her for the night. As Renee was sleeping, she was having a terrible nightmare. She could see Paul hanging from a cliff, and he was calling out her name and reaching for her hand. She tried to get hold of his hand, but she could not reach it. At that moment, he let go and fell into an abyss.

Renee awoke yelling Paul's name in a panic. The nurse came running in, trying to console her patient.

"Renee, it was just a nightmare. You're all right. You are at the hospital, and I am your nurse, Kathy. Settle down now before you hurt yourself."

Renee was so disoriented that she pulled out her intravenous. Kathy was having a hard time trying to calm her down, so she decided to call for help. As help arrived, they gave her something to calm her down, and Renee fell down on the pillow and returned to a restful state. The nurse placed the intravenous back in her wrist and decided to place restraints on her arms and legs so as not to get any resistance from Renee again.

***

Morning came, and Mr. Hamilton decided since he was up early, he would read the newspaper. The truth was, he wanted to see if the story of his wife's incarceration was still the big story of the day. He took the paper with him to the dining table, wanting to read as he ate his breakfast. He did not need to open the paper—the Hamiltons were on the front page again but not for burglary or imprisonment but for the cause of Renee Hamilton's so-called attempted suicide.

The headline read: *"Ted and Nancy Hamilton drive daughter-in-law, Renee Hamilton, to commit suicide."* The article went on to say that after the death of her son, Nancy Hamilton caused her daughter-in-law, Renee Hamilton, so much stress and grief that the poor girl had tried to commit suicide. Her father, James Clark, had found her dying on the floor and called 911. She had been taken to Winchester Hospital where she was admitted. Her parents, James and Christine Clark, were afraid of her emotional and physical state.

Ted could not believe what he was reading. He started talking to himself, "This is not journalism, but trash—a made up story to make us look like the villains. This girl is dragging our good name in the mud. This has to stop." He grabbed hold of the telephone and his address book, looking for James Clark's number. He then started hitting the numbers to James Clark's home phone.

When James answered the phone, Ted asked him, "What tricks are you playing now?"

Angered at this, James answered, "Ted, my daughter is in the hospital. She is frail and her body is tired. Instead of calling to see how she is doing, you call about how this situation is affecting *you*. I am sorry about the bad publicity you are getting, but do you not feel any compassion for my daughter? Don't answer. I know your answer to that question. I will ask you not to get in touch with my daughter; she needs her rest. That means no more stress, so please leave us all alone." Then he hung up on Ted.

Ted was furious and shouted aloud, "How dare he talk to me that way! Who does he think he is? It's just too bad that the bitch didn't succeed in killing herself, as these escapades are making *her* look like the victim and *we,* the guilty party. All this negative publicity makes us look bad. What must our friends and neighbors think?"

Ted believed Renee was more devious and conniving than he and his wife had all thought. Well, they never wanted to see or hear from Renee again. She was dead to them, as was their son.

Chapter 6

When Renee awoke, this time she was pleasantly calm, so the nurse introduced herself and took off Renee's restraints. Renee answered all the nurse's questions, and Kathy, her nurse, answered a few questions Renee had as well.

Renee wanted to know why she was here and why the restraints? Kathy explained how her father found her unconscious on the floor and how she was brought here to Winchester Hospital where Dr. Ross had admitted her for exhaustion and dehydration. The nurse left a tray of food for Renee to eat if she could manage it. She was not hungry but attempted to eat half a piece of toast and drink a little orange juice. It pleased the nurse to see she was trying to do what they had asked of her.

A lab technician came into Renee's hospital room to draw some blood. The doctor ordered a full panel of tests to be done to see if there may be some medical reasons for her illness and exhaustion. Renee complied with all requests, as she was too weak and fatigued to fight. She realized she had no fight left in her. She knew that the nurses were there to help her, not to harm her.

Dr. Ross came in to check on her. He was pleased to see she was up and had eaten a little on her tray. He mentioned how much everyone had been worried about her since her husband passed. He told Renee that her parents were with her for a while, but then they left to go home because they were very tired.

Dr. Ross advised Renee, "Your parents did call earlier this morning wanting an update on how you were feeling, and they were happy to hear you were doing better. They said to tell you they would be back to visit later on this afternoon because we told them we would be doing a few tests on you this morning. He paused before continuing, then said, "Renee, I have asked Dr. Sarah Chamberlain, our psychiatrist on staff, to come and speak with you. She is a great listener and has counseled those who have lost loved ones. She is a bereavement counselor and has many helpful strategies and techniques to help people like you cope with their loss. This is what this doctor recommends for you."

He saw that she was overwhelmed by all the information given to her, so he then said, "Renee, let's take this one step at a time, okay. Let's get your body strong, and then we will work on the rest. Does that seem to work for you?"

Renee just nodded and closed her eyes. She was so tired. The doctor left her to rest.

Chapter 7

Christine and James Clark arrived at the hospital at about twelve fifteen, just in time for lunch. One of the nurses asked them if they could wake Renee up from her sleep and get her to eat some of her lunch. Mr. and Mrs. Clark agreed to give it a try.

Renee's mom sat on her daughter's bed and nudged her, saying, "Sweetheart, it's Mom and Dad. We are here to visit you."

Renee whispered, "Oh! Hi, Mom, Dad, have you been here long? I was just talking to the doctor. I must have dozed off."

Christine then added, "Well, it's nice to see you up, sweetheart. You gave us such a scare. I have to say, you look like you have a little more color in your cheeks than when you were first admitted.

"Sorry, Mom, Dad, I don't even know how I got here."

Renee's mother replied, "How about we tell you the entire story while you eat up all that tomato soup and grilled cheese sandwich?" Christine got her child sitting up and her meal tray ready for Renee to eat. As Renee was slurping her soup, her mom began telling her how she came to be in the hospital.

"Renee, Dad went to check up on you and he found you out cold on the basement floor. Do you remember falling or taking any pills, sweetheart?"

"No, Mom! I remember going down to wash my bedding. I believe I vomited all over my sheets. I can't remember anything after that."

"Well, thank God, Dad found you and called 911. The paramedics came and that's how you ended up here," Christine said.

Renee then conveyed to her parents, "I'm so sorry. I don't know what's wrong with me. I just can't seem to cope with all this, I guess. But Dr. Ross has a plan to help me work through all this stuff I'm going through. Thanks, Dad, for getting me here and getting me some help. I need to get some kind of perspective and guidance on how to live my life without Paul. I can't just fall apart like this. I have to carry on. Paul would be so ashamed of me if he were here."

James tried to console her by saying, "Don't mention it, sweetheart. Your mother and I just hate to see you like this. You know we would do anything for you."

"I know, Dad. I'm just so scared to do this living on my own."

Dr. Ross entered the room and asked how the patient was doing. Christine said that her daughter was doing much better now that she had eaten all of her lunch. He was pleased to see she was holding down her lunch.

Dr. Ross asked Mr. and Mrs. Clark if they wouldn't mind stepping out for a while so that he could speak to his patient. They left promising to return later that afternoon. They kissed Renee and said goodbye to the doctor.

Dr. Ross came to sit by his patient and started talking to her about the bloodwork they had taken that morning and its finding. The doctor reported, "Renee, it seems that after testing your bloodwork, we found that you are pregnant. I would say about six weeks along, give or take. I see by the look on your face you did not know of your condition."

His patient was speechless, and when she finally found her voice, she asked him if he was positively sure about his finding. The doctor said he was one hundred percent sure of his finding.

Renee then burst out, "I'm pregnant, pregnant with Paul's baby? Doctor, thank you so much." She was so excited, she jumped up and hugged him, then started crying because she was so happy to have a piece of Paul with her but sadden as well—Paul would never get to meet his daughter or his son.

"Now, take hold of yourself. This is a good thing. You have to start taking good care of yourself. You have to eat right, exercise, and rest because you want a healthy baby. You know that Paul would want you to take care of yourself and his baby. Renee, you have to be strong now that you are with child. If all goes well, in about seven and a half months, give or take, you will have a baby in your arms. Never forget that your baby was made by the love you and Paul shared for each other," Dr. Ross stated.

She excitedly affirmed, "Yes, yes, you're right. I need to think of the baby that is growing inside me now. No more self-pity; the baby must come first. Thank you again, Dr. Ross. I will take good care of myself from this point on. Can you please do me a favor and keep this great news between you and I for right now? I just want to keep this bundle of joy to myself until I am ready to tell the world. I just want it to be our little secret for now. Do you understand?"

"Yes, I do, and we won't say a word," the doctor replied.

"Thank you, thank you so much. You have given me the best news I could have ever gotten."

"Now, you get some rest," the doctor advised her. "Dr. Chamberlain, the psychiatrist, will probably come and see you sometime this afternoon."

He left her alone with her thoughts and dreams of being a mother—Paul's baby's mother. She was thinking to herself how Paul would have been so pleased to have a child. He had wanted to have a huge family since they both had no siblings. Renee slowly dozed off.

Dr. Chamberlain awoke her sleeping patient. "Hi, Renee, I am Dr. Chamberlain. I was told you were expecting me."

Renee, still in a fog, answered, "Oh, yes. I'm so sorry. I must have dozed off."

"That's fine. I thought maybe you would like to chat for a while," Dr. Chamberlain stated. "Let's start with you telling me a little about yourself."

Renee started talking to her like she had known her for years. She divulged, "Well, I was an only child. My parents loved me and supported me in all that I wanted to do. I always loved children; I babysat for all the neighboring kids. I was in great demand, believe me. I was interested in becoming a nurse or an educator. I decided to study to become a teacher. I never regretted my decision because teaching makes me happy and I am told I am good at it. I teach Grade 4 at Shamrock Elementary school.

"I'm getting ahead of myself. After graduating and getting my teaching certificate, my friends and I made plans to go out to the beach to swim and tan. It was on that day, I met Paul, my husband. He was working as a life-guard for the summer. He had just finished school with a law degree but wanted one last summer on the beach, watching all the girls go by.

"Anyway, my girlfriends caught me staring at him on his lifeguard stand, and they dared me to play the drowning victim so he would have to come and rescue me. I didn't think much about it. I thought he was gorgeous, had a great body, and getting rescued by him and getting mouth-to-mouth sounded exciting. I have to tell you that doing this was something I would never normally do—ever. But I did that day. I swam out far enough to look believable and played the role of the drowning victim. The act worked quite well because he ran into the water and swam to me. I fell into his arms. He swam with me to the beach, holding my head out of the water, and on the beach, he started mouth-to-mouth. I placed my arms around his neck and started kissing him. My girlfriends started laughing and oohing. Paul was into the kiss. I felt it deep in my soul, but he then pushed me away saying that my friends and I had played a stupid dangerous game. Someone could have really been drawing while he was distracted by my stupidity. Someone could have lost their life because of our childish games. I felt quite ashamed at that moment and apologized. But Paul, very annoyed, ordered my friends and I off the beach.

"My friends all wanted to know if he was a good kisser, and I told them to stop it. I urged them to forget it, as it was a big mistake. Later that same day, I went back to the beach to apologize again, but he was not on duty. I asked the lifeguard working if he knew the name of the lifeguard that was on duty that morning and he told me his name was Paul Hamilton. He even told me where I could find him working most evenings. At night, he worked at Waxy O'Connor's, an Irish pub on Hartwell Ave. in Lexington. I thanked him and made plans with the girls to go bar hopping, making sure to stop at the Irish pub.

"I got all dressed up in my tight-fitted jeans, high heeled boots, and a tight T-shirt. I made sure I looked good because I was on the prowl. We visited every bar in town, and I made sure the Irish Pub was our last stop. I saw him right when we arrived, but I acted like I didn't notice him. My friends and I found ourselves a place to sit, and we were pleased to see they were playing contemporary music. We all got up to dance, made spectacles of ourselves, and got a little rowdy so that we were noticed. To say the least, we were noticed by everyone. I noticed Paul looking our way, so I told the girls I was thirsty and was going to get something to drink at the bar. One of the bartenders came to take my order, but Paul nudged him away so he could serve me. He asked me what I wanted and I replied, 'Whatever you have on tap please.' Then I acted surprised to see him working at the pub.

"He nonchalantly asked me if I wanted to play the drowning victim again, that it would be his pleasure to assist me. He would save me and give me mouth-to-mouth, anytime, anywhere, but only as long as he wasn't on duty. I laughed a little and told him I would take him up on his offer. He gave me this great big smile, and when he smiled, his striking smoky big blue eyes sparkled. His eyes and lips were mesmerizing. He honestly took my breath away. I truly stopped breathing for an instant, or maybe it was my heart that skipped a beat. I asked him if he would like to hook up some time and he said the pub would be closing at one a.m. We made plans to meet up at the beach where we met that same morning.

I went back to the girls, and we danced the night away. My friends and I left for home. When I arrived home, I put on my swimsuit under a sundress and grabbed a beach towel and a blanket. I arrived at the beach at about 1:30 a.m., and Paul arrived shortly after. He was riding a beautiful motorcycle. I complimented his cycle, and he asked me if I wanted to go for a spin. I asked for a rain check and he said, 'Sure any time.'

"We walked toward the beach and he took my blanket and placed it over the sand, and we sat down inches from each other. I asked him if he was up to giving me a few swimming lessons. He just looked at me with those eyes and shook his head saying no. He said he was off the clock but was more interested in practicing his CPR, the mouth-to-mouth part, if I wouldn't mind being his volunteer. I got up, took off my sundress and ran toward the water. He asked me what I was up to, and I said I am going to drown so a handsome young lifeguard can save me again. I played my part and he played his; he came into the water to save me. When he was swimming toward me, my heart was doing flip flops in my chest. When he carried me back to the beach, he pressed his lips on mine and started CPR. He showed me some serious passionate life saving techniques. We fell asleep on the beach in one another's arms.

"We were both awoken by squawking seagulls and barking dogs being walked on the beach. Paul got up on one elbow and lowered himself toward me. His lips touched mine. I remember thinking to myself what a great way to start the day, being kissed by this blond, muscular, well-bronzed Adonis. He was looking into my eyes, straight into my soul, with those mesmerizing eyes of his. I felt like I was under a trance. We fell in love on the beach that day, and we kept on seeing each other all summer.

"During that same summer, I was sending my resume to schools far and near and even some private schools abroad. I wanted to find a teaching job close to home because Paul was there, but I knew that was a long shot. I was lucky. By September, I was teaching a Grade 4 class at Shamrock Elementary School. I was so excited that I got a job close to home and wouldn't have to leave everyone I loved.

"Paul already had his job set up for him. He would be working alongside his best friend, Peter Lockwood. They had been friends since primary school. They were more like brothers; actually, they did everything together, even went to the same law school. They were inseparable. Peter and I became good friends, and I didn't mind sharing Paul with him. At times, I felt like the third wheel, but I believe Peter felt the same way at times too.

"Paul was to start working in September at the law offices of Lockwood and Sons. Mr. Lockwood Senior was retiring that January, leaving the firm to his son. Peter and his father had discussed bringing in a new partner, and the firm became Lockwood and Hamilton Attorneys at Law. Peter's father stayed on for a little while to help the boys with the existing cases. You know, he wanted them to get a feel of the place and the clients before he left. He wanted his existing clients to feel like they were getting the same exceptional service they always had.

"That summer, Paul wanted me to meet his parents. Our first meeting was to take place at the country club, as they were members there. I remember saying to myself that this is how the other half live. When I met his parents, I could see how disappointed they were in me. You can tell his parents did not like me much, and they didn't mind showing it either. As they talked amongst themselves, they just ignored me. They were talking about people and upcoming events that I knew nothing about. Paul must have sensed how out of place I felt, as he asked everyone to excuse us; he wanted to show me the gardens. I took hold of Paul's hand as he guided me outside. I started complaining the moment we stepped out into the garden. I told him that his parents hated me. They acted as though I wasn't even there. I don't think I was quite what they expected. I felt like, you know those old movies, where the rich boy falls in love with the common girl who lives on the other side of the tracks. I know they were hoping for a debutant or a girl that came from a well-to-do family. My family and his don't seem to hang with the same social groups.

"Paul was so ashamed at how his parents treated me, neglected me, and did not acknowledge my existence. He wanted me to not let them get under my skin. I know he was hoping that they would have shown me some kindness. Paul's parents believe that one marries for social advancement, and I am a social embarrassment to them. You see, Mr. and Mrs. Hamilton had always fixed Paul up with dates when he came home from school. He told me that he would go out to social events with these handpicked girls they had chosen for him because it pleased them. At that time, he wasn't looking for anything steady anyway.

"He loved his parents, but he needed his space. He said when he met me, he knew that I was different from those plastic Barbies he had always been set up with. I was that 'one in a million,' 'take your breath away,' and 'love at first sight' type of girl. He couldn't wait to introduce me as his girlfriend to all his friends and lastly his family.

"I took Paul to meet my parents after just a few dates, and they fell in love with him and him with them. My father was pleased with my choice and decided to adopt him as a son. Paul waited to introduce me to his parents. He wasn't ashamed of me or anything; he just didn't know how they would react. He was right on the money. His parents are boring stuffed shirts; they were nothing like Paul. He was hoping, for his sake at least, that his parents would show some decorum, being I was his guest at the club. I remember leaving the club, reassuring him that I didn't care if his parents didn't approve of me. I had told Paul that I was not dating his parents but him, and for him, I could look beyond his parent's dislike of me.

"We dated for a short time before he asked me to marry him. It was New Year's Eve. Paul had invited my parents, Peter, and myself, of course, to the country club as his guests. It was a dinner and a dance affair. All five of us were all dressed up like we were going to the royal ball. My mother and I had bought full-length gowns just for the occasion. My mother's dress was a beautiful apricot gown that just complimented her coloring and figure to a T.

My gown was a little risqué number that I would never have purchased in a million years, but my mother and the women selling us the gorgeous gowns said that the red gown was made for me. The dress was a long red strapless gown that fitted me like a second skin. My mother and the saleswoman said that everyone at the gala would be envious of me. The men would be envious of Paul, and the women would be envious that I am the belle of the ball.

"The night of the gala we Clark women were all made up. We had gone to the salon late that afternoon to have our hair and makeup done. When Paul arrived with a limousine, he looked so devilishly handsome, my legs felt like they couldn't sustain my weight. The best part was when he saw me coming down to join him from upstairs, his eyes were transfixed on me and I think he was salivating from the mouth. He took my hand, which was dressed in a long red glove, placed his lips on it, and said, 'My beautiful lady, your coach awaits.' At that precise moment, I felt like Cinderella and Paul was my Prince Charming. My mother looked stunning and my father looked dashing in his black tux. We all got into the limo, and off we were, on our way to the castle. Oh! I mean the country club."

Chapter 8

Renee continued with her story. "We arrived at the country club. A doorman opened our car door, and we debarked from our limo. Paul knew that my parents and I were out of our elements here, so we all followed Paul's every move. He squeezed my hand and told me that I was the most beautiful creature he had ever laid his eyes on and to please keep all the waltzes for him and only him." Renee laughed a little, remembering how happy she was that day. "I told him that I already had two requests for this evening's waltzes, and he looked at me in awe and said, 'Who the hell did you promise to dance with?' I whispered to him that I had promised to dance with the second and third best looking men in the club. He still couldn't guess, so I said, 'My dad and Peter, you fool!' I told him there were no other arms I would rather have wrapped around me than his. Then I kissed him playfully on the mouth. We entered the club and checked our coats and walked to the hall where all the festivities were taking place. The room was the most beautifully decorated room I had ever seen; it looked like we were walking into a frosty Neverland. Everything in the room sparkled like diamonds. We mingled a little before sitting down to an elaborate feast. Peter looked very dapper in his tuxedo, and his beautiful date, Carla, joined us at our table.

"We all sat down together, hoping to enjoy the evening festivities. I remember the menu included: a toss salad, smoked turkey, a delicious stuffing, mashed potatoes, corn, green beans, and homemade cranberry sauce, and for dessert, they had bread pudding with this marvelous creamy custard sauce drizzled on top. There was a bottle of wine on all the tables with refills as the bottles were emptied. After finishing our dessert, we all went out into the garden and waited for the tables to be emptied. When all was put away, a live band set up on stage for the second part of the evening to commence.

"Paul's parents were among the guests, but they did not make an effort to come see their son and his guests. Paul decided to introduce my family to his parents, and I was delighted to see that they were polite and welcomed them to the country club. Mr. Hamilton had then asked them how my parents liked their little country club and if they enjoyed the meal and were enjoying the music. My father responded, saying that everything was wonderful and that they had been very excited about coming to this glorious gala. He said they would have never had an opportunity to come to such an event like this if it wasn't for their wonderful son, Paul.

"After introductions, Paul asked me if I would like to dance to the first waltz of the evening. I remember I felt like I was floating on air. Paul was an amazing dancer; I could tell he took lessons. I was not a very confident dancer, but Paul made it very easy to follow his lead. I felt safe in his arms. We were dancing toward the garden when I said to him, 'Paul! You and I are like two pieces of a puzzle that fit perfectly together, don't you think?' He replied that he wanted our puzzle pieces to be joined together forever. As I was getting up on my toes to reach up and kiss him, he got down on one knee and took out this red velour ring box. As he opened the box, he asked me, 'Renee, would you do me the honor of becoming my wife?'

"I was shocked and blissfully happy, and of course, I said yes! He placed the beautiful huge princess-cut white-gold diamond ring on my finger, and we then kissed and embraced. It all felt like a dream, and I did not want to wake from it. But that special moment ended when Peter came out to the garden with Carla. They were each holding two glasses of champagne to share with their friends. Peter asked what we were doing out in the garden missing all the festivities when Paul shared with them the news. They were both very happy for us and congratulated us on the engagement.

"We all returned to the party laughing and cheering when my mother came toward us and jokingly suggested we perhaps slow down on our consumption of the vino. I then showed her my left hand with the engagement ring on my finger. She took hold of both our necks and wished us both the best. She then ran to tell my father, who was so happy about the news. I knew deep down he was happy to be having Paul as a son. Now, my father wouldn't need to adopt him, as he had suggested he would do on several occasions. The light in the hall came on so as to see what all the commotion was all about. Paul yelled out, 'The love of my life just agreed to be my wife!'

"Everyone started clapping and giving us their best wishes—but not Paul's parents. You could see that they disliked the idea. I saw Mr. and Mrs. Hamilton sneak out of the hall; I knew they did not want to wish their son and me their best wishes. You see, to them, this had to have been the worst news. I had mentioned to Paul that his parents did not look pleased, but he said to me that his parents would love me; they just had to get to know me better. Paul hoped they would eventually see in me what he had seen in me, but if they didn't, it would be too bad for them. He knew exactly what to say to make me feel better. Paul looked around for his parents but could not spot them anywhere. They had left without a word, and I think that was when he realized that his parents may never approve of me as his wife. Paul ran out to see if he could catch them, but he just missed them. I saw how upset he was that his parents left without even saying a word about their nuptials. He joined me just in time for the countdown.

"Everyone counted together: ten, nine, eight, seven, six, five, four, three, two, one. Then we all yelled, 'Happy New Year!' The song 'Auld Lang Syne' was played by the band, and I placed my arms around Paul's neck. We hugged each other and kissed like we were the only two people in the room. I then unlocked my arms around Paul's neck and wished everyone around us a happy new year. We all started blowing our horns and had a glass of champagne to toast the coming new year. Paul called for the limo right after finishing our champagne, and we all said our goodbyes, got our coats, and left in the limo. My parents thanked Paul for the wonderful evening and congratulated us again on their impending nuptials.

"After dropping off my parents, Paul asked me to go with him to see his parents. He wanted to know why they had left in such a hurry. We knew why, but he wanted to hear it from them. When we arrived at his parent's, he unlocked the door and we just walked in. We found them both together in the den. As we entered the den, Mrs. Hamilton turned around to face us. Paul asked his parents why they had left without congratulating them or saying their goodbyes to everyone. Mrs. Hamilton could not keep quiet. She shouted, 'Do you think we are happy about the news that you are going to marry beneath you! She can dress the part of a debutant, but she will never be one of us and we will never accept her as a daughter. We have introduced you to so many acceptable, proper girls and this is the one you chose to dishonor us with." I remember her exact words, she said, 'Shame on you! I will never accept her as being a part of our family. So if you marry this girl, it will be without our approval.' I immediately got up and thanked them for a lovely evening, then walked out. Paul ran after me and said how ashamed of his parents he was and that he wished that his parents could be more like my parents. I felt so bad for him. I knew it hurt him and it hurt me because I knew I would never be accepted as part of their family.

"You see, my parents liked Paul right from the first time they met. They accepted Paul into our home as part of our family. His relationship with my father was like father and son, and my mom just loved him. She thought he was a real catch compared to the other young men I had introduced them to over the years. My mom thought he was intelligent, charming, thoughtful, loving, respectful, and handsome. Most of all, she loved the way he made me so very happy.

"That summer we got married. His parents did not like it but did not want to lose their only son. They paid for the entire wedding. It was like being in a fairy tale. I arrived at the church in a coach drawn by two white horses. The church was decorated with flowers and candles. It was just splendid. It was a dream wedding any girl would wish for, but all I needed for this day to be perfect was Paul. When I walked down the aisle with my father at my side, all I could see was Paul and how handsome he was at the front of the church, waiting for me to reach his side. When he took my hand from my father's, he told me that I looked beautiful and he said that he loved me. The ceremony went on without a hitch; the rings were exchanged and then we kissed. Then the pastor introduced us to all our friends and family as Mr. and Mrs. Paul Hamilton. After the applause, Paul whispered, 'I love you, Mrs. Hamilton,' and I replied, 'I love you back, Mr. Hamilton,' and then we kissed again.

"We ate and danced. I threw the bouquet and he threw the garter, and then we left in a hurry to go and start our honeymoon. First, we drove off to a destination unknown to me. I had asked Paul where we were going, but he said it was a surprise. Then we parked in front of a big house and he said to me, 'Mrs. Hamilton, I bought this house for you, for us to begin our new life together. I thought, what better place to start our first night as husband and wife.' I was overwhelmed and shocked that we had a home of our own. He opened my door on the passenger side and carried me into this beautiful big house. He then carried me straight to the master suit, where champagne and chocolate-covered strawberries were placed next to the bed. We were not hungry for food, but we were hungry for each other. We made love over and over again that night, all over the house. We ended up sleeping on a blanket in the living room in front of the fireplace in each other's arms. I felt so happy and safe in his muscular arms.

"The next morning, he got up and brought coffee, orange juice, and croissants that he had purchased the day before for our breakfast. After eating our breakfast, we decided to take a bubble bath for two. We devoured each other in the tub while feasting on the chocolate-covered strawberries and drinking champagne. We towel dried each other, and then made love to each other again in our queen size bed. I didn't know that a person could be so deliriously happy being with another person. Our bodies reacted to each other's every touch. With Paul, I knew I was home, I was where I was supposed to be, and with whom I was supposed to be with.

"We went to Paris for our honeymoon. The food there, with its smell and taste, was just so darn scrumptious. The weight I would have put on from all the eating was lost in the many hours of love making each day. The people in Paris are so joyous, and they seem to live life in slow motion, like they have all the time in the world. Paris is the place for love or, as the French say, *amour*. Paul had promised me that we would go back to Paris on our fifth wedding anniversary, but that was another promise he wasn't going to keep.

"We came back home after our honeymoon to our new house and our jobs. We were going to live a normal life together. We were married for an entire month when he was asked to go to New York on business. Paul was there on the same day and in the same place as the attacks on the Twin Towers. My husband died that day, like so many others, and my world crumbled down like the Twin Towers. I had lost my best friend, my lover, my partner, and the father of my unborn child. Oh! Erase that last part, please! I don't want anyone to know that I am pregnant. I am not ready to tell anyone the good news yet, but when I am ready, I will tell them myself."

"Renee, I am obliged to keep our sessions confidential. I am sorry about your loss and congratulations on the good news of the baby. The baby is good news, isn't it?" Dr. Chamberlain asked.

Renee sighed, then replied, "Yes, it's great news. I already love him or her, and the baby is a great reason to carry on. I am afraid, though. How do I do this all alone? Am I ready to be a mom? I can't take care of myself; that's why I'm here. How am I supposed to take care of an innocent child? Am I a lost cause?"

"I think you are too hard on yourself and I believe that this baby is going to be very lucky to have you as a mother. I know you've had a rough few weeks, but with Dr. Ross, the nursing staff, and myself helping you, we will get you through this. I will prescribe you something for depression. Renee, you know that it is normal to be depressed when losing a loved one, right?"

"Dr. Chamberlain, I don't want to take any medication that will harm my baby."

"Renee, sometimes one needs to take medication to get well," the doctor replied. "If you decide not to take the medication I am prescribing for you, I really think your depression might just take over your entire being, and then your baby will not even have a fighting chance to take its first breath or meet his mother. Is this what you want for Paul's baby?"

Renee sighed. "No, you know it's not. I will do everything you and Dr. Ross tell me to do."

"Great, then I want to see you on a regular basis, starting tomorrow and then twice a week until we get you better. I will tell Dr. Ross that if he wants to discharge you, he can, and I will see you tomorrow. Here's my card. You call this number here and my secretary will set up a time for us to meet tomorrow. Here are two prescriptions that I want you to pick up at our pharmacy downstairs. So, I will see you tomorrow Renee at my office?" said Dr. Chamberlain.

Renee nodded.

***

After both doctors agreed on a plan of action, Dr. Ross went to see his patient.

As he walked into her room he said, "I'm very pleased that Dr. Chamberlain will be seeing you on a regular basis. We both think you are ready to be discharged. Renee, you have to take care of yourself. You need to eat because you are eating for two. The healthier the mother, the healthier the child will be. I also want you to take prenatal vitamins, as they are for expecting mothers. You have to take one every day, and you need to see your family doctor on a monthly basis, at least. Also I want you to sleep eight hours a day and exercise. You need to include the five food groups in your daily menu. I am talking about fruits, vegetables, proteins, breads, and milk. Do you think you can follow this regime, Renee? If you agree to all my demands you can go home as soon as you are dressed. Do you want me to get a nurse to call your parents to pick you up?"

"No! If they can just call me a cab. I'm just so ready to get out of here. Dr. Ross, I just want to thank you again for everything."

Renee left to take her cab home and to start her new life.

Chapter 9

Renee opened the front door and entered her home. As she closed the door behind her, she could feel the emptiness and the loneliness encircling her heart. She could not endure the pain that this house gave her, so she went directly to her bedroom, where she curled up in her bed and cried herself to sleep.

Later on that same evening, her parents went to visit their daughter at the hospital, but they were informed that she had been discharged earlier that afternoon. They wondered why she did not let them know that she had gone home. They decided to go check up on her before going home.

As James and Christine arrived, they tried the door, but it was locked, so they rang the doorbell and still no answer. James took out his key, and they entered the darkened home. James and Christine were beginning to get worried again. They called out to her, but no one answered. They started lighting up the house, as they could not see in the darkness. They began looking for Renee and found her sleeping in her bed, dead to the world. They decided to let her sleep and come back In the morning to check up on her.

***

Renee slept well all night. She was eventually awoken by the garbage truck picking up garbage on their street. She felt ill again and had to run to the bathroom. After vomiting, she felt a little better. She walked downstairs and noticed that the light on the answering machine was flickering. She pushed the message button on the machine and listened to the many messages that were recorded. She listened to her friends and neighbors calling to pay their respect and asking her if she needed them for any reason, as they would be there for her. One call was from her school asking much the same. The director wanted to know when she thought she would be back at work. Returning to work was the furthest thing on her mind.

Renee felt faint again, so she rested on the sofa to wait for the spell to pass. When it did, she got up but immediately felt ill again. She ran to the washroom and knelt head first in the toilet. She still had severe morning sickness, but it was more like all-day sickness. She hoped that this nausea would subside soon. The nurses had told her that after three months, which was the duration of the first trimester, her morning sickness should pass. They also advised her to eat soda crackers. It was something to settle her stomach when she felt ill. She could not wait for the second trimester to begin so that she wouldn't have to look at her sickly reflection in the toilet water. Her body was so frail that it took all of her energy to climb the stairs to her bedroom.

She rested peacefully until her parents awakened her later that afternoon. Her mother and father came over to check up on their daughter. Christine had asked if she had eaten today, and Renee told her that she didn't have the strength to make herself anything to eat and that she was still nauseated from the flu. Her mother said that she had brought her some nourishment. Her parents went out and got her some groceries. They picked up some milk, vegetables, fruits, eggs, and bread, as they knew she had nothing in her refrigerator. Christine had made her some chicken soup with dry toast and a steaming hot cup of tea.

Renee was grateful for her parents' help. Her mother told her that they would not leave her until she had eaten all the food on the tray. Renee had thanked her, but the smell of the food made her gag and she grabbed the waste paper basket and heaved bile since there was no food in her stomach.

Renee had not eaten anything since she left the hospital. James was worried about her and asked if she wanted to return to the hospital because she did not look well at all. Christine took the soup away but wanted her to try and eat the toast and tea. Renee started nibbling on the toast and sipping the tea so that her parents would worry less about her. She decided that perhaps it was the right time to tell her parents about the pregnancy.

"Mom, Dad, can you both sit here beside me? I have something to tell you."

They both sat down on either side of her, with worried faces.

"Mom, Dad, I want to tell you that the symptoms I am having—the vomiting, the tiredness, and the nausea—are normal symptoms of pregnancy. You are going to be grandparents."

Her parents were in awe. They looked at each other, then started yelling, "Oh my God, Renee! Why did you not tell us? How long have you known? Are you sure?"

"Yes, I am sure," Renee replied. "I was as surprised as you are now when the doctor gave me the news. I did not tell you right away because I needed it to sink in before I gave everyone the good news. I'm going to be a single mother in about seven months, and I am a little—no, more like a lot—worried about doing this on my own, without Paul's help."

Renee's parents locked their arms around her neck and hugged her; they were so pleased. Christine said to Renee, "Sweetheart, don't worry. We will be here to help and support you throughout your pregnancy and after you have this miracle baby. Won't we, James?"

"Yes, dear, whatever she needs. We will help our little girl out."

Relieved, Renee thanked her parents and said, "I really needed to hear that because, right now, I feel like I'm all by myself and it scares me to death."

Renee's father went over and whispered to her in her ear, "Sweetheart, you are never alone. Your mother and I are here for you, and I know that Paul is watching over you from heaven. Don't forget that God only gives you what you can handle and you are a strong woman. I believe you can take on any challenge or obstacles that are thrown your way. Don't forget, you work with a classroom of thirty students every single day and make it look easy. So don't you worry. You will do just fine. You will find that inner strength when you need it the most."

Her parents both kissed her and congratulated her on the wonderful news. Christine voiced, "You look so tired. I think your dad and I will let ourselves out and you get some needed rest. You call us if you need anything?"

Renee had asked her parents not to tell anyone about her pregnancy. She wanted to keep her secret for just a little longer.

"Whatever you want, dear. The secret is safe with us. Now, you go get some rest, and if you get hungry, there is soup in the refrigerator," Christine advised her.

Renee thanked them again. Her eyes closed before they even left the house.

***

Renee's parents were so happy for their daughter. Even though she had lost her husband, she would now have a part of him in this child. After leaving their daughter, they decided to go out to the restaurant to celebrate the news of them becoming grandparents. As they entered their favorite restaurant, they had to wait to be seated because it was busy. Fortunato's was known for being the best Italian restaurant around, so it was always busy, every day of the week. They decided to sit out on the patio until a table was available. They were so excited that this baby might be the only person that would make their daughter start to live again. They had been very worried about their daughter's well-being.

James and Christine were well known by the staff at Fortunato's since they were regulars. Their name was called out on the intercom; their table was ready. After being seated, their waitress asked them if they would like something from the bar and James said, "We would like to order an inexpensive bottle of red wine, please. We are celebrating tonight."

The manager sent them a very expensive bottle of Sangiovese on the house. Their waitress poured the wine for them. Then James raised his glass to his wife and made a toast, "To our daughter's pregnancy, that this child fills her with joy and takes away the hurt that she has in her heart." They touched each other's glasses and took a sip of their wine.

Then Christine made a toast, "To becoming grandparents!"

Then James made one last toast, "To Paul, rest in peace and keep watch over your family."

Tears began rolling down both their eyes when the waitress interrupted their teary eyed moment. "Sorry! Did I interrupt something? I can come back in a few minutes if you are not ready to order."

"No, we are ready to order," James replied. "We will have the special, vegetarian lasagna, and we would like to start with a side Caesar salad and some garlic bread, please. We're famished."

When the waitress left, James started remembering when his wife gave him the news that she was expecting their baby girl, Renee. "Christine, do you remember the day I came home from work and you wanted to go out for dinner at McDonald's? I thought to myself, 'Anywhere but there,' but you were adamant about eating there. So, we went to McDonald's and you ordered two Happy Meals for us, and I thought you were going crazy, that you must be going into your second childhood. I had asked you why Happy Meals, and you said soon we'd be eating here all the time with our own bundle of joy. I couldn't believe that we were going to be parents. We had tried for years, and I gave up hope, but the good Lord blessed us with our own little miracle."

"Yes, James! I remember. I was the one carrying that bundle of joy, did you forget?" Christine replied.

James took hold of his wife's hand and said, "Renee's going to be a great mother because she learned from the very best mother I have ever known."

Their salads arrived and they ate while suggesting names for this new life that Renee was carrying. They were wondering if it would be a girl or a boy.

James stated, "It doesn't matter as long as he or she is healthy and that this baby helps Renee come out of this depressive state she is in."

Christine lifted up the glass and said, "Here, here."

Their lasagna arrived and they ate, drank, and laughed over their meal.

The Clarks did not notice that Ted and Nancy were sitting at the bar, waiting to be seated. They were eating here instead of at their posh exclusive country club because they could not face their friends after all the smut printed in the local newspaper.

"Look at them, they are having a little party over there and the staff is treating them like royalty and we can't even get a table. In this establishment, we are treated like the riff raff. How RUDE!" Nancy said to her husband. "The Clarks don't seem to be too upset about losing Paul. I think that the speech James gave at Paul's funeral was all a big performance. That family never really cared for our son; they are all money hungry scavengers. They thought they won the lottery when Renee married Paul, but their meal ticket is dead and buried."

Ted conveyed, "Darling, they are probably celebrating getting Paul's life insurance policy. They should all die and go to hell for the shame they brought our family and the disrespect they are giving to our son. Paul is probably turning in his grave now that he sees the true colors of that family."

Appalled, they both got up and left the restaurant.

Chapter 10

On September 11, 2001, New York City was in complete chaos. Al-Qaeda terrorists hijacked four Boeing jets (two 767s and two 757s) on the way to Los Angeles and San Francisco. The first American Airline crashed into the North Tower of the World Trade Center. It was said that the hijackers took over the plane with as many as eighty or more passengers and crew. They were all killed on impact. The second American Airline crashed into the South Tower of the World Trade Center; this time killing more innocent passengers. The third plane crashed into the Pentagon, and the fourth plane crashed and burned in a field before it had a chance to get to its destined target—all because of the heroism of the crew members and passengers, who fought the terrorists and crashed the plane before reaching its destination. All the people on that plane died. This attack was a strategically coordinated terrorist attack on the United States of America.

Many American citizens were lost during this strike on American soil. The World Trade Center was the landlord to various government organizations and many financial firms. It also housed an underground shopping center, the Mall, which included many vendors and shoppers.

Many innocent people died in the burning building. The lucky ones who made it out of the building said that the building shook and was filled with smoke. Some survivors described their experience like being in a big tidal wave of smoke, making it hard to breathe and see where they were going. Many heroic first responders died trying to save and protect the good people trapped and injured in this crumbling inferno. The streets were filled with screaming, frightened people trying to escape the World Trade Center building in Lower Manhattan, New York City.

Paul was having a meeting with someone from the Cantor Fitzgerald Firm. This firm specialized in institutional equity, fixed income sales and trading and serving the middle market with banking and commercial real estate financing.

At the time of the first attack, people were frantically fleeing the building. People were frightened and running for cover. The people who worked in offices above the impact zone had no chance of fleeing the World Trade Center. Many good people died. Paul was in the towers during the attack, but luckily, he was away from the strike. Paul would have died if not for leaving a file in his rented car.

He was on his way down to fetch the file when the attack took place. He was just getting out of the elevator when the building shook as if by a massive earthquake. After exiting the elevator, people were running for the exits of the building. He thought how ant-like everyone seemed, fleeing from their home when being attacked.

As he was trying to follow the hundreds of people fleeing the towers to safety, he saw an old woman was trampled on as she tried to leave the building. He could not just leave her there, so he tore himself through the crowd of people and pulled the poor woman up. He then exited the building with her under his arm. As they left, the building was filled with smoke and they could not see the fireball of debris, much like a firing comet, soaring down from above and falling straight toward them. Gazers were shouting, "Watch out!" But Paul could not hear their warning cries. The old lady ran from under his arm as quickly as she could the moment they reached the light of day. Thankful that he was safely out of danger, Paul bent over and took a moment to inhale a well-deserved breath of fresh air, but all that he breathed in was dust and smoke. He had stopped only inches away from the fireball, which would have burnt him badly.

Debris from the crash continued to rain down. Although he was saved from being hit by the fireball, stopping for that single breath of air got Paul hit on the head. He fell to the ashy and glass-covered ground. A first response worker rushed over and carried him safely away from the collapsing building. Paul had lost consciousness for about five minutes before awakening. He was confused, dizzy, and his eyesight seemed blurred. The first responder stayed with him until he awoke and advised him to seek medical help. Paul told the first responder that he was fine, but asked if he could help him get up since he was still shaky. When back on his feet, Paul thanked his rescuer for all of his help and told him that he should go help those in need. Paul's head was throbbing and he felt dizzy.

Crowds of people were running to evacuate Lower Manhattan. Paul walked away from all the commotion he didn't know where to go but he just walked away from there. Now that he seemed to be at a safe distance away from all the noise, the screams, and alarms from first response vehicles, he found himself a quiet restful spot to rest his aching body and throbbing head for a few moments. As he lay his head down, he was out cold.

Chapter 11

Rachel was coming home from a busy day at the supermarket. She was watching the terrorist attack on the television. The store was very quiet; everyone wanted to be with their families in the safety of their homes. After Rachel was done with her shift, she walked over to the daycare to pick up her two-and-half-year-old son, Philip. Walking home, Rachel asked him about his day and he told her about playing outside with his friends, but that today, they did not get to go outside.

"Mommy, did you bring me a surprise from the store today?" Philip asked. "I was a good boy for Miss Carpenter." Rachel told him he would just have to wait until they got home to see.

When they arrived safely home, they were surprised and frightened to find a man sleeping on their welcome mat, in front of their screen door. Rachel put her son down in the safety of their fenced backyard.

"Philip, I want you to play out here while Mommy goes and starts dinner. Okay?"

"K, Mommy," Philip said.

Rachel made sure to latch the gate and went to see the stranger on her porch. Rachel tried to wake him from his sleep so he could leave the premises. Rachel spoke softly, "Mister, mister, wake up. You're sleeping in front of my front door. You have to wake up. Come on, get up."

She tried shaking him and even rolled him on his back, but he did not even move a muscle. She knew he was not dead because his chest was moving up and down. She also knew he was not a down-and-out kind of guy because he was wearing designer clothes and his shoes looked like they'd cost about what she'd make at the store in a week. This guy was what her friends would call "Grade A beef."

What was she thinking? This guy was a stranger and he had to go. She looked for any identification, but he had none. She thought that this man must have been one of the survivors at the towers during the attack. She decided to be a good Samaritan and take this poor man inside her home and see if she could help him out. She had trouble dragging him into the house, as he was somewhat heavier than she could carry.

When she got him settled on the living room carpet, she went out to get her son, who had been crying and wanting to come in. She consoled him and gave him a kiss and apologized for not coming to get him quicker. She placed him in his high chair and gave him some Honey Nut Cheerios and his sippy cup filled with milk.

Rachel told Philip, "Now, you be a good boy and eat this little snack as Mommy sees to a man."

Philip seemed content for the time being. Rachel thought she should call 911, but this guy might be thankful when he comes to and be appreciative for all her help. Maybe there would be some token of his appreciation, like money for taking care of him. She did need money; with what little she made at the store and the cost of daycare, she was broke. She had to give up her car because she could not pay for gas or the upkeep of the vehicle. Even if she got no reward, it was the right thing to do. She looked him over and saw a little blood and a goose egg on his forehead. She went to the kitchen, got an ice pack from the freezer, and placed it on the lump, then put a pillow under his head. He did not even stir.

She decided as long as this stranger was out she would go to the kitchen and look after her son. She would deal with his man as soon as her son was down for the night.

Chapter 12

Macaroni and cheese with cut up wieners was on the menu tonight. Thankfully, this was one of her son's favorite meals. He also loved pancakes, spaghetti with meatballs, McDonald's chicken nuggets and Happy Meals, and cheese pizza. She decided to make two boxes of mac and cheese just in case the man in her living room got up and was hungry. She wanted to be hospitable. Philip had just finished his supper when she heard her house guest moaning from the living room. She was afraid now that he was getting up from his slumber. Rachel washed Philip's hands and face and placed him in his playpen with a few of his favorite toys. She gave him a kiss on the top of his red curly head.

Rachel then took up all the courage she had and went over to see her house guest. She found him sitting up and looking a little lost in his surroundings. She walked toward him and introduced herself.

"Hi! I'm Rachel."

He just sat there looking at her like she was from another planet. Then he asked her, "Rachel, where am I?"

"You're in my home. What is your name if you don't mind me asking?"

Looking confused, Paul replied, "My name is . . . My name is . . . That's odd. I can't remember my name."

"Okay!" Rachel replied. "Do you know where you came from? Where do you live?"

He sat down on the sofa and looked dazed, then began holding his head and rocking himself back and forth.

Rachel sat beside him and tapped his shoulder, saying, "That's okay! You'll see, it will all come back to you. Were you at the towers today? You know, the terrorist attack?"

"I don't know what you are talking about. Are we at war? Tell me what's going on. Why can't I remember who I am and who you are?"

Rachel, trying to comfort him, said, "I don't know, but you have a big goose egg on top of your head. I think you may have a concussion, and I would guess you have amnesia because of it. I believe that's why you can't remember who you are or where you come from. Do you want me to call an ambulance? You need some medical help."

"Rachel, if I could just rest a little, I'm sure I'll be back to my old self, whoever that is. Would you mind if I stayed here and rested a while? Then I'll be out of your hair."

"I guess that would be all right, but I think you should think about going to the hospital," Rachel replied.

He closed his eyes, and Rachel's house guest was out again. She decided to look up concussion on the Internet. She typed in "concussion" and it read: *"A mild head injury, also known as mild traumatic brain injury, a concussion is the most widespread and least severe of traumatic brain injuries. It results in temporary, short-lived failures of mental function and is commonly caused by injuries involving a direct blow to the head or acceleration/deceleration forces. The signs of concussion include loss of consciousness for no more than thirty minutes, dizziness and confusion, vomiting, visual problems and amnesia."*

Rachel burst, "Amnesia, BINGO! That's probably what John Doe here has. Now let's see what this thing says about amnesia."

She read on: *"Amnesia—memory loss—is one of the most common symptoms of concussion and may be either retrograde (when you forget memories previous to the injury) or anterograde (when you lose memories formed after the incident.)"*

Rachel vocalized, "That's it! John Doe has a concussion. I remember someone at the store telling me that her husband had a concussion and they had to keep waking him up so he wouldn't fall into a coma. Oh my! I will have to stay up with you tonight, Mr. Doe, so that you do not fall into a coma on my watch. I hope you are worth all the trouble, handsome. John, you have to wake up."

After her prodding, Paul finally responded, "What do you want? Can't you see I was sleeping? Do you have something for the pain in my head?"

"I'll get you some aspirins." She ran to the kitchen to get him two pills and a glass of water, then came back into the living room. She gave Paul the two aspirins, hoping it would relieve his pain. Paul thanked her, then closed his eyes and rested his head on the sofa once more.

Chapter 13

Morning came very slowly for Rachel. She kept a watchful eye on "John" (Paul) all night. She didn't mind watching him because he was quite a beautiful looking man. She noticed that he did not have a wedding band on his left hand, not even a white band to say he had one but wasn't wearing it. His fingers were totally tanned; no sign of him being married. This man was single. She thanked God for answering her prayers; God must have put this man on her front porch for a reason. If she looked after him, he may start having feelings for her and who knows what could happen after that—Mrs. John Doe did have a ring to it.

But then she thought to herself that there were probably dozens of girls flaunting themselves at this attractive man on a daily basis. Rachel couldn't believe her luck. This gorgeous man was in her living room, and at the moment, he didn't know who he was, so maybe, just maybe, this nobody of a girl could turn his head just enough that she could be a contender in the race to win his heart. He probably goes out with girls that rank a ten on the sexy girl list, and Rachel knew she was maybe a seven or seven and a half on a good hair day. Rachel had curly red hair and was very petite and thin. She was a no-fuss, wholesome type of girl. She knew that she didn't have the curves that most men gaze at.

Rachel was a mother, and she was lucky if she got a moment to brush her hair or teeth before leaving the house for work. Philip was her life, and there was never time to go out with the girls or to find a man. There never seemed to be enough time in the day. Sometimes, Rachel was lucky and got to take a quick shower before she started her day, but only if she was up early enough. Then Philip would wait for her in his crib, ready to start his day. Every day was the same: they had a schedule to stick to or Rachel would be late for work.

Every day began with a change of a pull-up diaper and getting her little man dressed. After the toiletries, she would sit Philip in his high chair with some cereal and milk and some type of fruit. Rachel always found the time to drink a cup of instant coffee while getting Philip's bags ready for daycare. She needed the coffee to kick-start her day.

This morning was a little different, though. Rachel was exhausted because she had watched over the man all night. Usually, she got to Philip before he would wake up, but not today, she could hear him crying in his bedroom. He wanted out and he also wanted a dry pull-up diaper.

Rachel responded to his cry, "Okay! Okay! I am coming." When she got to him, he was sobbing. He then reached out his arms to her, wanting to be picked up. "Good morning, sweetheart. How was your sleep? I'm sorry Mommy is a little late this morning. She didn't get much sleep, but I know you don't care, do you? Well, let's get that wet, stinky diaper off and get you washed up and changed. Now, let's get back on schedule." She was hoping to get Philip potty trained soon, but diaper changing was so much easier. She made a little note for John to read when he got up. She checked up on him and he was still sleeping so she left him to start her day.

***

John got up after hearing the phone ring and began rubbing his head. His goose egg had shrunken down some, which was a good thing, but his head still throbbed. When he sat up, he found the note on the coffee table. He began reading it. The letter read:

Dear John (That's what I'm calling you),

Philip, my son and I have gone to daycare and work. We will be back home by 4:30. There is food in the fridge if you get hungry. Hope you are feeling better this morning.

Please make yourself at home.

Rachel

He could not believe that there were still people out there like Rachel. She looked after him all night and left him in her home alone. He could be a thief or a hardened criminal. He didn't think he was, but then again, he really did not know for sure since he still didn't know who he was. His memory did not come back as he had hoped. He was still a stranger to himself. He knew that the name "John" had to change because he didn't like it much. He thought to himself that he would rather be named Darren, but Darren who? He came up with "Darren Michaels."

Paul got up to find the washroom. After relieving himself, he looked at himself in the mirror and said to his reflection, "Hello, Darren Michaels! Yes! That name will do until I remember my real name. You, Darren, need a shower in the worst way. Rachel did say to make myself at home, so I guess I can take a shower."

The shower felt so good on his aching body. He stayed there for a long time, enjoying the heat.

Stepping out of the shower, he dried himself but did not want to get into his dirty clothes, which were piled on the bathroom floor. He would need to wash them before putting them on again. He would just have to wear the big bath towel until his clothes were washed and dried. He went out looking for a washer and dryer and found them in the basement, down from the kitchen. He put his clothes in the washer, put some laundry detergent in, and started the wash. *That was a simple task,* he thought to himself.

He marched up to the kitchen and looked into the fridge for something to eat. He was famished. He found some orange juice, margarine, milk, and some strawberry jam. He looked for the bread; he would have toast and jam for breakfast. He found the bread and then placed them into the toaster. While he waited, he enjoyed his orange juice. He would kill for a cup of coffee, though, and thought she must have a coffee machine somewhere. He did not find a coffee machine, but he did find some instant coffee in the cupboard, so he boiled himself a little water, then added it to his instant coffee. It was not a bad cup of coffee. He then went and lay down because his head was throbbing again.

Chapter 14

Rachel had dropped Philip at the daycare, but she had no time to talk to his teacher because she was going to be late for work. She gave Philip a kiss goodbye and ran off to catch the bus to the supermarket where she worked cash. She was lucky she got to the bus stop just in time, as it was about to leave without her. This meant she would be on time for her shift. She did not love her job, but it paid her bills and it worked out with Philip's daycare.

She put on her store blazer and was at her station, awaiting her first customer. Rachel was always pleasant when speaking to her customers.

"Good morning, Mrs. Blake, how are you doing this morning? I hope that yesterday's devastation did not injure anyone that you knew?"

Rachel knew most of her customers by name because she had been working there since she was pregnant with her son. She was the best cashier they had, as she was young and picked up quickly when new programs or machinery had to be installed. Rachel also worked extra hours or took a few more shifts during the week so that she had a little extra money for incidentals.

She was lucky her grandmother took her in when she had become pregnant, as her parents had kicked her out. Her poor grandmother died in her sleep months before she was due to have Philip. Every day, she thanked God for her, as her grandmother had given her the house she was now living in her will. If not for her, then Rachel and Philip would probably be living in a rundown, one-bedroom apartment somewhere less safe.

The house was located in Lower Manhattan. The small single-family home needed major repairs, but she could only do so much and could not afford to pay someone to work on it. To make ends meet, Rachel would buy day-old bread and meat, and vegetables that were bruised or a little sticky. Sometimes, Richard, the produce manager, would put aside produce that was not sellable to the public for her. Rachel was thankful for all the help because everything was getting more and more expensive, while her paycheck seemed to always have the same amount of money written on it. Rachel could use a raise, but the last person to ask for a raise was given less scheduled hours to work the following week. She needed this job. All the free food or extra hours helped tremendously.

During her lunch, Rachel often went to the nearby library, which was only a few blocks away, and read on medicine. She eventually wanted to work in a doctor's office or a hospital as a medical secretary or even an intake worker. Rachel had been planning to start college in the fall when she got pregnant and had to change her plans for her future. Rachel had done well in school, and she knew she would have succeeded at anything she put her mind to, but all that changed. Rachel's entire world changed when she was expecting Philip, but he was worth that change.

Someday when Philip was in school, and she didn't have to pay for daycare anymore, she hoped to be able to take night courses and get her degree in something. That was her dream but dreams change—her life was proof of that.

The afternoon passed by, just like any other day. At four o'clock, Rachel had to rush out to catch the bus if she was to pick up Philip on time.

Every hour of the day seemed to be scheduled for her. Every day, the same routine: wake up, get Philip ready to take him to daycare, catch the bus, get to work, work cash, go to the library if it wasn't raining, work cash again, run for the bus, pick up Philip, walk home, start supper, bath time, read bedtime story, put Philip to bed, tidy kitchen, wash up for bed, say her prayers, and fall to sleep. That was her boring life, but yesterday was a change in Rachel's routine and she liked it. She had worked it into her day too, so maybe, just maybe, this new stranger would make her life less boring and more exciting.

Rachel desperately needed more excitement in her life. She was only twenty-one. Twenty-one, and she was living like she was in her late thirties. She really had no life, at least no social life to speak of. Perhaps John would be that new something that would change her life. Rachel thought that this stranger was worth changing her life for. Even though Rachel didn't know this stranger very well, and he didn't know himself really either at the moment, maybe she would be the one to change his life too.

Entering the daycare, Rachel saw Philip with his coat and his backpack on already, waiting for his mother to take him home. He was always so happy to see Rachel when she walked in. He would run into her arms and give her a big hug and a kiss. Rachel looked forward to seeing her little man after a hard day at work. Philip had a good day; he was laughing and jumping all around, but he was ready to go home. Rachel was wondering how everything was going at home. Was John still there or was he gone? Did he remember who he was yet, or was he still "John"? She would see soon enough.

Chapter 15

Walking into the house, Rachel saw that it had been cleaned. All the toys had been picked up from the floor, and it also smelled like someone had been cooking, so it was safe to say that John was still there and he was making himself at home, just as she suggested in her note.

"Hi, Rachel! How was your day at work today? Now, who is this big fellow holding your hand?" John asked.

"Hi, John! I would like you to meet my son, Philip. My day went well, thank you for asking. How was your day? You seem to look better, and you are up and about, so that's a good sign," Rachel said.

"Yes! I am feeling somewhat better. I thought for your kindness, I would clean up a little and would prepare something for us to eat since you had worked all day and must be tired. I also thought that since I cannot remember my identity, that I chose a name for myself. I am now Darren Michaels."

"Thank you so much. No one has ever cooked for me and Philip before. This is so kind of you, Darren, to have even thought of doing something to help me out. I think I'm going to cry," Rachel stated.

Darren reached out and said, "Please, I didn't think I would make you cry by just preparing you a little stir-fry and rice. I promise I will not help you out again if it makes you upset."

"I'm not crying because I am upset you made me dinner. I'm crying because of the kindness that you have shown to my son and I. This is the nicest thing anyone has ever done for me since my grandmother passed." Rachel walked toward him and hugged him for being such a nice and decent man.

"Well, I think after the kindness that you have shown this stranger—taking me into your home and taking care of me last night—that I should be the one who owes you a debt of gratitude. Now, you two better wash up, and I will serve up some of my hopefully tasty stir-fry," Darren said.

Rachel picked up her son and said, "Okay, little man, let's get washed up. Looks like we are in for a treat tonight."

They both washed up and hurriedly returned to the kitchen to taste that sweet smelling stir-fry.

After Philip was safely sitting in his high chair, Darren started serving them their supper. Philip was not at all thankful for this supper; he did not like to eat vegetables, as they did not taste good. Just his luck, Darren also prepared some noodles with old cheddar cheese for Philip, just in case he was not a vegetable lover. Philip was so happy that he did not have to eat the yucky vegetables because he was always famished after a day at daycare.

Philip tasted the noodles and said, "These noodles are good, Mommy."

Rachel looked at Darren and started to laugh.

"Rachel, try the stir-fry and tell me what you think. If you don't like it, there is enough noodles for you as well."

Rachel took a mouthful and said to him after chewing her food, "Darren, you must be a chef or had been a chef in your former life. This is amazing! It tastes even better than it smells."

"Oh! I'm so pleased. I wasn't sure if you would like it."

"Darren, did you get some of your memories back?" she asked. "Do you remember making this recipe before?"

"I wish, but no. I found a recipe book from that shelf over there," Darren admitted.

"Philip and I want to thank you for this delicious meal you prepared for us tonight. Since you made supper, I will clean up and wash the dishes," Rachel said.

Darren refused and commented, "Rachel, you worked all day and must be tired. You go up and give Philip his bath and get him ready for bed while I clean up down here."

"Are you sure, Darren? I don't mind doing it."

"I'm sure. You go up and spend some quality time with your son. I got this covered."

Rachel walked over and hugged him. "Darren, you are the nicest man I have ever met, and if you have someone out there waiting for you, she's a very lucky lady. Thank you for all this. It means so much to me, you don't even know." Then she turned to Philip and said, "Philip, let's get you out of that chair and get you washed up and ready for bed." Then after a moment's thought, Rachel asked Darren, "Darren, when you are done down here, would you like to come up and join us?"

"Okay! I'll be up there as soon as I'm done cleaning up the kitchen."

Chapter 16

Renee was home resting as she always did since Paul's death. She had decided to take a sabbatical from work, being she was pregnant and still grieving Paul's death. Renee couldn't even get herself to watch television, as with Christmas around the corner, it was "Ho! Ho! Ho! Merry Christmas" this and "Merry Christmas" that when all Renee could relate to was with Mr. Scrooge saying, "Humbug." Thanksgiving came and went with no fuss and no festivities, and that was just the way she wanted it.

Renee wanted to take care of herself and the baby growing inside her, but she could not find the strength to do it. She was still very ill and could not keep anything down; she was just so lifeless.

That day, Christine came to visit her daughter, but when she rang the doorbell and got no answer, she took out her key and walked in. She called for her daughter with no answer. She ran up the stairs, her heart beating double time. She thought something must be wrong with her daughter since Renee was not responding when called. Christine ran to the bedroom and found her asleep in her bed. Finding her resting and not on the floor somewhere past out, Christine sighed in relief. She left her daughter resting and went down to prepare a little lunch for them.

Renee had not kept up her part of the agreement to visit Dr. Chamberlain or to see her family physician. Truthfully, her daughter did not keep in touch with her or her husband much since Paul's passing either. Christine was worried about her daughter and her grandbaby. She prepared some chicken soup and grilled cheese for their lunch. She did not want to serve Renee's lunch in bed, so she went up and woke her daughter to come and eat with her in the kitchen. Renee just shrugged her mother off.

Christine was determined. "Renee Hamilton, you get your sorry ass down stairs right now, and I mean now!" she ordered.

Renee opened her eyes a little and told her mother to go away. Her mother was getting a little upset with her daughter's attitude, so she filled a glass with water and then threw it in her daughters' face.

"Mom! What the hell was that for? You got me and my bed all wet. Are you out of your mind?"

"No! I am not out of my mind, thank you for asking, but I am getting tired of this pity party you have going on here. This thing here—all of this—has gone on long enough, do you hear me? Now, get up and take a shower, then come down to have something to eat and we will have a long talk. Do you understand? Well, do you?" Christine asked.

"Yes, Mother, I hear you. I am getting up and going to follow you to the kitchen for lunch. Are you happy now?"

"A little, but the day has just started for you, young lady."

Downstairs, Renee nibbled at her grilled cheese and played with her spoon in her soup. Christine was getting a little tired of her daughter's childish behavior. "Renee, is that all you are going to eat?"

"Yes! Mother, I am not hungry. I just want to go upstairs and rest, if you don't mind?"

"Well, if you want to know, I do mind. I mind very much because I love you and my grandbaby. Did you forget about that baby you are carrying inside you? Do you think that Paul would be happy about the way you are taking care of yourself or his baby?"

"To hell with Paul. I don't care what he thinks or doesn't think because he abandoned both of us. So, if I want to sleep for all of my pregnancy or my entire life that is no one's concern but my own. Do you hear me, Mother? You can let yourself out the way you came in, and thank you for the lunch, but I am not hungry these days."

"Well, I never thought my daughter would speak to me so disrespectfully. Renee, you may be too old for me to spank or wash out your mouth with soap, but I am not ever to be spoken to in that manner again. Now, get your tired ass up those stairs and get yourself into the shower. If you give me any resistance, I will carry you up those stairs and undress you and even get into that shower fully dressed and wash you, do you understand?"

"I'd like to see you try that, Mother." She started laughing so hard she got a stitch in her side.

"So, you think I am bluffing? Well, I'll just have to show you." Christine went over to her daughter and was just about to pick her up when her daughter started walking up the stairs to take her shower.

"Okay! Mother, you win. I'll take a shower, get dressed, and come and join you for a cup of tea."

Pleased with herself, Christine said, "Thank you, Renee. You've just saved my poor back from a visit to the chiropractor."

"Yeah, yeah, Mother! I will see you in a few minutes."

Renee had a shower, and the warm water touching her skin felt so good. She stayed in the shower for some time before dressing and marching down to have tea with her mother.

Her mother had made some tea biscuits and some chamomile tea when Renee joined her.

"Mom, did you make these tea biscuits?"

"Yes, dear, and they are hot out of the oven. I also made us some chamomile tea. The tea will help your body to relax, like a sedative. It also helps with anxiety, stress, and insomnia," Christine said.

"Mom, when did you get your medical degree?"

"Let me inform you, girl, that when one becomes a mother, you have to juggle being a teacher, a doctor, a chef, a housekeeper, a social director, and a taxi driver. That's where the saying, 'A mother's job is never done' comes from. Come, sit down. Let's have tea and we can have a mother–daughter talk."

Renee sat down and enjoyed the tea biscuits. She ate eight biscuits on her own, but her mother did not say anything, as she knew Renee had probably not eaten for some time.

"Mom, these biscuits and the tea just hit the spot. I didn't know I was this hungry. To be honest, this is the first thing I've eaten that hasn't made me want to vomit after eating. It must be the tea that is settling my nerves and allowing me to pig out on these delicious hot tea biscuits. Thanks, Mom! You always seem to know how to make me feel better," acknowledged Renee.

"That's right, and that's why your father and I are going to take you away from this house, the reporters, and the in-laws. We talked it over last night, and we decided that we all need a vacation. We are going to Punta Cana in the Dominican for Christmas. We thought that we would miss Christmas this year just like Tim Allen and Jamie Lee Curtis did in the movie *Christmas with the Kranks*. We watched that movie last night, and it gave your father the idea of missing Christmas this year and taking a trip. This trip will be your Christmas gift from us this year. Friends of your father's just came back from there and said it was a real paradise, so pack your swimsuit! We are leaving tomorrow morning, rain or shine."

"Mom, you must be joking? Christmas is still a few weeks away, and I can't just pick up and go just like that."

"Yes, you can, and Christmas, my dear, is only a few days away. You wouldn't know what day or month it was since you never get out of bed. You are coming with us, like it or not. Your father has already paid for the three of us, and there is no way to get refunded for the trip now. You need to get out of this house, darling, and maybe getting away to an exotic island is just what your doctor would prescribe. You know, a change in scenery can be very therapeutic. Plus your dad and I have not gone on a holiday in years, and we need to get away too. With everything that has been going on around here since Paul's death, we have been stressed out too. Your father and I need to get away. We need a break from our day to day life, but there is no way in hell we could enjoy ourselves while worrying about you the entire time. So, do you think you can muster enough energy and selflessness to take this vacation with your dad and I so that we can have a nice relaxing time away that we all need and deserve? Renee, can you please do this for us?" Christine pleaded.

"Okay," Renee sighed. "Now, tell me when we are leaving again?"

"Sweetheart, we are leaving early tomorrow morning to take our plane to Punta Cana. Your dad called a travel agent and set us all up to leave tomorrow. I will clean up here, and you go up and start packing. Now, let's go, girl. We need to pack your bags, and then you will come home with me. You can sleep in your old room. Tomorrow morning, we have to be up at the break of dawn, and if you sleep over, we don't have to make a special trip to pick you up."

Renee was feeling a little anxious and replied, "Okay, Mom! Let's go get my suitcase and pack my things for our well-needed break from life."

"That's my girl."

Renee went up and started packing. After cleaning up downstairs, Christine went up to help her daughter. She found her daughter on her knees crying.

"Sweetheart, dry up those tears, and let's start packing your suitcase."

"Mom, my entire life changed in a heartbeat, and I feel so dead inside."

"Renee, your life is not over, but your life with Paul, sorry to say, is. Life goes on, like it or not. You carry on the best way you can, and each passing day, life will become easier to manage. I promise you that, yes, things are not going to be as you expected them to be, but you are strong and you will find another reason to wake up every morning. Every day that passes will become easier for you to face."

Renee rested her head on her mother's shoulders and asked, "You promise, Mom? Because right now, all I feel is this emptiness inside me. Mom, I feel so lost without Paul."

"That's why this Dominican vacation is what we all need," Christine replied.

Renee wiped her tears. "You're right, Mom. Maybe getting away is what we all need. Help me get this suitcase packed so we can get out of here."

Chapter 17

Early the next morning, the car was packed and they were on their way to the airport. They arrived at the airport to take their flight to Punta Cana, Dominican Republic. The airport was filled with passengers going home for the holidays. They got through customs and stopped for a coffee and a croissant at one of the many airport vendors. The flight was supposed to leave by ten a.m., but it was now delayed for two to four hours because of engine problems. This vacation was not starting out well at all.

While they waited, the Clarks and Renee were entertained by carolers singing joyful Christmas classics. The travelers in the airport were joining in song, but Renee, Mrs. Scrooge, wished they would stop. Thankfully for Renee, a woman's voice called out on the intercom informing them that the plane was ready and that they would commence boarding in a few minutes. She apologized to the many passengers for the lengthy delay.

Christine got up and said, "Okay, Let's go, you two. We are beginning our tropical vacation."

They all boarded the plane at about two p.m. that afternoon. Renee remembered how not so long ago, she and Paul were boarding a plane to Paris for their honeymoon.

As they entered the plane and found their seats, Renee asked her father, "Dad, do you mind if I sit by the window? I like looking outside at the clouds."

James let his daughter through to sit by the window, while he took the aisle seat and Christine sat in the middle. Before sitting, Renee reached over and kissed her father on the cheek. Shortly after everyone was seated, the plane started moving and they were off.

It was too late to change her mind now. Renee held her mother's hand so tightly because she hated flying. As the plane leveled out, Renee became less nervous. The stewardess demonstrated what to do in case of an emergency. They showed everyone where the exits were located and how to use the air masks and the life jackets in case of an emergency. Then they came around with a complimentary glass of wine. Renee accepted the glass of wine.

"Girl, you are pregnant. You should not be drinking in your condition," Christine stated.

Renee replied, handing it to her mother, "I know, Mom. I only took the wine for you. You know that I would not drink in my condition. I wouldn't do anything to harm my baby."

"I'm sorry, sweetheart," Christine said. "I know you wouldn't harm your baby, not intentionally."

"Because of that, Mom, I am giving the glass of wine to Dad."

The airplane attendants came around with free headsets so everyone could hear the movie they were about to show. So far, it was a pleasant flight. Renee took off her sweater to use as a pillow and leaned her chair back a little, but not so much that the passenger behind would mind. Christine and James were enjoying the film while Renee listened to soft music and drifted off to sleep; she was exhausted.

***

Renee awoke when the captain asked the passengers to fasten their seat belts because of turbulence ahead. Renee squeezed her mother's hand again, and with the other hand, she held her belly. Renee's motherly instincts were kicking in. She was trying to protect her unborn child.

"Sweetheart, don't worry. This will pass." This was James's fatherly instincts kicking in trying to comfort his little girl.

The seat belt sign came off, and the stewardess came around with pre-moistened wipes to wash up before serving the meals. It was about five p.m. when the flight attendants came around with their cart. Passengers could choose between a three-cheese pizza or a chicken and cheese sandwich on a cranberry roll. Christine and James decided on the pizza, and Renee tried the sandwich. The meal was filling and quite good for airplane food. Renee really enjoyed the vanilla ice cream they served as dessert.

Renee closed her eyes after eating and fell asleep again. Christine knew that the forever vomiting and tiredness did not make her daughter's pregnancy enjoyable. Both Christine and James knew that even though this pregnancy was emotionally and physically hard on their daughter, she was thrilled to have a little part of Paul still with her.

The seat belt sign came on, and the plane started its descent. As the plane was descending, Christine awoke her daughter so as to put on her seat belt. Christine grabbed hold of her daughter's hand for that bit of comfort that she needed. Renee started feeling a little noxious as the plane descended. Thankfully, the plane landed and they were now at a complete stop. Everyone on the plane clapped their hands, happy that they arrived safe and that they were about to start their vacations in sunny Punta Cana.

Now that the plane stopped the travelers were getting out of their seats and grabbing their carry-on luggage from the compartments above. As the travelers were getting anxiously ready to disembark, Renee looked at her dad, who was helping others get to their bags. Her father grabbed their three bags and insisted on carrying them out for his ladies. James was the last of his breed, a true gentleman. Renee then thought of her baby and how her father was going to be a good role model in his or her life. It was too bad that Paul's parents wouldn't be in her child's life, but they made that choice when they kicked her to the curb. The stewardesses guided everyone off the plane and wished them all a beautiful stay. Everyone thanked them and walked off the plane in haste, wanting to begin their fun in the sun vacation.

Chapter 18

As the Clarks and Renee got off of their plane, Renee now knew how that chestnut felt on the open fire. The air was hard to breathe. The heat from the sun must have been a good forty degrees. It was going to be a hot seven days, but she felt this might be the exact place to get her life back on track. Perhaps this was to be a new beginning for this widowed mother and for her parents, who needed to have some fun and time away from always worrying about her. Renee needed to show her parents that she could stand on her own two feet and that she could enjoy herself again because if they thought she couldn't, it would ruin their vacation.

In the terminal, everyone waited at the carousel for their luggage. Then they went through customs quickly and found their tour bus. The bus ride took 45 minutes to get to their resort. The bus had a guide, who welcomed everyone to the Dominican. He introduced himself as Raymond and the bus driver as Miguel. Renee did not mind the bus ride at all because the bus had air conditioning and the seats were more comfortable than the plane's.

Raymond, the tour guide, had suggested possible outings outside of the resort to the tourists. They could tour the town and find many vendors, tour Saona Island, take a sunset horseback ride, parasail, snorkel, and swim with the dolphins. He also informed everyone that it cost twenty-five pesos to leave the country. Raymond directed everyone on the bus to some of the other resorts, the golf courses, and other interesting sights. He was a very funny man. He loved to tell jokes and also sold beers, which he called *cerveza*, on the bus for five dollars from a cooler he had in the front seat.

James purchased two cold beers and lifted his beer up to make a toast. "So, our vacation in the sun begins. Cheers!" Everyone who also purchased a beer yelled out cheers back.

Renee laughed to herself. Her parents were acting like university students on spring break. Renee wished she could be just like them: fun-loving and happy to be with each other. She had had that when Paul was alive but lost it when she lost him. Nevertheless, Renee aspired to one day be more like her parents again.

As they arrived at Hotel Riu Palace in Punta Cana, Renee finally felt a little excited to be here. This had been a great idea after all. Just like her parents, Renee believed this vacation would be exactly what she needed to get out of this rut she was in.

They got off the bus and went to the reception desk, which was nicely decorated for the holidays. Everyone from their bus all lined up and awaited their turn to get checked in. James offered to stay in line to let the women sit, as it may be a little wait before getting checked in.

Renee loved the decor in the grand entrance. The entrance had marble flooring and big vases holding huge colorful floral arrangements. The architectural design was unique. From the ceiling hung beautiful cascading chandlers. The color scheme was white marble and blue. There were sounds of birds chirping and water running from the fountains outside. The tourists were tanned and dressed in bathing suits, shorts, and sandals.

Once James checked in, he asked if someone could help them with their luggage. A porter put all their luggage in a big white golf cart and chauffeured them all to their rooms. As they were being transported to their rooms, they saw the beauty of this magical place. They could hear music playing on their drive. Their driver pointed out where the buffet was and he told them that the buffet was open for breakfast from seven a.m. to ten a.m., the lunch buffet was open from one p.m. to three p.m., and the dinner buffet was open from six p.m. to nine p.m. every day. There was also a beach grill that was open for twenty-four hours, where they served hamburgers, hot dogs, and fries, which were very good.

When they arrived at their rooms they were pleased to see that they had an adjoining balcony connecting their rooms. James thanked the driver for the ride and his help with the luggage, then tipped him.

Renee was pleased with her room. It was clean, nicely decorated, had a great balcony, a beautiful view of the ocean, and had a nice bathroom, with a deep tub and a shower. When Renee finished unpacking her luggage, she went out on the balcony and knocked on her parents sliding door. "Hey, guys, I hope you don't mind, but I'm exhausted, so I am taking a hot bath and going to bed. You go out and have fun. I will see you in the morning."

"Renee, you have to come with us for dinner. You have to eat a little something," Christine said.

Renee was a little short with her mother, saying, "Mom, please I'm not hungry. Can you just leave it for today? I promise I'll eat lots tomorrow. I'm just exhausted from the long day."

"Okay, dear, I won't pressure you, we will see you in the morning."

Renee went back to her room, closed the curtains, and got ready for a long soak. She fell asleep in the tub. When she awoke, the water was cold, so she got out and dried herself off. She put on her pj's, got into bed, and fell asleep as her head hit the pillow.

Chapter 19

The next morning, Renee's mother knocked on her sliding door to wake her daughter up so that she would join them for breakfast.

Renee answered, "Okay, Mom! I'm coming." Renee opened the door to find her mother dressed in shorts and a tank top, ready and eager to start her day.

"Darling, you're not up yet? Dad and I are going down for breakfast. You get yourself dressed, and we will meet you downstairs. Hurry up, dear."

While they ventured downstairs, Renee hurried and got dressed in a pair of stretchy shorts, a baggy T-shirt, and her comfortable sandals. She thought to herself that she would make the best of this vacation—if not for herself than for her parents, who had paid for it. They deserved to have a little fun. It was only going to be seven days; she could fake having a great time if only for them.

As Renee opened her door, the heat hit her face. She hurried downstairs to meet up with her parents.

"Hi there, sleepy head, did you sleep well?" her father asked.

"Yes, Dad, I slept like a rock. Now, let's get some grub. This pregnant woman is famished."

They all walked happily to the buffet for breakfast. Renee couldn't believe the variety of food they were serving. The buffet consisted of pancakes, French toast, bacon, sausages, ham, cereal, fruits, vegetables, cheeses, and breads. There was a chef preparing eggs or omelets for the tourists to their liking. The buffet looked scrumptious, but the smells coming from some of the foods made her ill.

Renee groaned, "Mom, I can't stay in here. The smells are making me ill."

"Okay! But you have to eat something. How about I make you a plate? What would you like to eat?"

"I would like two pieces of whole wheat toast and a glass of orange juice, if you don't mind, Mom?"

"No problem, sweetheart. You go back to your room, and I'll bring breakfast to you after we're done eating."

Walking back to her room, she enjoyed listening to the birds singing and smelling the fragrant flowers. The grounds were well cared for and the colors of the flowers were bright and vibrant. This place was a true paradise. There were workers that kept the resort well landscaped. Renee was greeted by many of the locals who worked for the resort; they greeted her with *"Hola"* or *"Buenos dias."* Everyone seemed to be so pleasant and happy working at the resort. There were even workers that climbed up to the top of the palm trees to pick coconuts. The locals made their livelihood on the tourists who visited their country. They survived on the tips that the tourists gave them for services rendered.

When Renee got to her room, she decided to rest for a spell because who knew what activities her parents had planned for them to do today. She would rest her head just until her mother arrived with her breakfast. Renee hoped that she would be able to join her parents for lunch at the buffet because she wanted to try the Dominican cuisine. She wanted to embrace all of the Dominican culture: the music, the food, the people, and the dancing. She wanted to take part in the activities that the resort had to offer like water sports, tennis, exercises by the pool, bingo, dance lessons, the spa, shopping, and the shows that the staff put on for the guests every night. Who was she kidding, though? She would probably just stay in her room or sit on the beach or by the pool and read one of the many books she had brought with her.

Christine knocked at Renee's door with her breakfast in hand. Renee sure hoped that this simple breakfast would stay down. After eating the toast and drinking the juice, Renee felt much better.

"Sweetheart, your dad and I are going out to sit by the pool. Will you join us?"

"Yes, I think that would be very nice. I'll just get my swimsuit on and meet you both by the pool."

***

Renee's father had found three lounge chairs for them next to the pool. Renee wore a two-piece suit, and you could see her baby bump. She was confident that everyone would just think that she just had a little fat around her midriff. Renee didn't have to conceal the fact that she was pregnant because no one here knew her, and she was certain that the people that she would meet would probably never see her again. This made her pleased to know there would be no gossiping.

There were many couples at this resort and tourists of all ages. The pool was so enticing that Renee had to go in. The water was a little cold, but her body quickly got used to it. She dove in and it felt so refreshing. Renee always loved the water. As a child, her mother had her in swimming lessons. Renee lived at the public pool or at the beach.

Renee's parents were like magnets—random couples their own age came around and started conversations with them. It was amazing, seeing them talking and joking with random people they had just met. As they enjoyed their mingling, Renee enjoyed swimming and getting a little exercise. When she exited the pool, her mom introduced her to Mr. and Mrs. Reynolds, a couple they had met last evening. Renee was very pleased to meet them; they seemed to have a lot in common with her parents. They were all about the same age and seemed to enjoy each other's company.

Just then, a younger couple, about Renee's age, joined them at the pool. Mrs. Reynolds introduced them as her children: Jo-Ann and Matthew. James then introduced his daughter, Renee. The Reynoldses' children were very gracious and even invited Renee to join them to go paddle boating.

Renee's mother nodded her head and said, "I am sure Renee would love to join you. Wouldn't you, Renee?"

Renee accepted their gracious invitation.

She put on her shorts and top, then joined them down by the beach. They walked together and picked up shells that were pushed onto the beach with each wave. The beach sand was so white, and the ocean was so clear, you could see the bottom of the ocean floor. Renee took off her sandals and ran in the ocean, and her two companions did the same. Matthew, being a boy at heart, started splashing the girls. They ganged up on him, though, and splashed back. They were having so much fun. Renee couldn't remember when she laughed and enjoyed herself like this—it had seemed like forever.

They walked on the beach for a while. They were inquisitive and very chatty, but all in all, the siblings were Renee's kind of people. From their first encounter, Renee knew they would be great friends, and she believed they felt the same about her. Renee was having a great time. She had thought she would feel like the third wheel, hanging around with her parents for this entire vacation, but now, having befriended the Reynolds family, she would have two adults her own age to hang out with. She felt like a teenager again, spending time with two best friends.

The beach was so beautiful, with its white sand and its blue ocean. Renee noticed it was the exact same color as Matthew's blue-teal eyes, and she immediately felt awful for even noticing his eyes. What kind of person was she? Paul, her husband, has just died and here she was noticing another man's eyes. She gave her head a shake and rethought her comment to herself. She retracted what she had said and specified that her friend Matthew had eyes that *other* women could lose themselves in—not her. His eyes could pull you in like a wave returning to the ocean after rolling itself onto the warm beach—that still sounded like a teenage girl crushing on a boy she had just met hours ago. Renee had to stop overthinking this. He was just a friend, just like his sister was just a friend.

The sound of the ocean had a very calming and welcoming effect. The three friends walked toward the paddle boats and borrowed one. Jo-Ann asked Renee if she wanted to sit in front and paddle.

"I would rather be chauffeured, if that is all right," Renee replied.

All three laughed. Then Matthew and Jo-Ann got into the front seats ready to paddle, but their paddle boat was stuck on the beach. The man in charge of the boats assisted them by pushing them off. They thanked him, and then off they went, paddling on the ocean, enjoying themselves.

Renee asked Jo-Ann and Matthew, "Is this your first time in the Dominican?"

"We have traveled to many different countries, but we like coming here at the RIU Palace in the Dominican because the people are very friendly. They become part of your family while you are here," Jo-Ann answered.

"So, you travel with your parents and each other all the time?" Renee asked.

"Yes, we do. Our parents have always taken us on vacations since we were little. We have always traveled together. We enjoy each other's company, and we have the freedom to do things on our own if we wish to. Matthew and I started staying in our own rooms when we became adults so that we could have privacy. So, once a year, we take time off from work to go away with our parents."

"So, you leave your own families at home then?" Renee asked.

"No! Neither Mat or I have a family of our own, we are not married and have not found our significant others as of yet. We do hope to find that special person to share our lives with one day, but for now, we are single with no prospects in sight." Then Jo-Ann remarked, "I see from your left hand that you are not married either?"

"No, I am also single at the moment with no prospects in sight, but . . . I was married not long ago. I am recently widowed. I am not wearing my wedding ring because they were being engraved and I forgot to pick them up," Renee replied.

Matthew said empathetically, "We are so sorry, Renee. Do you want to talk about it?"

"No, thank you, I came on this trip because my parents booked and paid for it without my knowledge. I didn't want to let them down; they needed this trip."

"Maybe you also needed this trip to distract you from all the hard times you must have gone through with your husband's death. Renee, look at this vacation as a breather or time to rejuvenate yourself for just a short week before going back to real life," Mat acknowledged.

"I have to say, meeting your family is probably going to make our vacation a lot more bearable and a lot more interesting."

"We will make it our mission to show you a good time," Matthew promised.

Renee playfully replied, "You know how you can show me a good time? Start paddling this thing so we can move."

Matthew exclaimed, "Oh! You're the bossy type then?"

"Not usually," Renee said with a smile.

They all started to laugh, then picked up the paddling, enjoying their afternoon on the water.

As they paddled to shore, Renee shared with them, "You know something, you both might be exactly what my doctor ordered for me."

Jo-Ann laughed, saying, "That's funny because Mat, my father, and I are all doctors. We specialize in different fields. Mat is an ob-gyn, my father is a surgeon, and I am a psychiatrist, who specializes in mental health and mental disorders."

Impressed, Renee said, "Wow, so I guess I should watch what I say around you?"

"No, I'm off duty this week. This week I am just a tourist, just like you," Jo-Ann assured her.

After paddling, they walked back to the pool where their parents were enjoying a cold *cerveza* at the swim up bar. Renee thought her parents were so cool and easy going; they blended in with all classes of people. Renee wanted her child to be just like them, and she thrived to be more like them too. Renee knew that if her child took after her parents, Paul would be so proud of him or her. Renee knew for a fact that Paul wouldn't want his child to be like his parents: snobby and stuck up.

As Renee got comfortable on a lounge chair, she whispered to herself, "Stop it, Renee. You need to relax and have some fun. That's what this week is about. And I have to stop talking to myself, or Jo-Ann will think I need her services."

A worker from the resort came around, asking the tourists to come and participate in the water aerobics, which was to start in five minutes at the shallow end of the pool. Andre, one of the social directors, grabbed Jo-Ann's arm and pulled her up from her lounge chair, telling her to come and show the newbies how much fun they could have exercising in the pool. Jo-Ann said she would if he could get her friend Renee to join them.

Andre knelt next to Renee and said, "Beautiful, Miss Renee, please will you join us at the pool? I promise you we will have lots of laughs and fun." He then grabbed her by the hand and kissed it so gently.

Christine urged her daughter, "Go have some fun. You don't want to hurt Andre's feelings now, do you?" She winked.

Renee got up off her chair and grabbed hold of Andre's offered hand, and they walked in the direction of the music and the many other women waiting for their fine-looking aerobics instructor to begin the lesson.

The music enticed their bodies to move, and the instructor enticed each student to watch and follow his every instruction. Renee had to admit she was having the best time. Everyone laughed, played, and flirted with Andre. Renee knew this was how he was with all the female tourists, but he still made her feel special and like a young desirable woman again. Getting a little attention was doing a lot for her ego. After the aerobics class was over, Jo-Ann went back to her lounging chair, but Renee stayed in the water and just floated around enjoying its coolness.

Mat decided to come and join her in the pool. Mat swam over to Renee and told her, "Your parents are overjoyed that you are having a good time. Renee, can I tell you something without you getting upset with me?"

"Sure, what's up?"

Mat continued, nervously clearing his throat, "I know I haven't known you for that long, but I'm starting to have romantic feelings for you. When Andre was flirting with you in the pool, I was a little jealous, like someone was making a move on my girl. I know it's crazy. I'm a grown man, but I feel like a teenager around you. I can't explain it. I care deeply for you and I hope that maybe you feel a little something for me too?" He waited for some kind of response, but she said nothing. Instead, Renee walked out of the pool, walked toward her parents, grabbed her wrap and her towel, and excused herself.

She walked to her room in shock of the declaration of admiration that Mat had just sprung on her. How could this have happened? She didn't think she was leading him on, but maybe she was without even knowing it. How could she show her face to him again? She was ashamed of herself. She decided to stay in her room for the rest of the duration of her holiday.

Then Renee heard a knock on her door. She did not want to open it, but Mat's voice told her to; he wanted to talk to her. She got up and hesitatingly opened the door. Mat entered and asked if they could go out onto the balcony to talk for a moment. Shyly, she walked and showed him to the balcony.

They both sat, and Mat started by saying, "Renee, I didn't tell you how I felt to scare you off. I understand that I was quite forward about my feelings toward you, but I understand it if you don't feel the same way about me. I didn't come on this vacation in hopes to find the girl of my dreams. I've been on many holidays and have flirted and enjoyed many female companions, but never have I felt so drawn to someone, to the point of professing my endearing love to a woman."

"Mat, it isn't that I'm not flattered by your sentiments, but I cannot relay the same feelings for you at this time. You know that I have been married, but what you don't know is that he was the love of my life and he died in a fire on September Eleventh. Paul, my husband, was on a business trip at the Twin Towers and he never made it out. So, I am a grieving widow and I cannot even fathom having someone new in my life at this moment. It would not be fair to you. I cannot say that I don't have feelings for you because I do, but I just can't be in a relationship with anyone right now. Mat, if I would have met you during a different time in my life, I would have been all over you. I hope you understand where I am mentally right now, but I hope we still can be friends?"

"I'm so sorry, Renee. I feel like such an ass for my behavior. If friendship is all I can have for now, then you have a friend in me. If in a year from now I still feel the same way about you, I will look you up, Renee—and that I do promise," Mat said.

"That's a deal, Mat, but your friendship and your sister's friendship mean a lot to me. Mat, let's get out of here and go ask the gang if they want to join us for lunch. I'm famished."

Chapter 20

It was Christmas morning, and in most homes, families were getting up and unwrapping gifts from under the Christmas tree left by Santa Claus. Renee was getting a little melancholy, thinking about how Christmas was supposed to be this year. Tears started to run down her face as she thought that this would have been Paul and her first Christmas together as a married couple.

Renee shook her head and thought to herself this was not helping things. This was supposed to be a fun-filled Christmas vacation; crying and feeling sorry for herself would not do anyone any good. She decided to stop her pity party and enjoy the beautiful morning.

Renee had decided to start her day by having a good healthy breakfast, hoping she could hold it down, and then get ready for the eleven a.m. aerobics class. Joining the many women every day to exercise was exhilarating and refreshing all at the same time; it made Renee feel better about herself and it gave her more energy for the activities that the Reynolds siblings had planned for them. Andre, the pool instructor, came out to the pool wearing a red Santa Claus hat and wished everyone a Merry Christmas. He played a few Christmas songs for all to enjoy while exercising.

Mat and Jo-Ann then kept Renee busy and entertained all day. She enjoyed spending time with the Reynolds family, and they seemed to enjoy her company as well. Even though they were well to do and had prestigious careers, they never treated her like she was less worthy. This showed Renee that Reynoldses had class and they slowly became part of her extended family.

Later in the afternoon, Mat came over to the pool to surprise Renee with a Christmas gift.

"Mat, you shouldn't have gotten me a gift. I didn't get you one in exchange. You see, my parents and I decided to skip Christmas this year, and that's why we are here instead of at home, exchanging gifts."

"That sounds a little drastic, but I wanted to get this for you and I wasn't expecting one in return. Now, open it if you please. I hope you like it because when I saw it, it reminded me of you."

Renee opened the package and found a lovely necklace with a flower as its pendant. The flower's center was a blue stone, the stone of the Dominican Republic, and the petals were covered with little diamonds.

"Mat! This gift is exquisite. Please tell me the stones are not genuine, are they?"

"Please, I would never give a girl a gift with fake anything. I saw it and had to purchase it because . . . this flower is as exquisite as you are. You are so beautiful, and I have strong feelings for you, as you know, and I wanted you to remember me when you are at home in Boston. I don't want you to forget me, as I will never forget you, Renee."

"Firstly, thank you for the compliment, and secondly, are you out of your mind purchasing something so expensive for me? You could have given me a key chain from the gift shop and I would have been just as appreciated, but this expensive necklace . . . I cannot accept it. She handed the box back to him.

"Renee, I will not take the necklace back, and it is rude of you not to accept this token of our friendship. It would please me if you kept it." He then gave her a puppy face look, with his lips turned down to show her how upset he was that she did not want to accept his gift.

"Okay! Okay! I will accept the beautiful expensive Christmas gift, but you must promise, no more gifts."

Mat declared, "I promise not to buy you any more gifts while we are on vacation. Now, we need to walk toward the beach if we are to be on time for lunch. You do remember that our parents planned for us to meet at the beach grill for lunch. We are going to try out the fish and chips, which everyone seems to be raving about. Our parents said we should all meet up at the grill by noon."

"Now you mention it, I am a little hungry. I'll just grab my things and put my shorts and top on over my swimsuit before we go."

Everyone was pleased to see the pair coming to join them for lunch. They had put two tables together and sat down, awaiting their server. She was a beautiful middle-aged woman, who spoke some English. She took their orders: the fish and chips and *cervezas* for the group and one *agua* for the pregnant lady. Renee loved the ocean air, but it was a little too breezy. The wind picked up, and the napkins on their tables flew away. Mat remarked that it was kite-flying weather. He then suggested, "Hey, girls, how about we do some parasailing after lunch?"

The smell of the fish and chips began to make Renee noxious, but she did not want anyone to get wind of how she felt. When the fish and chips were served, she had to excuse herself, as she was going to be ill. She did not want to vomit in front of everyone, including the Reynoldses. They asked what had happened, and Christine asked if Mat wouldn't mind following Renee to see if she was all right. He got up and ran after Renee to see what the problem was and if there was anything he could do to help her. Christine then decided to tell the rest of the Reynolds family what was going on. The Clarks were tired of lying about Renee's condition to their new friends. The Reynoldses understand now why Christine asked Mat to go after Renee; Mat was an obstetrician after all.

When Mat caught up to Renee, he asked her what was going on. Renee did not want to tell him, but she didn't want to lie to him anymore either. Renee divulged her secret.

"Mat, I am four months pregnant and have been ill almost every day. I didn't want to tell anyone because I can't believe it myself. I'm sorry, Mat. I should have confided in you when I told you I was widowed, but how can I be happy and ashamed all at the same time?"

"Don't worry about it. It's a lot for two parents to handle so don't be so hard on yourself. Renee, with all that you have been through, I'm amazed you are doing so well."

"Mat, I haven't really been doing so great. I was hospitalized for a while because they thought I was suicidal. It was during my stay in the hospital that I learned I was in the family way."

In disbelief, Mat said, "You tried to off yourself? Why?"

"No, no! You don't understand. My father found me on the floor of my basement unconscious. He thought that because I was so depressed, that

I tried to 'off myself,' as you say. I was out cold because I was dehydrated and undernourished—that's all. This vacation was all my parents' idea. They wanted to get me and themselves away from all the negativity of home and try to enjoy our life a little again. I was doing fine, but the smells of some foods made me ill, like the smell of the fish and chips we were having for lunch."

Mat was very understanding and suggested, "Renee, how about we skip the beach front grill and head for the buffet? There is so much more variety for us to eat at the buffet. If the smells in the buffet area bother you, I can prepare both of us a plate and we can eat our food on one of the tables outside of the buffet area."

"Mat, you are a true friend, and I have to say I wish you were my obstetrician. You have a great bedside manner. I bet you have a long waitlist of women trying to make appointments with you. Have you ever watched the television series *Grey's Anatomy*, where all the male doctors are real hunks? You Dr. Reynolds put those doctors to shame. Are you blushing? You must know that you are the best-looking doctor that I have ever seen. I bet you have more than one little black book with numerous young ladies' phone numbers."

"Okay, that's enough, little lady. I do not want to talk about this part of my private life with you. Now, if you want to eat lunch at the buffet, let's get going," Mat exclaimed.

"Okay! I will mind my own business, but thanks again for brightening up my day. You have this way of making me laugh, and I don't remember the last time I laughed, really laughed like this; it seems like forever. Dr. Mat, I have to say that you are the best medicine to make this pregnant women feel better."

"This doctor thinks you need to eat, and after lunch I would like to give you a quick once over to see if all is well with my two new patients. Don't look at me that way, Renee. You know darn well how much I care for you, so please let me check you over, and then if all is well, the subject of you being my patient is over. Okay?"

Renee agreed. "Okay, Doctor! I think if you check me out I may feel less anxious about how the baby is doing. Now, if you don't mind, get me something to eat. I'm starving."

***

After lunch, Renee went to Mat's room and he had her sit on his bed to check her over. Mat asked, "So, Renee, has this pregnancy been hard on you?"

"Yes! It has. I have been sick for all of my pregnancy so far. I read after the first trimester, the morning sickness should dissipate, but not for this gal."

"Renee, for some of the unlucky few, morning sickness lasts throughout their entire pregnancy," Mat informed her.

"Isn't that great; five more months of this."

"Renee, on your last visit to your family doctor or your obstetrician, what did they say about your health?"

"To tell you the truth, Mat, I've been too ill to leave the washroom. I didn't want anyone to suspect that I was expecting. I haven't seen a doctor since my hospital stay, but I do take my prenatal vitamins every day, and I am trying to eat but not much stays down. I have been joining Andre's aerobics class in the pool most days to keep myself fit."

"Okay! Renee, I am going to take your blood pressure, then your heart rate, and see if I can get a reading on the baby's heart rate." A little over a minute later, he said, "All right, all looks good. I think you should maybe take it easy this afternoon. Why don't you rest in your room or under an umbrella or those little huts on the beach? Let's not over do it today. That's what this doctor and your good friend suggest for you to do, just for today. How about you and me take a good book and rest under a hut on the beach this afternoon? What do you say, Renee?"

"I would like that very much."

"Now, you go to your room to get yourself a book, and then we can walk down to the beach and find a place to relax." He helped her up and led her to the door.

***

That afternoon, Renee relaxed and slept for a while under the hut. When she awoke, Mat was no longer sitting with her. She saw him in the pool and said to herself, "This has been a great day. The woman that gets Mat's heart will be a very lucky gal. Wait a minute, I am the gal who has Mat's heart. What should I do? If I have him wait for me to be ready, he may lose interest in me. But if I jump into a relationship that I am not ready for, it would not be fair to Mat, or Paul. I know I have feelings for Mat, but is it too soon for me to be with someone else? I am so confused, but maybe now that Mat knows that I am carrying Paul's baby, he may not even want me anymore."

The Reynolds family had invited the Clark and Hamilton family out to an Italian *a la carte* dinner, with a dress code. They were told that everyone had to get dressed up to go eat at these "a la carte" restaurants. Renee got dressed up in a lovely strapless white dress, which was short in the front to show off her legs and long in the back. It looked elegant, and the white color of the dress really showed off her great tan. She didn't need to wear much makeup either, but lengthened her eye lashes with mascara and applied a little red lipstick on her lips. Renee didn't get the chance to dress up too often, so this was a treat and it made her feel more feminine. She had decided to wear the stunning necklace that Mat had given her that morning as a finishing touch.

When Renee and her parents arrived at the Italian restaurant, the Reynoldses were waiting for them at the entrance. The moment Mat saw Renee, his gaze never left her.

He took Renee's hand and whispered to her, "You look beautiful tonight, Renee. The necklace looks pale in comparison to your beauty."

"Thank you, Mat, and you look very handsome tonight as well," Renee said truthfully.

They all entered the restaurant and were welcomed by a young man handing out a nonalcoholic punch, which Renee enjoyed. They were then seated at their table and told they could start serving themselves to the small antipasto buffet of cold meats, cheese, bread, salads, and olives. Renee's plate was overfilled with meat, cheese, bread, and olives. It was so good and did not make Renee nauseous, as there was no odor to this first course. They then had a choice of lasagna, a fettuccine noodle with a rose meat sauce, or, for the vegetarians, a pasta dish that included mixed vegetables. Renee ordered the lasagna, while her mother and father ordered the fettuccini with meat sauce. The Reynolds's all ordered the fettuccini as well. Renee's lasagna was very flavorful; everyone else at the table enjoyed their meals as well. Both sets of parents seemed to really enjoy the wine that was served with their meals. They had finished three bottles of red wine before the dessert menu came out. For dessert, Renee ordered a piece of chocolate cake, while the others were more daring and tried the tiramisu and the flan. The meal was a success.

Renee enjoyed every morsel and was pleased she kept it down. After the meal was over, Jo-Ann offered to take the drunks back to the front lobby. She told Mat and Renee that she would be right back to walk with them on the beach.

When Jo-Ann returned, she announced, "Our parents would like us to meet them at the theatre to watch the show later tonight."

They all agreed and began their stroll on the beach. The beach was deserted, a great time to talk and be listened to. Jo started asking Renee all sorts of questions; it felt like Renee was on trial.

"Jo-Ann, I am not one of your patients, and you said no work while on vacation," Renee uttered.

Jo-Ann replied, "Touché, Renee! I know you are not my patient, but I consider you to be a very good friend. I am asking as a concerned friend."

"Look guys, I am a pregnant widow who has been grieving her husband and who has been suffering morning sickness twenty-four seven. I am doing the best I can, so please drop it. I promise that if I need your help guys, I will ask for it, fair enough?"

"We understand, but maybe talking about the grief and whatever else is going on with you, could help. Just know we are here for you should you need us," Jo-Ann replied.

"Okay!" Renee sighed, then said, "The short version of my biography is as follows: Fell in love with Paul Hamilton, whose family is well to do in Boston. Paul died four weeks after our wedding. His parents hate my guts because they blame me for their son's death. I took Paul's death very hard and was a basket case. One day, my father found me out cold on the floor, and I was taken to the hospital. I was notified from the doctor on staff that I was pregnant. I am keeping my baby a secret from my in-laws because I don't want them to hurt me or this baby, ever. I'm on this trip because my parents booked this vacation without my knowledge. So, to make them happy, here I am."

"I like the condensed version, and I think you are doing great, considering all you have been through," Jo-Ann stated.

"Thanks, I'm really trying to keep it all together. I want this baby, and I don't want to do anything to harm him or her."

"As we are the doctors here, we prescribe that you relax and enjoy yourself for the rest of your stay here in the Dominican. Do you think you can follow these simple instructions?" Mat asked.

Renee answered, "If you both help me, I know I can do it. Now, let's go back and see what trouble our parents have caused." All day, Renee had been looking forward to the Michael Jackson Tribute show.

Jo-Ann said, "I hear the guy who plays Michael is one of the best impersonators and that the entire performance is really great."

They all walked back together toward the theatre, where their parents had saved seats for them in the front row. The performance was fantastic; the performers jumped on the audience and grabbed them to dance. It was a great night of fun and laughter by all. The group walked back to their rooms and made plans to meet for breakfast the next morning. Renee took a hot shower before climbing into bed. After confiding in her friends, she slept well that night.

***

During the rest of the vacation, the parents enjoyed spending time at the pool, drinking, swimming, and playing cards, while the kids were inseparable, doing everything together. They were adventurous: they swam and snorkeled in the ocean, rented mopeds, and went sightseeing. They had tried all the different restaurants the resort offered.

Jo-Ann, Mat, and Renee were known around the resort as the three amigos. Mat was always doting on Renee, like she was a porcelain doll that would break because she was so fragile. Renee knew Mat still had feelings for her, even though she was having Paul's baby. Jo-Ann went clubbing every evening when the rest of the gang turned in for the night.

It was their last night in the Dominican Republic, and Renee was upset. The next day, she knew she had to go back to the real world, and her world back home was ugly, dark, and cold compared to this beautiful, sunny, and warm place. She wished she could stay here for the rest of her life, but life was not a permanent vacation. It was sometimes pleasant, but it was also awkward, hard, ugly, cold, depressing, and challenging. She decided for her last night she would walk along the beach before turning in for the night.

Mat knew that this might be his last night, or last time even, to get to be with Renee. He insisted on accompanying her, like the gentlemen he was. As they walked on the white-sand beach, they took in the sound of the water splashing on the beach and the full moon's reflection glistening on the water. Surrounding that beautiful moon was the backdrop of thousands of stars, completing the most romantic setting. As they walked side by side, Renee lost her footing. Before she tumbled to the ground, Mat caught her in his muscular arms.

"Are you okay, Renee? "Did you hurt your ankle?"

"No, I'm fine, Mat."

His touch felt like a little electrical current going through her entire body. He guided her arms around his neck and then placed his arms around her lower back. He gazed into her eyes and felt like he was looking straight into her soul.

Thank goodness Mat's arms were around her because, all of a sudden, her legs gave way and she felt like she was ready to fall. Renee's body was shivering, and it wasn't because it was cold out. It was because of this man.

Mat gently bent over and whispered into her ear, "Renee, I was wondering if you would honor me with a dance?"

Renee nodded her head in affirmation, not able to speak. It was lovely. They could hear the faint sound of music from the resort, and they started swaying to it. Renee slowly placed her head on his shoulder, as she could not take his gaze any longer. Renee then realized that she hadn't danced with another man since before Paul.

She should have pushed Mat away, but for some reason, she couldn't. It felt so good being held by a strong man again, plus he smelled so good. Renee could not tear herself away. Then, she felt a pang of guilt, and tears began to flow down her face, wetting Mat's shoulder. Mat looked at her face and dried her tears with his fingers.

"Renee, are you alright? Did I do something to offend you?"

"No, Mat! This has nothing to do with you. I guess I'm just a little emotional and hormonal that's all. Mat, I am so happy I came on this vacation and got to meet you and your wonderful family. You are the most decent and charming man I have had the pleasure to meet. I hope that the girl who wins your heart knows how lucky she is to have found a one-of-a-kind treasure in you, Mat."

With that, Mat kissed her so tenderly, and by her amazement, she kissed him back. Renee shocked him because she kissed him like she had been starving for his loving embrace. Renee then pushed herself off of him and apologized while touching her full, wet lips. He looked at her, not knowing what to say, so he said nothing.

"Mat, you must think I'm crazy. I've been telling you I'm not ready for your advancements and then here I am, jumping your bones."

"I would be lying if I told you I wouldn't enjoy you jumping my bones, Renee, but the gentlemen that I am will escort you back to your room and say good night. I know, Renee, that you are not ready for an emotional or a physical relationship at this time, but I hope you know that I am not giving up on us without a fight."

"Fair enough, Mat, but do you really want to waste your time on a girl with a ready-made family?" Renee asked.

Mat blurted out, "This is my answer to your question." He then turned Renee to face him and kissed her hungrily this time.

Renee threw her arms around him and kissed him back. "Mat, I hope we do keep in touch. I consider you a good friend, and when I am ready, I am coming for you," she said.

"I hope you mean that, Renee. I will wait for you, forever. I am a very patient man. Now, you need your rest, so . . . good night."

When Renee walked into her room, she felt like she was floating on air. She felt so blessed to have met two of the most wonderful men on earth and that they both wanted her. With their time in the Dominican ending, Renee was sad. She had made two really good friends and so did her parents.

***

In the morning, they all had breakfast together and exchanged addresses, emails, and phone numbers so they could all keep in touch. Mat offered to help Renee bring down her luggage when she finished packing. Renee thanked him and promised to call him as soon as she had everything packed.

Mat knocked on Renee's door, and when she opened it, he grabbed her and kissed her like it was the last time, and that saddened her.

"Mat, you're just in time. I just finished packing the last of my things" acknowledged Renee.

"Great, I hope you know how much this is hurting me. You are not gone yet, and I am already missing you," Mat replied.

"I know how you feel, Mat. I have had the time of my life here with all of you. I can't tell you how much I will miss the walks on the beach, the witty conversations, and the most fun I have had in a long time. I really needed this vacation. It was medicinal for me. I rested, exercised, ate good meals, and made great friends. I couldn't have asked for a better vacation."

She paused and thought to herself that she wished Paul could have enjoyed it with her, but that was not ever going to happen. Thinking about Paul at this time was not fair to Mat; she knew it was Mat and not Paul who had made this vacation one to remember. Before embarking onto their bus, the two families said their last goodbyes and left for the airport. The Reynoldses were leaving for home later that afternoon.

Chapter 21

After a two hour wait at the airport, the Clarks and Renee boarded their plane for home. The flight was fine. They were served a light lunch on the plane. Christine and James watched a movie, while Renee opted to rest instead. After their plane touched ground, everyone got up and walked off the plane in the direction of the carousel to pick up their luggage. Renee's family took a shuttle, and it dropped them close to where James had parked his car. Renee's dad dropped his daughter off first and helped her with her bags. Renee thanked him again for the wonderful trip and waved them off.

When Renee stepped into her dark and silent house, in the pit of her stomach, she felt empty, lonely, and desolate. She couldn't step inside, so she called her mom on her cell phone and asked her if she would mind a house guest for the night.

"Darling, you know you are always welcome to come and stay with us. Our home is your home, and we would be happy if you spent the night. Dad said he will double back and pick you up."

"Thanks, Mom! Tell Dad not to bother. I will drive myself and I'll be right over."

Christine told James that Renee was coming over to spend the night. "I think that she is afraid to be alone in that house. It brings back sad memories for her," she said.

James replied, "Christine, I think we should ask her to stay for a while so we can keep an eye on her. I know that you would worry about her alone in that house, and so would I. I think we should talk to her about maybe selling that house and starting fresh, a new beginning."

The Clarks and Renee arrived home, and James carried their luggage into the house while Christine ran to Renee's old room and opened the drapes and the windows to get some light and some fresh air into the room, ready for Renee's visit. Not long after, Renee walked into her parents' home and her mother gave her a great big hug.

Christine asked, "Sweetheart, are you hungry? I can prepare something for you?"

"No, thanks, Mom. I'm not really hungry."

"Well, I think I'll make soup and grilled cheese sandwiches for everyone anyway," Christine replied.

"Okay, thanks, Mom! That sounds good. I'll just put my bag in my room and wash up, then I'll come right back down to eat with you and dad."

Christine prepared her family a light meal while Renee was upstairs. After being pampered at an all-inclusive resort for an entire week, Christine thought cooking felt like a chore.

Renee entered the kitchen and found her meal and her parents waiting for her at the table. "Mom, that smells so good, real American food again. What's going on? You both look so serious."

"Sweetheart, come and sit here and eat your meal. Dad and I have been thinking that perhaps you should move out of your home for a while. You and the baby are more than welcomed to stay here for as long as you want. We don't know what your plans are for the future, so maybe it's time to get rid of the house. You don't need a big house like that for just the two of you," Christine said.

Thinking for a while, Renee replied, "Mom, Dad, right now I just want to take it one day at a time. I don't want to rush into doing anything until I figure out just what my next move is going to be."

"Okay, Renee! We won't push you to make any decisions, but you know, this baby is coming soon and that's a fact. Decisions will need to be made."

"Yes! I know, Dad. Don't push me to make any decisions, okay? We've just come back from a great vacation, and I just don't want to come back to reality yet. Can't you both see how hard this is for me?" She started crying big sobs at the kitchen table.

James said softly, "Renee, sweetheart, we are just concerned about your future. Mom and I won't push you anymore to make any decisions. Instead, we will support you and help you when you need us. Now, wipe those tears and eat up. You're eating for two now, you know?"

Renee blabbered, "Thanks, guys! I'll need your support. I don't know if I can do this on my own. FYI, Dad, eating for two is just a myth."

"Renee, you won't have to. Dad and I are here for you and that grandbaby of ours. Just because you are having a child of your own doesn't mean that we stop being your parents. Renee, you will always be our baby girl," Christine replied.

Renee and her parents were all exhausted, so they got up to go to bed.

"Good night, Mom, Dad. See you in the morning."

"Good night, sweetheart. Sleep well, and if you need us, we're just next door," Christine said.

As Renee crawled into her bed, she prayed, "Dear God, please help me be a good mother to this child and please, please, let this little miracle be healthy." She then drifted off to sleep.

Later that night, her cell phone started to ring, startling her. She answered, a little groggy. She was surprised it was Mat.

"Hi, there! Did I wake you?" Mat asked.

"Yes, but I'm glad you did," Renee replied.

Mat confessed, "I've been missing you all day. Does that make me sound pathetic?"

"No! Not at all, it makes you sound like a man missing his very good friend."

"Just a good friend, is that all I am?"

"Yes!" Renee replied. "For now, that's all you can be . . . but just for now."

"You promise?"

"Yes, I promise. Now, this girl is tired, so good night, Mat. Thanks for checking up on me; you're sweet."

Mat whispered, "Good night, Renee. I'll keep in touch and sweet dreams."

Renee thanked God for sending this man into her life. He was being so supportive and a great friend when she really needed one. She then dozed off again.

Chapter 22

Paul was getting stronger and feeling better each day. His feelings for Rachel and her son, Philip, had intensified as well. Rachel worked hard every day at the grocery store to put food on the table and pay the bills. Paul felt useless staying home while Rachel worked. Yes, he fixed all that needed fixing in Rachel's home and that kept him busy, but now he had nothing left to do.

He felt it was time to find where he belonged. He wanted to know if there was a family out there somewhere searching for him. He knew that he was not married since he had no ring on his left hand, but maybe he had a girlfriend out there pinning for him. He must have parents and maybe some siblings looking for him, they must be worried about him and missing him. He had so many questions, but no answers.

He put out some flyers around the neighborhood with his picture and a message saying, "Do you know this man? If yes, please contact Rachel Barry at . . ." He used Rachel's cell phone number, as he did not have a phone, and anxiously waited for someone to contact her. He even checked with the police department to see if they had any missing person that fit his physical description in their database. There were no matches in the computer for a man of his age and physical description missing anywhere. He did not want to lose hope, but things did not look good.

After weeks of waiting and with no calls, he lost hope of finding out who he was. It seemed that unless his memory came back, he would never know. He read up on his condition on the library's computer. It said that some patients with amnesia never retrieve their memories, while others do in time.

Rachel had been a good friend to him and supported him in all of his decisions. She secretly hoped that he would always be Darren Michaels. She knew it was selfish of her, but she was falling for this guy and knew her son loved him like a father. She dreaded answering her cell phone every time it rang, knowing it may be someone who knew Darren from his past life. Rachel was relieved that she received no calls about that, even though Darren was disappointed. He was no closer to discovering his true identity.

While having breakfast one morning, Darren told Rachel, "I think it's time that I get a job so that I can find myself a place of my own. I know that you must be tired of having me live in your home."

Rachel was shocked to hear his announcement and replied, "Darren, what are you talking about? Philip and I love having you live with us. To be honest, I am thankful for all your help and your friendship. Philip would be heartbroken if you were to move out."

"How about you, Rachel? Would you be heartbroken if I moved out?"

"Yes, I would, if you need to know the truth."

"Well, I am thankful for your hospitality and I do have a fondness for you both as well. "If I stay here, I want to help you out. I want to be able to contribute monetarily, so that's why I need to find myself a job."

"I will bring home the newspaper tonight after work, and you can look through the classifieds. You can also go to the library. There are sites you can search on the Internet for employment," Rachel suggested.

"That's a great idea. I will walk with you and Philip this morning and continue to the library. I do hope that today's going to be my lucky day, and I find something right away."

The weather has been getting colder in New York every day. Christmas was just a few days away. The 9/11 attack was now just a bad memory for Darren; for Rachel, though, that day was a blessing.

After dropping off Philip at daycare and Rachel at her work, Darren walked to the public library. He sat at a computer and typed in "New York job bank." Every job that he thought he would enjoy asked to email them a resume. Darren didn't have one, and if he did, what would have been written on it? Darren knew he couldn't lie to potential employers. He couldn't tell them that he didn't have a resume because he didn't remember his identity.

He didn't know what he was qualified to do because he couldn't remember anything about his life.

After many wasted hours of browsing the Internet, he decided to give up and walk home. After arriving home, he did some housework, trying to forget about his wasted efforts of finding employment. He vacuumed the entire house, washed the kitchen and bathroom floors, and then did the laundry. He took a shower before Rachel came home, then found the ingredients he needed in the pantry and freezer to make a spaghetti sauce with small meatballs for dinner. Philip liked spaghetti and meatballs; it was one of his many favorites.

When Rachel entered the house with Philip, she was pleased to see that their dinner was prepared and the table was already set for them to eat. She was exhausted and starving because one of the other cashiers did not come into work and Rachel had to stay on cash with no lunch or breaks. Rachel took Philip to the washroom, and they both washed up for dinner. They all sat at the table to enjoy their meal together as a family.

"Hey there, buddy. How was your day? Guess what I made for you for dinner?"

Philip was happy to see his favorite meal being served on his little table. "I love s-ghettis" as he called it.

"I know, little dude, that's why I made it. I made it just for you."

Philip turned to his mother and told her, "Darren made s-ghettis just for me, Mommy."

"Yes, I see, Philip. You are a lucky boy to have a friend like Darren, who makes you your favorite foods."

After Darren served them all their meals, he sat down to join them at the table.

Rachel was anxious to ask, "Darren, how was your job search today? I've been thinking about you all day, wondering if you had some success in finding a job."

"Well, I found lots of jobs that I was interested in," replied Darren. "But with no resume and no knowledge of my past employment, I had no luck at all."

"That's too bad. I asked some of my regulars today if they knew of any job openings at their or their spouse's workplace for a hard working guy, and

Janice O'Hara told me that her husband, Ron, is looking for someone to tend the bar and wait tables at his pub, It's called the O'Hara's Restaurant and Pub. Now, if you are interested, she gave me Ron's cell number. I told her you would phone him tonight if you were interested."

He was so pleased with the news that he got up from his chair, pulled Rachel out from the table, and gave her a big kiss. Rachel knew it was just a kiss between friends, but she wished her heart realized it too. Darren exclaimed, "Oh, Rachel! You just made my day. Forgive me. I didn't mean to make you feel awkward by kissing you."

She was speechless and was trying to gasp for air.

Darren felt like Rachel was not opposed to the kiss, so he asked her, "Rachel, could I try kissing you again?"

She just nodded her head to let him know she was willing to let him kiss her again and again as often as he wanted. He kissed her tenderly and then with more passion and hunger than she had ever felt in her entire life. She wanted the kiss to go on forever because she knew now that this man owned her heart and had owned it since the day he had entered her home.

Darren stepped away from Rachel and gazed into her eyes. He knew that it was probably a mistake kissing her. It was just not fair to Rachel. He was a man with no knowledge of his past. The last thing he wanted to do was to hurt her. Yes, he cared deeply for her and Philip, but was there someone who had a claim to his heart waiting for him somewhere in this city that he could not remember? He thought that if there was someone special in his life he would be able to sense it. He had to stop this before there were amorous feelings between them; he did not want to give Rachel the wrong impression. If only he knew that there was no one waiting for him or loving him somewhere else; only then could he give his heart to another.

He sat down to finish eating his dinner when Philip yelled out, "More s-ghettis, please!"

Darren and Rachel both laughed, happy of the distraction. Darren told Rachel to go up and take a shower while Philip and he cleaned up. She thanked him for the delicious meal and for keeping Philip busy while she took a hot shower. Darren gave Philip a few plastic containers and a clean washcloth for him to help out with the cleanup.

***

Rachel was all confused about all that happened in the kitchen at dinner. She thought that he was really into her, but then he seemed like he had second thoughts. What was she to do with that? She loved Darren and wished he loved her in return. She would love for Philip to have a man to call dad, a man to also raise him.

She dried herself off and wrapped herself and her hair in a towel, then went to dress in her room. She knelt on the ground with her elbows resting on her mattress and pleaded to God.

Rachel prayed, "Please, God, let this man love me and my son because I know you know how much we both love and need him. Why would you bring this man to my doorstep if not for us to be together, to be a real life loving family?" She then got up, lay down on her bed, and rested her head on the pillow for a moment. She fell fast asleep.

***

Darren heard Rachel go to her room, so he brought Philip up to take a bath. He knocked on Rachel's bedroom door, but she did not answer, so he peeked inside and saw that she was sleeping. Darren decided he would give Philip, the spaghetti monster, his bath tonight. He also decided to join Philip in the bathtub so they could both get cleaned up at the same time. Darren made sure to put lots of soap so there would be clouds of bubbles for Philip to enjoy. Philip did enjoy his bath time; he didn't want to get out.

Rachel awoke to laughter. She put on her robe and followed the laughter to the bathroom. The door was unlocked, and she just walked in not expecting to find them both in a bubble bath together. She started laughing at the sight. Darren had bubbles all around his face; he looked like Santa Claus, and Philip looked like an old dwarf.

"Well, well, don't you two look like you're having fun?" Rachel remarked.

Darren asked, "Did we wake you? It's hard to get this guy to use his indoor voice."

"No! I'm glad I got to see this," answered Rachel. "Wait there, don't get out. I want to get my camera. This is a candid shot, one for the mantel if I had one."

When she came back, she took a few shots of them in the tub. They were perfect; it was something a real father and son would share.

This was what Philip was missing, being he had never had a father figure in his life. Did Darren realize how much he had changed their lives? He had brought so much joy to them, and Rachel and her son would cherish and be grateful to him for the rest of their days.

"Okay, Rachel! Can you leave us guys some time to get rinsed off and get dried and dressed without any more pictures being taken?" Darren asked.

"Okay, you party poopers, I'll let you do your male bonding thing. When you two are ready, I'll meet you in the living room with some hot chocolate and mini marshmallows and animal crackers for Santa and his little elf. If you are interested, Darren, maybe you can get a position as a mall Santa." She left them laughing at the idea.

When Philip and Darren came down to the living room, they had found three cups of hot chocolate and a plate of animal crackers. They enjoyed listening to Philip guessing the animals and making the sound of each animal before devouring the cracker.

Darren was pleased to see a roaring fire in the fireplace and said, "Rachel, this fire makes the living room so cozier and inviting."

It was time for Rachel to put her excited child to bed. She asked Philip to run upstairs and pick out a book or two for his bedtime stories. Philip did as he was told because he was very tired.

Rachel gave Darren the piece of paper with Ron O'Hara's phone number before joining her son upstairs. He decided to call while Rachel and Philip were busy. It was the perfect time to call, as the house was now quiet. He rang the number and reached Ron on his third try. It was hard to hear Ron speak because of the music and the chattering noises from the pub in the background.

Ron said that he was hoping to hear from Darren and that his wife highly recommended him for the job. Ron asked, "Would you be able to come down and help me out tonight? I'm sort of shorthanded."

Darren excitedly answered, "Sure, give me the address and I'll take a cab down."

"You're really helping me out of a jam," Ron said. "You get a receipt from the cab driver and I'll reimburse your fare, and by the way, you're hired. We will talk after your shift tonight."

"Thank you! I'll be right down." After he hung up, Darren ran up the stairs two at a time and walked quietly into Philip's room and gestured for Rachel to come out. Darren reported, "Rachel, I got the job and I start right now, tonight, so don't wait up for me because I don't know when I'll be home. Thank you again for helping me get this job. With my first paycheck, I'm taking you out for dinner and a movie, so you'll have to find a sitter." He kissed her quickly on the mouth and ran down the stairs to call for a cab. He then waited outside for his ride to arrive. The evening air was crisp. Winter was surely here.

Rachel was so happy for him. He was so excited and ready for this new chapter in his life. She hoped that she and Philip would have major roles in that chapter.

Chapter 23

As Darren arrived at the pub, he walked in asking the first waitress he saw if she could be kind enough to direct him to the owner of the establishment. She pointed to the man behind the bar. Darren walked over, zigzagging through the crowd, and introduced himself to his new boss. They shook hands, and Ron told Darren that he would be shadowing him tonight behind the bar. Darren was eager to learn, and he wanted to please his new boss, Ron. Darren was amazed that he needed no help from Ron or the cocktail book on how to prepare fancy drinks. He seemed to be an old pro at this, like he had done this kind of work before.

Ron came over to Darren and said to him, "You've tended bar before it seems."

"I guess I have in the past," Darren replied.

"Okay then, Darren! You are the full-time bartender here at O'Hara's Restaurant and Pub. I'll make you a work schedule, and it will be ready for you tomorrow afternoon. Now, do you think you can manage alone for a few minutes? I want to check in with the kitchen and maybe take a short break."

"Sure, I've got this covered. Do what you need to do, boss," Darren said.

"Darren, I think you are doing a great job for your first-time bartending here, but please no formalities. We all go by our first names or nicknames here at O'Hara's."

The pub started thinning out at about eleven p.m. Darren guessed everyone had jobs to go to in the morning since it was only Monday night. He started cleaning up the place to close up for midnight. He put all the bottles back on the shelf where they belonged and put the dirty glasses in the kitchen to be washed in the dishwasher. Darren was getting a little tired. He was usually in bed by ten p.m. because Rachel had to work in the morning. After all was cleaned and the chairs were placed on the tables, they closed up and everyone wandered home.

When Darren entered the house, it was after one a.m. He did not want to wake anyone up this late in the evening, or this early in the morning— whichever it was. He walked up to the bathroom, then off to bed he went.

***

He slept soundly, as he did not hear Rachel and Philip get up and get ready for their day. Rachel tried to keep Philip quiet as they got ready. She knew Darren had come in late last night and that he must be tired. She missed not having him up, as he usually prepared the coffee, cereal, and toast for them before they would go off to work and daycare. It saddened her that she did not get to see his beautiful face and smile before going off to work.

When Darren got up at ten a.m., he found the house too quiet. He was used to hearing Rachel in the shower or singing in her room before descending to the kitchen with her energized son. He got up and found himself alone in this usually busy kitchen. Rachel had left him a note on the table saying:

Dear Darren,

Hope all went well at the pub last night. I am anxious to hear how the job turned out. We missed seeing you at the table this morning, but I didn't want to wake you, knowing that you had come in late last night. We both wish you a great day. See you after my shift tonight. I thought maybe we could spring for a pizza some night this week when you are off work to celebrate your new job.

Fondly yours, Rachel

Darren was a lucky man to have found a wonderful and caring woman like Rachel to share his life with. He cared deeply for her and Philip. He decided to let his old, forgotten life be forgotten. It wasn't like anyone was missing him; he had pinned up flyers everywhere and even got the police involved, but nothing had come of it. Now, he had to decide what he wanted to do next.

He now had a job that he enjoyed and that he was good at. He had a son that loved him like a father. All that was left for him to do was to convince Rachel that she loved him or at least could love him in time. He knew that his feelings for her were more than friendship or sisterly love. He hoped in time, they could become a real family. He was even hoping that in the future, perhaps Rachel would consider having children with him. He wanted to have a big family, and he didn't think it was fair to Philip, being an only child.

He decided to make a plan to woo Rachel into caring for him. He would court her like the good old fashion days. Now that he would be getting a weekly check, he could help her with the financial burden of caring for Philip and the upkeep of the home. He also wanted to take her out on romantic dates and go out on family outings.

He had a great idea. He would prepare a picnic lunch for the two of them to enjoy today since he did not get to see her this morning. Afterwards, he would pick Philip up early from daycare and go to the park. He prepared two chicken salad sandwiches and a few slices of watermelon. He planned on stopping along the way somewhere to pick up a bottle of sparkling wine for their lunch.

After preparing their lunch, he cleaned up the kitchen and then left the house to go pick the wine for their romantic lunch. When he stopped for the wine, he decided to get another bottle for that celebratory dinner they would have on his night off from the pub. He decided to stop at the florists to pick Rachel a nice bouquet of assorted flowers. He thought it would be a nice gesture to thank her for all the help and support she had given him. He had found a new life here with Rachel and Philip.

When he arrived at the grocery store, Rachel was still working the cash. He came into the store and walked directly to her station, surprising her with the flowers and an invitation to a picnic lunch. Everyone started commenting on how romantic he was. She thanked him for the beautiful flowers and told him that she would just finish up with her customer and then gladly meet him in the front of the store. He left her and awaited her arrival.

She quickly finished up with her last customer and happily joined Darren, who was waiting for her with a picnic basket in hand.

"Rachel, do you know if there is a place nearby where we can enjoy a quiet picnic? I know you have only an hour before you have to return to work."

"Yes! I have just the place. Behind that little church there are picnic tables where we can have a quiet lunch together. I have to say, this is the nicest surprise anyone has ever given me."

"I hope to surprise you like this for years to come."

Rachel held her breath—did Darren just propose marriage to her? No! He only meant he would do nice things for her because they were friends. Yes! That was what he had meant to say and that made more sense as she thought about it.

Darren opened up the lunch basket and passed her a chicken sandwich, then took out two plastic wine glasses and poured them both some sparkling wine.

"This is too much. You are going to spoil me with all this attention," Rachel said.

"Rachel, you deserved to be spoiled. You are the most selfless and giving person I have ever met. I mean, that I can remember ever meeting."

They both had a good laugh at his correction.

Rachel asked, "Darren, how was your first night working at the pub?"

"It went quite well. It seems I have what it takes to be a bartender. I think in my past life I must have worked as a bartender because I knew how to make all the different alcoholic beverages people were ordering from me."

"So you think you were a bartender before losing your memory?" Rachel asked.

"I think I might have been. The job comes naturally to me, and I seem to know the ins and outs of it."

"So, we uncovered a little piece of the puzzle of your real identity!"

"I guess we have," Darren declared.

"Does working at the pub bring on any memories of your past life?"

He shook his head no. Then Darren said, "Rachel, I was thinking that if you wouldn't mind it, I would like to start courting you? That's only if you want to; if not, I understand, and will not ask you again."

Rachel leaped up and put her arms around Darren's neck and kissed him, then said, "Yes!" Then she kissed him. "I would love, love, love to be courted by you. What made you decide that you wanted me? I thought you didn't want to make any romantic connections in case you had someone out there that you may remember one day."

"Yes, that is what I had thought too, but I decided that life is too short and one must live every day to the fullest. There's no one out there looking for me, I know it. So, I decided to start my new life today as Darren Michaels, eligible bachelor and bartender at the O'Hara's Restaurant and Pub."

"Well then, I want to make a toast to you, Darren. I want to congratulate you on your new job and the beginning of your new life as Darren Michaels." Tears fell from Rachel's eyes. She was so happy for him, but mostly for her and her son. She looked at her watch. She had to run because her lunch break finished five minutes ago. "I'm sorry, Darren, but I'm late for work. I want to thank you for doing this for me and for including me in your life."

"Oh! Before you go, Rachel, I was wondering if it would be okay with you if I picked up Philip on my way home so we can have a little male-bonding time?"

"He would love that. I'll call the daycare when I get into the store and tell them that you will be coming to get him," Rachel answered.

He then kissed her tenderly on the mouth and said, "See you tonight." Then he went on his merry way.

***

Back at work, Rachel realized she had had the most wonderful lunch she had ever had, and with the most caring and wonderful man she had ever met in her entire life. Today, he proclaimed his feelings toward her and told her he wanted to share his life with her and her son. She had wished and prayed all her life to be lucky enough to find someone just like Darren, and here he was—a man who wanted her as much as she wanted him.

***

Darren arrived at the daycare where Philip was waiting impatiently for him. Philip's friends came over to meet the man who was picking him up.

The kids asked Philip, "Is this your dad, Philip?"

Philip then looked up at Darren with a sad look on his face.

"Yes! I am Philip's dad," Darren said.

Philip looked like a peacock strutting off his feathers. Philip was so happy and proud to be Darren's son, and Darren was also happy and proud to be Philip's dad.

When they left the daycare, Darren asked Philip, "I know it is cold out, but I was wondering if you would like to go to the playground and then we can stop and get a hot chocolate on our way home."

Philip did not answer.

Darren asked again, "Is going to the playground and getting a hot chocolate a good plan, son?"

"Darren, can you be my dad?" Philip asked.

"Philip, would you like me to be your dad?"

"Yes!" Philip answered happily.

Darren replied, "Then I am your dad."

Philip excitedly cried out, "Yippee! I have a dad, and we are going to the park, and then we will get hot chocolate!"

Darren picked up Philip and placed him on his shoulders with the pride of a new father. After enjoying their afternoon together in the park, they walked home hand in hand.

When they arrived home, Philip asked his new dad, "Let's take a bubble bath together. It's lots of fun!"

"Sure! Let's get your swimming trunks on first," Darren answered.

***

Rachel ran home, excited to see her family. She found them enjoying a bubble bath again. Philip was so excited to tell her the news. "Mom! Me and dad went to the park today, and we got hot chocolate. I sat on Dad's shoulders."

"That sounds like you both had a wonderful day. While I go start dinner, you both get dried up and dressed and meet me downstairs," Rachel said.

The moment she left them, she ran to her room, with tears gushing down her face. Darren wanted Philip to be his son, and she knew how much Philip wanted a dad. She knew he wanted a dad, like his friend Tyler's dad, who took him fishing, go-kart racing, kite flying, and played ball with him. He wanted to experience all the different things fathers are supposed to do with their sons.

Rachel left her room and went down to start their dinner. When Philip and Darren arrived in the kitchen, the macaroni was boiling on the stove and there were hot dogs on the table. After all was devoured, Darren excused himself from the table, as he had to call a cab to drive him to work.

"Rachel, dinner was great, one of my favorites," Darren admitted.

Philip agreed, "Mine too, Mommy, my favorite."

Before leaving for work, Darren gave them both a kiss and wished them both a good night.

After he left, Rachel tidied up the kitchen and then she and Philip watched a little television before his bedtime. Philip fell asleep watching TV. He had had a busy day with Darren. She carried him to his room and placed him into bed. She kissed him on the forehead, closed his light, and walked quietly out of his room.

Now that Philip was out for the night, she decided to take a relaxing soak in a hot bubble bath. She played her favorite spa CD and lit up a few vanilla scented candles. She was in her bath soaking, daydreaming of her and Darren making love. She was getting a little hot and bothered when the phone rang. It startled her and made her lose her train of thought. She decided to let the machine take the message, as she was not quite ready to leave the warmth of the tub. When she came out of the tub, her skin was prune like.

After drying herself off, she dressed in her robe, then walked to her bedroom to see who had called and left a message. She was a little upset she had missed Darren's phone call. He called to say good night and for her not to wait up for him because he would be home late. She then slid under the covers and fell fast asleep.

***

Rachel and Philip left the next morning for daycare and work. They missed not seeing Darren in the morning, but they knew they would get used to it. When Darren got up, he also missed not seeing his little family. He always enjoyed having breakfast ready for both of them and talking to them about what plans they had for the day.

He remembered the morning when Rachel had said, "I feel like today's going to be my lucky day. You see, boys, my knight in shining armor is going to come and whisk me away from the store and bring me to his castle. He is going to be so rich that I will not need to work and we will live happily ever after just like in your books, Philip."

Rachel and Darren had started to laugh but not Philip, he had started to cry.

"What's going on, buddy?" Rachel asked Philip.

"Mommy, I don't want you to go away. I want you to stay with me and Darren."

"Oh, Philip!" Rachel burst out. "Mommy is just teasing. I would never leave you because you are my little boy and we belong together."

"What about Darren, Mom? Does he belong?" Philip asked.

Rachel had just looked at Darren, not knowing what to say, so Darren answered for her, "Yes, Philip, we all belong together. We are a family and families stick together, right?"

"Yes, Mom! We are a family, so you can't leave us ever."

Darren recalled how she had responded, "Your right, buddy, a person who belongs to a family never leaves."

Chapter 24

Darren was pleased that he did not need to work tonight. His boss gave him the night off, knowing that the weekend would be busy with Christmas only a few weeks away. Darren would have to work overtime with the Christmas parties and the yuletide festivities.

Darren decided that he would take Rachel out for dinner and a movie. He called his boss, asking him to suggest a place close to the theatre so that he could take his girl out. After calling to make reservations, he called the daycare to see if they could suggest a sitter to watch over Philip for the evening. The director of the daycare suggested one of their own student employees, Susan Dark, who worked there with the after school programs. Darren asked for Susan's phone number and called her. Susan was happy to help out. She could walk over after finishing at the daycare that afternoon.

Susan advised him, "I will need a ride home afterwards because it's not safe to walk home alone after dark."

Darren kept himself busy; he changed the bedding, did the laundry, dusted, vacuumed, and washed the floors, with time to spare for him to shower and change.

When Rachel arrived at the daycare, she was surprised when Susan told her she was coming home to sit with Philip tonight. It seemed like Darren had planned for them to go out on the town tonight. She did not ask any questions but was wondering what Darren had planned for them this evening. She wanted to run home, anxious to see what other surprises awaited her, but it was slow going since Philip had short legs and did not want to be carried.

When Rachel arrived home, she walked into a very clean house and saw a handsome, impatient man waiting for her to show up.

He greeted the both of them and ordered Rachel to go up and take a quick shower, get dressed, and come downstairs to join them. She obeyed his every word. She felt like a teenager on her first date.

While Rachel was upstairs getting ready, Susan arrived and Darren asked her what she liked on her pizza.

"My family usually orders the deluxe pizza," Susane replied.

Rachel descended the stairs, wearing a beautiful knee-length black cock-tail dress. Darren whistled at her in admiration. Susan commented on how lovely she looked as well. Rachel thanked everyone for the kind compliments.

Darren asked, "Rachel, could you phone a pizza place and order a deluxe pizza for the kids?"

She left the room to phone for an extra-large pizza, with everything on one half and plain cheese on the other, to be sent to her address. When Rachel returned, she told them that she ordered a pizza and it should be there in forty minutes.

"Mommy, did you get cheese pizza for me?" Philip asked.

"Yes, Philip! I got you half a cheese pizza and half a deluxe pizza for Susan."

"What's a lux pizza?" Philip asked.

"No, Philip, it's called a *de*luxe pizza and it has all kinds of different meats and vegetables on it."

"Yuck! I just want my cheese pizza, Mommy. No lux pizza for me," Philip replied.

"Okay! Okay! No lux pizza for you Philip, just for Susan." Rachel gave Susan the money to pay for their pizza and gave Susan her cell phone number in case of an emergency.

Darren had called for a taxi to take them to the restaurant. When the cab arrived, Darren hurried Rachel along, as he had reserved a table for six thirty. She was like a mother hen worried about her chick. She had never left Philip with a sitter before, but she knew Susan from the daycare. Her son was in good hands. Philip was pushing his mother out the door. He wanted her to leave so that he and Susan could play a game of Candy Land before the pizza arrived. Darren tried to reassure her that Philip was in excellent hands.

Rachel said goodbye and good night to her son, then followed Darren to the cab.

Sitting in the cab, Rachel asked, "Darren, what made you decide on taking me out tonight?"

Darren answered, "Well, firstly, I want to say how beautiful you look this evening. Secondly, I want to thank Ron for giving me the night off. Thirdly, I wanted to take you out on an official first date. I wanted to celebrate having found a job and thanking my lucky stars that you and Philip want me to be part of your family."

She was getting emotional again, so Darren sat close to her, put his arms around her, and told her, "That's enough of that for tonight, sweetheart." Suddenly he got a flashback of his past. He was calling someone "sweetheart," but it wasn't Rachel—it was another woman. But who?

Rachel felt him tense up and looked up at him. "Are you all right, Darren? You zoned out for a moment."

"Yes! I'm fine, just getting a little emotional as well, but enough of the emotions. Tonight, I want everything to be special and I want us to both have fun. No worries, no problems, just a woman and a man on a date celebrating his good fortune."

Rachel remarked, "You mean, our good fortune? I feel as lucky as you do, as I have found the love of my life and a father for my son."

He grabbed her tightly and kissed her tenderly but with passion. She wished that they were embracing in the privacy of her bedroom.

The cab stopped at the restaurant. Darren took Rachel by the hand and guided her inside. As they were being seated, he asked for a good bottle of champagne, as they were celebrating tonight. Rachel blushed; she had never been on a real date before and she did not know how to act in a fancy restaurant. She had only been to restaurants like McDonald's, Harvey's, Pizza Hut and Dairy Queen—the restaurants that were kid friendly. At this restaurant there were tablecloths, glassware, and silverware. She thought to herself, *Dorothy, you are not in Kansas anymore*, and she started to chuckle.

Darren asked to be excused; he needed to use the men's room. But in reality, he needed to get outside and breathe in some cold air. He was confused about what had happened to him in the taxi cab. The flashback he had in the cab—did it mean he was getting his memory back or was that just a one-time thing? Who was that lady in his vision and what connection did she have to him? Darren walked into the restroom and splashed a little cold water on his face before returning to his table.

Their server poured each of them a glass of champagne and gave them each a menu to look over. Darren asked their server what he would suggest for them to try. Their server suggested the beef tenderloin, with baked potato and sautéed mushrooms. Darren looked at Rachel, and she nodded her head, so he ordered two of the beef tenderloin and asked for two garden salads to start. The waiter jotted their request and went off to the kitchen to deliver their orders.

They enjoyed each other's company and the bubbling champagne. The waiter placed two garden salads and excused himself from the table. After the salads were finished, the main course arrived and it smelled heavenly. The odor of their meals triggered another flashback of a family enjoying a meal together. Darren zoned out again while Rachel kept on talking to him, without noticing he was not listening.

Darren wondered who the family was at the dinner table in his vision. Was it his family? But he did not see himself at the table, so who were these people in these images he was getting? The waiter arrived and asked them if they would like some coffee and some dessert. Coming back to reality, Darren asked Rachel if she would like anything else and she said, "No, I'm stuffed. I couldn't eat another bite."

Darren asked the waiter for the bill, and he took out some cash from his pocket. Rachel asked him, "Darren, where did you get the money?"

"I asked Ron for an advance on my pay. I wanted to take you out on a real date, so he advanced me enough money to pay for an expensive dinner and to pay for a sitter."

"Well, that was nice of him, but you shouldn't spend your hard earned money on me."

"I beg to differ," Darren replied. "I think my money was well spent."

After paying his server and giving him a nice tip, they walked to the movie theatre and decided to go see a comedy. They opted not to get popcorn because they were stuffed from their delicious dinner. They found a spot to sit. Darren then put his arm around Rachel's shoulders, and she leaned in close to put her head onto his chest. She loved this man more than she had ever thought a woman could.

The movie started, and it was all it was hyped up to be, as they laughed and enjoyed their time out together. When the movie ended, Rachel called for a cab to take them home. As they entered the cab and advised the driver where they wanted to go, they snuggled and made out in the back seat. Rachel didn't care if the driver was watching because she was enjoying Darren's passionate kisses and his touch. He stopped himself before he exploded. They were both panting heavily. The taxi stopped them at their door, and Darren asked the driver to wait because he had another fair for him. Rachel entered the house and saw Susan reading a book on the sofa.

"Susan, did you have any problems with Philip tonight?" Rachel asked.

"No, he was a little darling. If you ever need a sitter again, please don't be afraid to ask."

"Thank you, Susan. Darren has a cab waiting for you outside."

Susan got herself ready and walked out the door. Darren paid Susan for sitting with Philip, and he gave the cab driver enough money to take Susan home. He thanked her again for helping him out tonight and wished her a good night.

Rachel looked in on her son, and he was sleeping soundly. She went downstairs to be with Darren. She sat on the sofa, and Darren joined her. She wrapped her arms around his neck and gave him a memorable kiss.

"Wow! What was that for?" Darren asked.

"That's for making my son the happiest little boy in the world and for making his mother feel again. In the short time he has known you, he has become so attached to you. At times, he looks at you as if you were a superhero. Philip loves you like a boy loves his father, Darren," Rachel replied.

"That's great because I love him like a son. I felt like that kiss was more than an appreciative kiss, Rachel. Rachel? Am I correct in assuming that it meant something more?"

"Okay, yes!" Rachel admitted. "You're right in assuming that the kiss meant so much more than just appreciation. It meant thank you for helping me and Philip, for fixing what needed to be fixed in the house, for pitching in with the day-to-day chores, for the cooking, and mostly for bringing joy and laughter into our dreary lives. I did the best I could without any help from anyone and that was working, but when you joined our little family, I now just cannot phantom how we did it without you. If you were ever to leave us, I don't know how we would manage without you. Do you even know how much you've changed our lives for the better?" She started to cry again.

"That's all nice and dandy, but I was hoping you were going to tell me that you had romantic feelings for me; that's all," Darren replied.

Rachel added, "Oh! Did I forget to say that I also kissed you like that because I've fallen head over heels for you? Now does that answer your question, Mr. Michaels?"

"I knew that kiss meant more than appreciation," Darren said.

Rachel punched him in the arm for teasing her.

"I'm relieved in hearing that your falling for me because I would feel stupid telling you that I love you and Philip very much if you felt nothing for me," Darren said.

Rachel was afraid of what she was thinking about doing. She had not been with a man for a very long time. She wondered if she remembered how to be a seductress, and what about Darren? Would he remember how to please a woman, she thought to herself. She was melting in his embrace, so she decided she was going for it.

Rachel whispered in his ear, "Darren, I want you so badly right now. Would it be too forward of me to take you by the hand and guide you to my bedroom?"

He looked at her, and she was blushing. "It would not be forward of you at all," Darren replied. "I was just wondering how to ask you the exact same thing. I want to show you how much I care by making love to you and devouring your naked body."

Rachel thought it was funny because he was now the one blushing. Smiling, she grabbed him and pulled him forcefully up the stairs to her bedroom.

Loving someone and making love to someone were like riding a bike. Something one's body does not forget. To be honest, Rachel had never been loved or been devoured by any man like this. Darren made her feel more alive and more feminine than she had ever felt in her entire life. He did things to her that she had never thought possible. She climaxed for the first time ever, which was not overrated by any means. He made sure that she was in ecstasy the entire time. She loved that he took time to hold her and caress her naked body. He suckled on her breast, which drove her crazy, and made sure to be very gentle when entering her and making love to her. He was a very patient and selfless lover. She now felt saddened, as she had never experienced this most amazing sensation before.

Darren showed her how much he loved her by his every touch. Her body now craved Darren's touch and his love making techniques with all of her being. She did not want to seem selfish, but she wanted him to take her again and again. She could not get enough of this man; she was like a sex-crazed animal, and Darren loved making Rachel squeal. She loved how much he wanted her. They could not get enough of each other.

Darren stopped abruptly when he felt a sudden pain in his heart as if he was having a heart attack. He couldn't catch his breath. There was something wrong with him, but he could not fathom what it could be.

"Darren, are you alright? What's going on with you?" Rachel asked worriedly.

Darren did not respond, as he could not hear her from the loud beating of his heart. His heart was beating so loudly that it had drowned out her voice. Rachel phoned 911 and asked for an ambulance to be sent to her address. She frantically clothed him as well as she could, but he was deadweight, though he could hear her speaking to him now.

Rachel was telling him that she had called for an ambulance and that they should be arriving any minute now. Rachel uttered, "Please, Darren, don't you die on me. I couldn't take it." She started sobbing.

He could tell she was afraid of losing him, so he calmed her down by telling her that he was feeling better now. "Rachel, I want you to know that I love you so much. Making love to you tonight was the most natural and wonderful feeling I had ever experienced in my entire life." After proclaiming his love to her, he started having sharp pains in his heart again.

Rachel could hear the ambulance coming from blocks away and she ran to open the door for the paramedics. She ran right back to be by Darren's side. The paramedics checked their patient over and asked her about his medical history, which she did not have. She told them that he had never been sick since she had known him. They took his vitals and said that his heart was beating quite fast. They put him on a stretcher and strapped him in, then rolled him into the ambulance. Rachel thought to herself that he was much too young to have a heart attack. She looked on as the ambulance took Darren away. She ran upstairs and got Philip out of bed. He was still very tired, but she got him dressed and phoned for a cab to pick them up and drive them to the hospital.

The emergency team hooked Darren on the ECG machine while in transit. When they arrived, the doctor on call checked Darren over and told him, "Darren, you are not having a heart attack but an anxiety attack. It would be hard for you to differentiate an anxiety attack from a heart attack if you've never experienced an anxiety attack before. Be glad you're not having a heart attack because the outcome is never a positive one. We administered a sedative that should help you rest. We're not admitting you so you are free to go home. I suggest you go home and get a good night's rest. If you get another episode, I suggest you go see your doctor and maybe he can prescribe something for you to take if these attacks come on regularly."

Darren voiced groggily, "Doctor, this is the first time that this has ever happened to me. Well . . . that I know of."

Rachel and Philip had arrived when Darren was exiting the emergency. Rachel ran into Darren's arms, asking, "Darren, are you okay? I was so afraid for you."

I am fine. The doctor informed me that I just had an anxiety attack. "I just need to go home and rest. I should be as good as new in the morning. Hi, Philip! Shouldn't you be in bed?"

"Mommy got me up. She said you were sick. Did the doctor give you a needle?"

"Yes! One little needle, but it did not hurt. How about we call a cab to take us home and go back to bed. What do you think, kiddo?"

"I'd like to go home, Dad." Philip wanted Darren to carry him out to the cab, but Rachel said no to that idea. They both took him by the hand, and they all walked out together.

Back home, Rachel put her son back to bed, then put Darren to bed. She slept next to him, keeping a watchful eye on him throughout the night. She was so thankful that he was alive and back home.

***

The next morning, Rachel was awoken by the phone. She let the machine get it because she was too tired to reach for it. She was shocked to hear it was her boss.

Her boss asked, "Where are you, Rachel? You are late for work. I hope since you did not answer your phone that you are on your way to work now."

Rachel got up in a hurry, looking at the time on the clock. She was an hour late for her shift at the store. She had never been late before, so she hoped that she wouldn't be in too much trouble. She was sure that after explaining to her boss the events of last night that he would be a little forgiving. She had no time to take Philip to daycare, so she woke Darren up and asked him if he could take Philip to daycare for her. Darren felt badly, as he knew it was his fault she was late for work.

"Rachel, you call the daycare and tell them that Philip won't be in today because he is staying home with his dad. Now, if you don't want to get fired, you had better get ready for work. I'll call you a cab so that you get to work a little quicker," Darren proposed.

She thanked him and then kissed him goodbye before rushing out to work.

Philip crawled into bed with Darren and snuggled close. Philip was told by his mother to be quiet because Darren was still sleeping. Philip started poking Darren in the face, saying, "Daddy, are you awake yet?" Darren did not respond, so Philip tried to open Darren's eyes with his fingers, asking him, "Daddy, are you awake now? Daddy, it's time to get up? I'm very hungry. My stomach is making a hungry sound."

Darren opened his eyes and grabbed him. "Hello, Philip! What can I do for you on this beautiful sunny morning?"

"Mommy came into my room this morning and told me to stay in my room until you came to get me, but I am hungry. Daddy, my tummy is rumbling. It's so hungry like when Winnie the Pooh is hungry for honey."

Darren started to laugh at his son's comparison.

"Do you think you are awake enough to make me some pancakes?"

"You know what, Philip? I'm hungry for pancakes too. What if we get up and we both make some pancakes for our breakfast?" Darren suggested.

Philip yelled, "Okay! Let's go." After all had been eaten and the kitchen had been cleaned up, they both decided to watch a movie.

Darren had fallen asleep on the sofa while Philip was watching his movie. Darren was dreaming of a woman who was reaching out for him, but as he was just about to grab hold of her slender fingers, she started falling out of his reach. He could not save her. He got up frightened for this woman whom he thought he recognized from the past. He got up sweating as if he had a fever. He did not know who she was or how he knew her, but it felt like she was haunting him. His memories were starting to resurface, a little at a time. He wondered if he would get all of his memories back. Darren wondered if he would ever remember this person in his dreams and how she fit in his life.

Chapter 25

Darren went out one morning in search of some long overdue answers. One of his regulars at the pub told him that he did investigative work, so Darren decided to look him up for personal reasons. He found the address to this building in the phone book. As he entered the building, there was a directory of various names and offices of the people who work in the building.

The office of Doug Hansen of New York Private Investigators was on the fifth floor of the building. Darren took the elevator up and walked into Doug's office. He was greeted by Doug himself. Darren told Doug about his life since 9/11 but wanted to know his true identity. Doug said he would be happy to look into finding Darren's past. Doug took out his camera and took a picture of Darren. He thought that he would show the picture around to the employees who had survived the 9/11 attack to see if anyone recognized Darren.

"That sounds like a great plan," Darren said. "If you find anything at all, you can reach me at the pub."

Walking home, he wondered if asking Doug to look into finding his past history was a mistake. He loved his new life with Rachel and Philip, and he didn't want anyone to disturb that. He just didn't know what the correct decision was.

When he arrived home, he decided to start tidying up so that Rachel had the evening to relax. When Rachel and Philip arrived home, they found the house had been cleaned. Darren had surprised them by ordering a pizza, half cheese and half deluxe, for them for dinner. Darren did not need to work that evening, so he decided to make tonight a movie night with pizza, chocolate milk, and wine.

There was a roaring fire in the fireplace. They ate the entire pizza, then Darren came out with dessert. Philip was excited when he saw the sticks and marshmallows.

"Daddy, are we gonna cook those marshmallows in the fireplace?" Philip asked.

"Yes! We are Philip and we are going to make s'mores."

Inquisitive, Philip asked, "What are s'mores, Mommy?"

Rachel answered, "S'mores are made up of two graham crackers, with chocolate and marshmallows in the middle."

"See, Philip, let me show you," Darren said while demonstrating. "First, you take a marshmallow and you cook it in the fireplace on a pointy stick. Then, when they are to your liking, you place the marshmallow on one cracker. And then, you place a piece of chocolate on top of the marshmallow and mush it all together with another cracker. It's like a sticky delicious campfire sandwich."

Philip shouted, "Wow, Mommy, it's like going camping. I have never been camping before. I think, when I grow up, I want to go camping, Mommy."

"Philip, what if, when your mommy takes her holidays in the summer, we go camping as a family?" Darren said. "We will get a tent and sleeping bags and sleep under the stars. We could even go fishing if you want."

"Mommy, do you think we can go on a vacation?"

"That sounds like a plan," Rachel answered.

"Mommy, do you think Santa will get me a fishing rod and a sleeping bag for Christmas if I ask him?"

"You know what? I think that's a great idea, but don't forget, Santa only delivers gifts to the good little boys and girls."

They all ate a few too many s'mores because they were so addictive. Then they washed up and started their movie. Rachel and Darren enjoyed drinking the wine while watching the movie. Philip couldn't stop yawning, as he was ready for bed. He had had a very busy day with his indoor campfire.

"It's time for bed, little man, so say good night to Darren and off we go."

"Mommy, can daddy tuck me in tonight and read me a story?"

"You bet, son! I would love to tuck you in and read you a book if it's okay with your mom?"

"Is it okay, Mommy? Can daddy tuck me in?"

"Yes! Of course, he can. You both go ahead while I clean up down here. I'll come up in a few minutes and kiss you good night."

While Rachel was cleaning up, she felt like her life had become a fairy tale. The three of them were like the three bears: the papa bear, the mama bear, and the baby bear. She hoped that this fairy tale ended like all of the Disney fairy tales—happily ever after.

Darren caught her humming happily while tidying up the kitchen. He sneaked up on her and grabbed her from behind.

"You startled me. Is Philip sleeping all ready?" Rachel asked.

"Yes, I didn't even get to finish the book before he fell asleep. The little guy must have been exhausted from his busy day. You look tired too, Rachel."

"Yes, I guess I am. I think I'll turn in too. Do you want to join me?" Rachel asked.

"Sure," Darren replied.

"Darren, you sound hesitant. Is there something wrong?"

"No . . . I guess I'm just a little tired too. Let's go to bed."

They both got ready for bed and got under the covers. Darren turned and gave her a quick kiss good night, then got himself comfortable under the covers.

Rachel was a little upset; she thought that they would make love or at least hold each other and snuggle. Since there was no movement on his part, she positioned herself close to his bare back and started giving little kisses on his back, but he did not respond. She turned around and wept silently, wondering what was going on with him.

Darren was trying to control himself. He had felt each and every kiss and wanted so much to turn around and make love to her, but he was afraid of hurting her. He felt like he should wait before committing his heart and soul to Rachel because of that darn woman who had been tormenting him in his dreams. He loved his life as Darren, but he now needed to know who he really was. That woman may be his mother, his sister, or maybe a girlfriend, but he had to know for sure that his heart was free to give to Rachel.

Chapter 26

Things were getting a little uncomfortable at home for Darren. He seemed to be somewhere far away when he was at home. He was still a loving father and a loving partner, but he was reclusive. Rachel did not want to ask him what was going on with him, but she was hoping that he would talk to her and let her in.

With Thanksgiving the next day, they were going to spend an entire day cooking and eating. Philip was excited about spending the day with his two parents. Darren did not need to work, so they could enjoy each other's company, watching movies and playing board games. He was also going to watch the Thanksgiving parade on the television. Philip knew at the end of the parade Santa Claus would make his appearance. He would have to send his letter to Santa Claus soon.

Thanksgiving was like Christmas morning for Philip. He got Darren and Rachel up early so as not to miss the parade on TV. Darren made French toast for breakfast while Rachel was making a pumpkin pie for their dessert for that night. After eating breakfast and with the pie baking in the oven, they watched the parade. It was great fun to see how excited Philip was. Darren wished he could see the parade through Philip's eyes.

After watching the parade, Rachel went into the kitchen to check on her pie, which smelled heavenly. The pie was ready, and it was time to get her turkey stuffed and shoved into the oven to cook. The odors in the house made Darren remember something of his childhood. He remembered watching football with a man while similar smells came from the kitchen in that house. That man must have been his father, or was the man himself watching the game with his son while his wife was in the kitchen preparing their Thanksgiving feast? No! He couldn't be the father, as he believed that he would remember having a child. Philip was not his own flesh and blood, but Darren could not fathom not remembering him. The bond between father and child is a powerful force, and he believed he would know in his soul if he had a child. The man must be his father. At that exact moment, Darren began missing a father he could not even remember knowing.

Dinner was a feast. They all relished: the mashed potatoes, the yams, the peas and carrots, the turkey and its stuffing, the gravy, and the fresh pumpkin pie with whip cream. Darren thanked Rachel for the best meal he had ever eaten. He told her that since she had slaved all day preparing their Thanksgiving meal that he was on clean up duty.

"Rachel, you go and put up your feet and finish drinking your coffee in the living room while I clean up," Darren said.

"Me too, Mommy. I'll help daddy clean up."

"There you go, Rachel," Darren acknowledged, smiling. "It has been decided that the men of the house will clean up the Thanksgiving dishes."

"Well, I thank you both, and I will be in the living room, enjoying my coffee," Rachel replied..

While the men were cleaning the kitchen, Rachel fell asleep on the sofa. When the dishes were washed and dried, the men came out to sit with Rachel but found her fast asleep. Darren put his finger to his mouth and said, "Shhh," to Philip so that he did not wake his mother's slumber. Darren covered her with a blanket and turned off the lights. Thanksgiving was over, and he carried Philip upstairs to get him ready for bed. While Darren was reading his son a bedtime story, they both fell fast asleep.

Chapter 27

Now begins the hectic and busy time for all retailers, the countdown to Christmas. With only a few weeks before Christmas, Rachel worked crazy hours at the supermarket. Darren was also busy at the pub with all of the Christmas parties. Rachel and Darren did not see much of each other, as one worked days and the other, nights.

Philip was so excited that Christmas was nearly here. He asked his mother to write his letter to Santa while he voiced it to her, and then asked her to mail it for him since there was a mailbox next to the store. His letter said:

Dear Santa Claus,

My name is Philip Martin. I have been a very good boy this year. I have a big favor for you. Would you be able to make my mommy marry my daddy?

My mommy is my real mommy, but Darren is not my real daddy, and I want him to be my daddy forever. I know he loves me and I really love him and I don't want him to ever leave.

I would also like a tent and a fishing pole so my dad could take me fishing like all my friends' dads do.

Please Santa Claus, please use your magic to make Darren marry my mom and stay with us forever.

I will leave you some cookies and milk and some carrots for your reindeers.

Thank you, Philip Martin

***

A few days before Christmas, both Rachel and Darren had a day off so they planned to go pick a tree from a tree lot and decorate it while listening to Christmas music. Philip was so excited to go pick out a tree this year. Rachel had a fake tree that they put up each year, but this Christmas was different because Darren wanted the real thing. Philip wanted his Christmas wish to come true so badly because everything was better since Darren came into their lives. Mommy was happiest when she was with Darren too. She wasn't sad or grumpy or too tired anymore, and that was all due to Darren. Rachel told Philip that Darren was their Christmas miracle.

When they arrived at the tree lot, Darren made Philip the tree picker; he could pick any tree he wanted. There were so many to pick from, but he wanted a big humongous tree, the biggest they had. Darren pointed a tree out for Philip to judge, and he said, "No way! That tree is like the tree Charlie Brown picked out, remember?"

They all started laughing and Darren replied, "You know what, Philip. I think you're right."

After looking at about a hundred trees, Philip found the perfect tree. Darren paid for the tree, and the owners tied it to the top of their cab.

They were all singing Jingle Bells on the drive home. Rachel chose the spot where the Christmas tree would be placed, and then it was time to decorate it. Darren had brought all the decorations down from the attic that morning. He and Rachel untangled the lights, then put them on the tree. Philip was given the honor of placing the first decoration on the tree. They enjoyed decorating it and singing along to the Christmas music playing on the TV.

Darren was asked to place the Christmas angel on the top of the tree, as he was the newest member of the family. Darren was honored, but when he placed the angel on top of the tree, he had a flashback from what must have been his past. He looked down from his father's shoulders, where he must have been sitting, and put the Christmas angel on the top of their tree. He could see a roaring fire and feel the heat that the fire was giving. After the vision, Darren fell to his knees before placing the angel in its rightful place. Luckily, he protected her from breaking during his fall.

Rachel ran to his side. "Darren, are you ok?" she asked. "Do you want me to call the ambulance?"

"No, don't, I'll be fine. Can you get me a glass of water, please? I am quite thirsty," Darren said.

Rachel ran to get him his water. When she returned, he was sitting on the sofa with a flushed face. He thanked Rachel for the water, then drank it.

"Can you please tell me what that was all about?"

"I just got light headed, that's all. Now let's forget it. I have to put this angel where it belongs," Darren replied.

Rachel was concerned for Darren because he was getting a lot of these episodes. Perhaps she should have taken him to the hospital the day she found him on her front porch. What if the concussion he endured was more serious than she had first thought?

As if reading her mind, Darren commented, "Rachel, stop worrying about me. I am fine now, so let's not ruin this wonderful day." He walked toward her and kissed her tenderly on the mouth. He whispered in her ear so that only she could hear him, "Rachel, Philip is enjoying this day so let's not ruin this for him, okay? Now, dry up those tears and let's start singing again."

After the tree was entirely decorated, Darren brought the unused ornaments and the empty boxes back to the attic.

"Mommy, when can we make our cookies for Santa Claus? Christmas is coming soon. I promised Santa cookies and milk in my letter, remember? All of my friends at daycare made their Santa cookies and shared some at daycare."

"I guess now that the tree is up and decorated, we can make our Christmas cookies. Darren, do you want to help with the cookies?" Rachel asked.

"Would you mind terribly if I passed on the cookie making? I am tired and would like to take a short nap, but I will help with the eating of those cookies."

Concerned, Rachel asked, "Are you sure you're alright?"

"Yes! I am sure everything is fine."

"Then I guess, Philip, the cookie making will be our job. Now we have to be extra quiet since Darren is trying to nap," Rachel said.

Darren's brain was working overtime. He was having all these memories, but he could not join the pieces of the puzzle together. While Rachel and Philip were in the kitchen, he decided to call Doug, the private eye.

Doug picked up the phone on the first ring.

"Hey, Doug, this is Darren Michaels here. I was wondering if you had found anything on my identity?"

"I'm sorry Darren, but so far it has been a dead end. I'm not giving up, mind you, but I will continue my search after the holidays."

They both wished one another a Merry Christmas and a Happy New Year before they hung up. Darren was nowhere closer to finding out his identity. He promised himself that he would not think about it again until after the holidays, as he did not want to ruin Christmas for Rachel and Philip.

***

Darren awoke with a sweet smelling aroma enveloping the entire house. The smell of cookies baking in the kitchen had brought fond memories to him. The aroma gave him a warm feeling inside. He probably made cookies with his mother when he was a young boy. He wished he could just remember. He wondered if his family was missing him during this festive season, as it was a time for family and loved ones to come together.

Darren walked into a messy kitchen, a little boy covered in flour, and a tired-looking mother. He saw all the cookies on the counter and said to them, "I guess you both have been busy little elves. Look at all those delicious-looking cookies. Do you think Santa would mind if I ate one of his cookies?"

"Daddy, the cookies are not all for Santa. Most of the cookies are for us to eat," Philip acknowledged.

Darren took a cookie and said, "Yum . . . these cookies are just yummy. I think these are the best cookies I have ever eaten. You and your mommy should open your own cookie store and call it the Yummy Cookie Store."

"No, I don't think so. I just make these cookies for the ones I love," Rachel replied .

Darren suggested that she should go up and take a bubble bath or a shower and a cat nap while he and Philip tidied up the kitchen. After all was cleaned up, Darren took Philip up to a bath too, which he surely needed.

Philip was yawning. He was tired from all of the events of the day. When Philip was fast asleep, Darren entered Rachel's bedroom and snuggled next to her. She awoke from his touch. She turned to face him, and they started kissing so passionately and hungrily that sex was inevitable. He loved holding her naked body next to his; it felt so right, like they fit together and became whole, but for some reason unknown to him, it felt so totally wrong as well.

They both got up from their love making, just before Philip awoke from his nap. Darren had suggested that they all go out for dinner, then maybe go see the Christmas tree at Rockefeller Center to see it all light up.

Philip was all but ready before Darren finished his suggestion.

"I guess that means you agree with me then?" Dareen said.

"Mommy, Mommy, can we please go to McDonald's for dinner?"

"Philip, if you don't mind, I would like to go eat at the pub where I work. Every night until Christmas, they have a variety of singers singing Christmas carols until about eight p.m. I am in the Christmas mood after decorating the tree and eating Christmas cookies" Darren said.

"Okay! But does the Pub serve chicken nuggets and French fries because that's what I eat at McDonald's."

"Philip, you are in for a treat—the pub serves animal-shaped chicken nuggets and French fries."

"Really! I have never eaten animal-shaped chicken nuggets before. Mommy, hurry up and get ready because I am really, really hungry."

They arrived at the pub, and the atmosphere was very Christmassy. Rachel and Darren ordered the fish and chips, and Philip ordered his animal-shaped chicken nuggets with fries. As they listened to the entertainment and enjoyed drinking a bottle of wine, which was sent to their table, compliments of the owner. Philip was enjoying his fruit juice in a fancy glass with a little umbrella that was made especially for him. When their food arrived, Philip was amazed that the nuggets were really shaped like animals.

Philip announced, "Mommy, I am a dinosaur and I am going to eat all of these animals for my dinner."

Rachel put on a frightened expression on her face and said to him, "I hope that the dinosaur only eats animals and not mommy and daddies!"

"Of course not, Mommy. You're not made of chicken."

"I am thankful for that," Rachel replied.

They all enjoyed their complimentary dinner, another gift from Darren's boss. Darren loved working at the pub, as his employer and the employees were a great bunch to work with. He felt so comfortable working there; maybe it was because he knew that bartending was something he did in his past life.

After thanking his boss for the delicious dinner, they caught a cab to Rockefeller Center. They were amazed at the size of the tree and of all the twinkling lights it held on its branches.

Rachel asked, "Philip, isn't this tree the most beautiful tree you have ever seen?"

"Mommy, this tree is nice, but our Christmas tree at home is even nicer."

"You know what, Philip? I think you're right. This tree is the second most beautiful tree we have ever seen," Darren said.

They stopped to look at the skaters doing their pirouettes, spins, and jumps. They were so graceful, it was like watching ballerinas on ice.

When they arrived home, Philip was already fast asleep. Darren carried his son up to bed. He couldn't believe that Philip did not awaken from his slumber while undressing him and then dressing him in his pajamas. He kissed his son gently on the head and whispered, "Sleep well, my little one."

Darren loved his son and Rachel so much it frightened him. He was afraid that if Doug found out who he really was that he may lose more than he thought to make. This boy needed a father, and his mother needed to be loved and cared for. They needed him more than he needed to know his true identity. He would contact Doug after the holidays and have him stop searching for his identity. He walked to Rachel's bedroom, and she was fast asleep. He got himself undressed, got under the covers, and rested his weary body next to hers. Like working at the pub, sleeping next to Rachel was a right fit. He rested his head on the pillow and fell asleep, listening to her every breath.

Chapter 28

The days seemed to fly by with all the hustle and bustle of the holidays approaching. It was already Christmas Eve. Rachel was hard at work, and Darren was off work for a few days since the pub was always slower just before and right after Christmas. Everyone was short on cash after buying all their Christmas gifts.

Darren was glad to have the time off so that he could take Philip shopping for a Christmas gift for his mother and buy a few more surprises to put under the tree. He and Rachel had bought Philip a few gifts already and surprises and candy to fill his stocking, but Santa was bringing him all the big items on his Christmas list.

Philip tried to explain to Darren, "Daddy, I don't have to get mommy a gift because I already asked Santa to get her a gift."

"Philip, Santa only brings gifts for little boys and girls, not for the mommies and the daddies. What if you tell me what Santa was to bring your mommy and we can buy it ourselves?"

"Are you absolutely sure, Daddy?"

"I am absolutely sure, Philip, so why don't you tell me what you asked Santa to bring your mommy for Christmas."

"Well, I asked Santa to marry Mommy and you. I want you to stay with us forever. I need Santa's help because I know that's what Mommy wants and I want that too, Daddy."

Teary-eyed, Darren said, "I see. Philip, you are sure that marrying your mommy is all that she wants for Christmas?"

"Yes, Daddy, I am sure."

Darren thought to himself what he should do. He then decided what the hell—why not get engaged on Christmas Eve? Darren then asked. "Philip, what if you and I buy your mommy an engagement ring for Christmas."

"Okay, Daddy, but that's not what I asked Santa to bring Mommy for Christmas."

"This is exactly what you asked Santa for, Philip. Giving your mommy a ring means that I promise to marry her," Darren insisted.

"You mean it, Daddy? You will promise to marry Mommy and be my daddy forever and forever?"

"I do, Darren answered.

Philip was the happiest boy alive at that very moment. Darren and Philip picked out a princess-cut, one-carat diamond ring, but the diamond was not a real diamond but a zirconia fake diamond. Darren hoped that Rachel would not be angry that he could not afford a real diamond. He promised himself that one day, he would replace the fake stone with a real one. He had the sales clerk wrap up the ring in its velvety box, and then they walked home. Darren could not buy Rachel any other gifts like he had planned because the ring took up all of his cash.

***

Rachel had arrived home after work tired but excited as well. She was off for a few days and would have time to relax and enjoy her first Christmas with Darren, the man that she loved. *This was going to be the best Christmas ever,* she thought to herself. When she got her coat and boots off, she followed the scent of pizza.

In the living room were two handsome men waiting for her with pizza and what looked like champagne. They were serving her one of her favorite meals. Darren had made a fire in the fireplace and had lit up the tree. The warmth and glow of the fire and the twinkling of the lights in the Christmas tree made the living room feel warm and inviting. The moment Rachel sat down next to Darren, he took out a small branch of mistletoe, held it above her head, and then kissed her.

He took Rachel's breath away. Philip then pushed the play button on the DVD player and they watched *Home Alone* while eating pizza and sipping champagne.

Rachel lifted up her glass and made a toast, "I hope to celebrate Christmas Eve like this every year—with the two most important men in my life."

After the movie was over, Darren said, "Rachel, would you be willing to go to church with me tonight? I feel like it would be a great way to start our first Christmas together. I called a few of the churches close by to inquire about the times of their Christmas Eve masses. There is one at eight p.m. that I am interested in attending, which is near the pub. What do you say Rachel, want to join me?" Rachel was surprised that Darren wanted to go to church, as he had never asked to go before.

"Darren, do you really want to go out tonight in this cold weather?"

"Yes, I do, but if you don't want to go, I don't mind attending church alone."

"No, I don't mind going, Darren, but what brought this need to attend church?" "Are you remembering something from your past life? Remembering that you are a religious man who attends church on Sundays?"

"No, I am not remembering anything from my past life. I just thought it would be more Christmassy to go and listen to the Christmas Story and the Christmas music, that's all. I also thought it was the right place and the right time to give thanks for all the blessings I have received since I have come to live with you and Philip."

Touched, Rachel said, "Well, if you want to go to church as a family, I better go upstairs and change into something a little churchier. Can you get Philip tidied up and get him dressed in some clean clothes?"

"Rachel, I am mostly thankful for you and for Philip, without whom I would not be here having the best Christmas ever," Darren divulged.

"Now, I think I really need to go to church with you so I can also give thanks for you coming into our lives and changing it for the better," Rachel voiced.

As they entered the little church, they were amazed by how full the church was. It was beautifully decorated and had a well-lit manger set up in the front of the church. Philip wanted to go see the manger, so Rachel and Darren walked him over to see the nativity scene.

Philip whispered, "Mommy, this is the family that Miss Carpenter read a story about. The baby's name is Jesus, and he was born in a barn with farm animals. That lady is the mommy, and that man is the step-daddy. They had no money for food and no place to stay because no one wanted to let them rest in their house. Mommy, if they came to our house, you would let them stay with us, right? Just like Daddy?"

Darren answered for Rachel, "Of course, your mommy would have taken them in because she is a nice lady who cares about people, and she would have never let a lady with a baby stay in a barn."

Philip smiled at his mother and said, "You are the best mommy and lady in the world, Mommy."

Rachel bent down and gave her son a big kiss and a hug. They decided to find themselves somewhere to sit before all the seats were taken.

"I guess all these people were thinking the same way you were, Darren. I guess they have come to give thanks for all their blessings as well," Rachel declared.

The music was so beautiful; there was an entire orchestra accompanied by the church choir. Darren thought that this must be what angels sound like when they sing in heaven. Rachel looked at the beauty in the charming little church. Everyone had been given a candle, and they shut off the lights in the church. The entire church was lit by candle light.

***

After the mass was over, Rachel felt her spirit was uplifted in some way.

"So, tell me, Rachel, did you enjoy the Christmas mass or did you hate it?" Darren asked

"Darren, I can honestly say that it was amazing. I want to make this a Christmas tradition. Going to church was a fantastic idea. I don't think I have ever felt this serene. I would also like to start attending church on Sundays as a family."

"I am so pleased you enjoyed it because I really enjoyed the priest or minister's sermon. I think a little religion is a good thing for everyone to live by," Darren said.

Darren called for a cab to take them home, as Philip had started walking with his eyes closed. When they arrived home, Darren took Philip upstairs and got him ready for bed. He kissed him good night, then closed the bedroom door. He then joined Santa's helper in the living-room.

Rachel had Philip's stocking filled with candy and small Hot Rod cars that he enjoyed playing with his friends from daycare. Darren helped her take out all the other gifts that were hidden away in the basement. Darren ate up the cookies and drank the milk that was left out for Santa Claus. The carrots were put back in the crisper in the refrigerator.

Rachel whispered to Darren, "I'm going up to bed because Philip will be up before the birds do. Will you be coming up soon?"

"I'll be up in a moment. I just want to check if the back door is locked." He checked on the door, but he wanted to place Rachel's engagement ring in her sock. He also put a few other gifts that he got her weeks ago. He then joined Rachel, who had already fallen asleep. After shutting the light from his side table, he too fell asleep.

***

It was early Christmas morning when Philip came running into Rachel's bedroom yelling, "Santa was here! Santa was here, Mommy, and he left lots of gifts for me."

"How do you know the gifts are for you, young man?" Darren asked.

"Daddy, I just know," Philip answered. "Mommy, Daddy, hurry up! I want to unwrap all of my presents."

Darren was having fun with Philip by making him believe he fell back asleep and snoring very loudly.

Getting annoyed, Philip shouted, "Daddy, wake up it's Christmas morning. Mommy, Daddy isn't waking up." Philip got up on Darren's stomach and started jumping on him.

Darren grunted, "I'm up, Philip, I'm up! Let's go down and see what surprises Santa left for you."

They were all seated around the Christmas tree, and Rachel started passing out the gifts.

"Here is one for Philip. It says to Philip from Santa Claus."

Philip yelled, "Yippy! That big one is for me. I wonder if it's a tent!" He ripped the wrapping paper and was overjoyed that it was his tent. "Daddy, look! I got my tent so now we can go camping in the woods, like my friends."

"That's great, son, but we will have to wait for the summer, though," Darren replied.

Philip opened another gift from Santa. This gift was long and skinny; Philip knew that it had to be his fishing pole. He was correct—it was his fishing pole. He then got a sleeping bag and a fishing box, with hooks and fake worms inside. "Mommy, Santa Claus must be a fisherman because he knew all the things to go camping and fishing. I will have to give him a thank-you letter!"

Rachel then asked, "Now that we are done with the Santa gifts, can we start on the other gifts?" Rachel handed out a gift to Darren from Philip; it was a T-shirt that said, "World's Best Dad."

"I love it, Philip. I should have gotten you one that says, 'World's Best Son.'"

Rachel then handed Philip a gift, and it was a life jacket.

"Thank you, Mommy and Daddy! Now, I can go close to the water or be in a boat and if I fall in, I won't drown." Philip then asked his mother, "Mommy, give that one to daddy. It's from me, Daddy. I picked it out just for you."

As Darren was opening it, he realized how wonderful it was to have a family to share all these special moments with. Inside the small box held a Hallmark ornament that said, "Family," and it had a little frame that held a miniature picture of the three of them together.

"I love it," Darren said. "I will place it on the tree and on all the Christmas trees to come."

Rachel had received from her two special guys a watch, dangly earrings, sexy undergarments, fluffy slippers, and a beautiful dress that she could wear out on dates or even wear to church. She was so thankful for all of the beautiful gifts she had received.

"Now, let's take down our Christmas stockings and see what treasures we will find inside," Darren suggested.

Philip was happy to get the Hot Rod cars, and he already had a candy cane in his mouth.

Rachel put her hand into her stocking and found nice smelling perfume and soaps, and then she took out a little box beautifully wrapped up. She couldn't believe her eyes, as inside held a gorgeous diamond ring. When she looked up, she found Darren kneeling on one knee. He took the ring from the box and placed it on her finger.

"Rachel, would you make me the happiest man alive and agree to become my wife?"

Rachel was speechless; she never would have imagined this moment happening to her. Tears of joy came flooding down her happy face. She jumped into him and placed her arms around his neck, saying, "Yes! A thousand times, yes! I would love to be your wife."

She had always wanted to say that phrase; it was from her favorite movie, *Pride & Prejudice*, when Charles Bingley asks Jane Bennet to marry him. Rachel kissed Darren with such passion and force that Darren could not but reciprocate the same hunger.

"Mommy! Daddy and I picked this ring for you. Now, this means that Daddy is going to stay with us forever and ever," Philip announced.

Darren agreed, saying, "Yes, that's exactly what it means, Philip. How about you take some of your toys and put them in your room. I would like to talk to Mommy alone for a minute?"

Philip took his fishing pole and his fishing box up to his room.

"Rachel, the stone in that ring is not a real diamond," Darren confessed. "I would have loved to buy you a real diamond for your ring, but funds are tight right now. I promise that one day I will replace the stone with a real diamond."

Rachel held his face with her small hands and said to him, "Darren, I never want to take this ring off my finger again. I love this ring, just the way it is. Fake stone or not, it's my engagement ring and I love it. No one will ever know the difference, as it looks exactly the same as would a real diamond. How did you know that I have always dreamt of having a princess-cut diamond ring?"

At that precise moment, Darren had one of his flashbacks—this time, he was purchasing a princess-cut diamond ring for someone. She was a special someone from his past, but who?

Breaking his thoughts, Rachel declared, "Well, I have to say, Darren, I love the ring you picked out for me. It's just so beautiful. I had no idea you were even thinking about marriage, but I promise you, I will try each and every day to make you happy."

"Rachel! You have already made me a happy man by accepting my proposal. Now, do you think we can have some breakfast, then go back to bed for a nice Christmas nap?" Darren asked. He gave Rachel a little wink, which meant no nap but love making.

"Do you want those two demands in that exact order?" Rachel asked. "I thought I would model those sexy undergarments for you." She saw the hunger in his eyes, so she ran up the stairs to her bedroom with her man right behind.

Darren looked inside Philip's bedroom to see what he was doing. Philip was playing with his play dough on the floor. "Philip, Mommy and Daddy are a little tired, so we will be napping in our bedroom if you need us. You be a good boy and play in your room until we get up."

Philip was so engrossed with his playing that he just nodded his head to let them know he was listening.

When Darren entered Rachel's bedroom, she was in the bathroom. He got his clothes off and got under the covers, waiting to see the show. Rachel came out wearing the sexy, flimsy red two-piece garment and high heels. She walked around the room, modeling her outfit. Darren was so excited, he could not contain himself. He jumped up, grabbed her, and flung her on the bed, then quickly undressed her.

Rachel commented, giggling, "Why buy these sexy undergarments when all you want to do is tear them off me?"

He didn't answer; he just kissed every inch of her entire body. Rachel wanted him to take her, as she was so aroused that she could not wait anymore and she climaxed.

"So, you couldn't even wait for me to finish what I was doing?" Darren asked.

Rachel answered, "I'm sorry, but you were driving me crazy. Now, it's my turn to drive you crazy."

"Rachel, just touching you drives me mad."

Rachel then touched and kissed her man until he was as fulfilled as she had been a few minutes ago.

They both just lay in bed together when Philip entered their room and said, "Mommy, are you up yet? I am very hungry. My tummy is rumbling just like Winnie the Pooh bear's tummy rumbles when he is hungry for honey."

"I'm sorry, Philip. I will be down in a minute and make us some pancakes," Rachel said.

"Okay, Mommy! I'll go sit on my chair and wait for my breakfast."

After Philip left the room, she kissed Darren once more, then got dressed and ran downstairs to her starving son. Darren came down to a stack of hotcakes waiting for him on the table. He was so hungry after this morning's gift opening and what had taken place after that.

"I forgot to wish you both 'Merry Christmas' this morning," Darren said.

Rachel and Philip wished Darren a, "Merry Christmas to you too, Darren, Daddy."

After eating all of the pancakes, they went into the living room to watch a Christmas show that was playing on the television—*It's A Wonderful Life* with James Stewart. This was one of Rachel's favorite Christmas movies, and she always watches it on Christmas day; it was a Christmas tradition for her. Philip wanted to go up and play with his toys instead of watching the movie. Darren was willing to watch the program with her.

The movie brought on memories for him of watching this movie with a special someone from his past. He wished that he could remember who this woman was. Rachel snuggled next to him and watched the entire movie, which was a long-ass, depressing movie. When the movie ended, Rachel went into the kitchen to start preparing the turkey. Darren followed her and gave her a hand in peeling the potatoes and the carrots. She had bought a cherry pie from the bakery for dessert.

While the small turkey was cooking in the oven and the table was set, they both went to play with Philip in his room. Philip was tired and fell asleep on the floor. His parents left him to rest and decided to go to their room and do the same.

***

Rachel awoke from the smell of turkey cooking in the oven. She wiggled herself away from Darren's hold and went down to check on the turkey and start cooking the vegetables.

Rachel thought to herself, *What a perfect Christmas this has been.* Who would have thought that she would be engaged to the man she had found on her front porch months ago. Today, she could honestly say that she was the happiest she had ever been in her entire life.

When the boys got up from their nap, the food was already on the nicely decorated table. The turkey looked perfect and was waiting for Darren to carve it. Darren mentioned to Rachel how great everything looked and smelled, and he even commented on how lovely she looked. They all sat down for dinner, and Darren took hold of both Rachel's and Philip's hand and bent down his head to make a Christmas blessing.

"Dear Lord, I would like to thank you for this wonderful feast on our table this evening and I hope that everyone around the world is as blessed as we are tonight, being with those we love. Amen."

Rachel and Philip repeated, "Amen," as well, and then Rachel commented, "Darren, that was such a beautiful blessing."

Darren carved the turkey and served a slice to each of them. After they had finished with the cherry pie and ice cream, they all helped out with the kitchen clean up. When all was washed and put away, they sat in the living room, enjoying the cozy fire in the fireplace and watching *The Santa Clause* with Tim Allen. Philip had the pleasure of choosing this movie selection. They all enjoyed watching the movie.

Chapter 29

Back in Boston, Renee was staying close to home because she did not want the Hamiltons to know that she was with child. The baby was growing at a faster rate, and she now had a sizable, noticeable baby bump. She had to stay in to conceal her pregnancy. Who knows what her in-laws would do if they knew that she was carrying Paul's baby? She must keep this baby a secret.

Renee's parents had been on Renee's case again. They wanted her to have all answers to all life's questions. At this point in her crazy life, she could honestly say she had no answers to any questions.

Christine had prepared Renee's favorite breakfast: her delicious blueberry pancakes. The moment Renee sat at the table, her parents started nagging her again. Her father asked, "Renee, have you made any decisions on what your next move will be? You know that you can't just stay in your room or this house indefinitely. You have been hiding in that room for over two months now. This baby is coming, and that is a fact. Decisions have to be made."

"Dad, don't push me to make decisions right now. "I just can't do it." Then she started to cry.

"Sweetheart, we are just worried about you. You know that we love you right? While we were on vacation, you were your old self again and we were hoping that your old self would come back home with us, but sadly, she did not. We are concerned that you haven't seen a doctor other than Mat and that was while we were on vacation. Have you been taking your prescribed medication? Sweetheart, you have been hibernating in this house for two months now; we are worried about your health. You look sickly. We will try not to push you, and we will support you and help you with anything you need, but you have to show us you are trying to go on with your life. If you do not get help, we will have to take drastic measures and get you admitted into the hospital. Now, please stop crying and eat a few of my blueberry pancakes. I made them especially for you," Christine said.

"Thanks, guys, I hear what you are saying, but all I need from you is your support. I don't know if I can do this on my own, but you need to give me time and space to get through this," Renee responded.

"Dear, you won't have to do anything on your own," Christine told her. "Your dad and I are always here for you. How about getting out today?"

"I think I may go out today and see if Dr. Chamberlain, the psychiatrist on staff at the hospital, can find time to see me."

"That sounds great, Renee. Did you want me or your father to join you?" "Thanks, Mom, but I think I'll be okay on my own." Renee ate a pancake, then washed her dishes and excused herself, as she wanted to call the doctor to make an appointment.

Renee was lucky because Dr. Chamberlain had an opening at ten a.m. that morning. Renee decided to wear her blue jeans and a pullover since it was very chilly out. She was shocked that she could not get into her jeans. It seemed that it was going to be very difficult to keep this baby a secret for long. She decided to wear her baggy sweats, as that was all that fit her comfortably.

When Renee was ready to leave, her mother asked, "Renee, are you going out to your appointment in your jogging suit?"

"Mom, I have no other choice. I don't fit into any of my clothes. I am a whale."

"You don't look like a whale but a beautiful expectant mother. We will have to go shopping for some maternity clothes. How about we go out later today and pick you some nice clothes that fit?"

"Sure, but we have to be very discreet. I don't want the news of the baby to leak out to you know who," Renee answered.

***

When Renee got to Dr. Chamberlain's office, she could not make herself get out of the car, so she decided against going in. She reached into her purse and took out her phone and decided to call Jo-Ann Reynolds, the friend she met in the Dominican Republic.

Jo-Ann answered the phone on the first ring. "Good morning, Dr. Jo-Ann Reynolds. How can I assist you?"

"Well, don't you sound professional. Hi, Jo! This is Renee. I hope you don't mind me calling you, but you did say I could call anytime."

"Renee! It's nice to hear from you. We were just saying last night how we want to stay in touch with your family. My parents had the best time in the Dominican because of your parents. I'm happy to hear from you. What's up?"

"I am calling you for your professional advice. Jo, when I was on vacation with you all, I felt so alive and happy, but since I've been home, I am starting to get in my old slump again. I am afraid for the baby. I don't want it to suffer because of me and my depression. Jo, I haven't gotten out of bed for two months now. I try to force myself out of the house, but I am frightened. I am afraid someone will notice that I am pregnant. I am frightened to think of what the newspapers will say and what my in-laws will do."

Concerned with Renee's well-being, Jo-Ann stressed, "Renee, I am worried about you. You need to go see a psychiatrist or someone there who can help you with these feelings."

"I know, Jo. That's why I made an appointment with a doctor this morning, but I am so afraid someone will see me in my condition and tell my in-laws. Jo, I need your professional advice. Can you please help me?"

"Okay, Renee, we can work this out. Now, tell me, what brought on all of this stress?" Jo-Ann asked.

"My parents want me to make all these decisions. I could not go back home after our vacation to the Dominican Republic, so I am living in my old room at my parents' place. They asked me about selling my house, but I don't want to rush into anything and make the wrong decisions. I'm not ready to get out of the house, so how can anyone expect me to go back to work or even function as a responsible adult. I still am nauseated most days, so I am constantly tired. Can't my parents see that I am not fit to make life-changing decisions at this time?" Renee was in tears.

Jo-Ann saw the gravity of the situation and insisted, "Okay, Renee, you have to calm down. All this anxiety and stress is not good for you or the baby. You could lose this baby if you don't start taking care of yourself. You have to decompress yourself, girl. You are having a complete meltdown. I think you need to be admitted into the hospital so that they can monitor the baby and get you the help you need."

"I can't go to the hospital! They know me there, and I don't want to worry my parents any more than they do."

"Renee, I have an idea. What if you come to New York and I admit you into the hospital here?" Jo-Ann suggested. "You could tell your parents that Mat invited you to visit since he misses you so much—you know, you wouldn't be lying."

Renee hesitated, then said, "If I accept this invitation, I don't want Mat to know why I am there."

"If that's what you want, I'll agree not to expose your whereabouts to anyone. Renee, when do you think you can get away?"

"I have a few things to do before leaving but would tomorrow be too soon?"

"Sounds great. You let me know what flight you are on and at what time you'll be arriving, and I'll be there to pick you up. We'll go straight to the hospital and get you admitted," Jo-Ann said.

"Thank you, Jo, you are a true friend."

Chapter 30

Renee went to her home and packed a suitcase for New York. She did not like being in the house anymore. The house felt eerie, lifeless, cold, and spooky to her now. She realized that she did not want to raise her child in this mausoleum.

When Renee arrived at her parents' house, it was quite late. As she entered their home, she had found two parents waiting for her, with worried looks on their faces.

Renee's mom asked, "Where have you been? We have been worried sick about you. Dr. Chamberlain called to see if you were all right since you did not make your appointment with her."

"I'm sorry if I worried you, but I am fine. I did not make the appointment because Jo-Ann Reynolds called and asked me to come to New York for a visit. It seems that Mat is behaving like a love sick puppy, and she thought that a surprise visit from me would get him out of this funk he's in. I accepted her invitation; it's come at the best time since I am in a funk as well," Renee stated, then added, "I need to get away from here for a little while. I think spending some time with Jo and Mat would give me the time I need to sort out my pathetic life. Jo is even willing to take me shopping for maternity clothes and maybe even start shopping for this little one. She said they have really nice boutiques for pregnant mothers. I'm sorry to have worried you both. I'm late because I went home to pack my bags. I booked myself a flight to New York for tomorrow morning. My plane leaves at nine a.m."

"This is all of a sudden, don't you think? We were hoping you would return to work and get back on track with the real world," Christine said.

"Mom, Dad, the real world will still be here when I get back from New York. Dad, I decided to sell my house, so if you know of a good real-estate company or agent that can sell it for me, that would be great. I decided I can't live in that mausoleum of a house anymore. Now, I am tired, so I'm off to bed. Good night mom, Dad. I will see you both in the morning."

Her parents replied, "Good night, sweetheart."

As Renee crawled into bed, she said a prayer to God, "Heavenly Father, please help me get through this pregnancy. Please help me to carry my innocent baby to term. God, please help me be a good mother to this child and please let her or him be healthy."

Then she drifted off to sleep.

***

James and Christine sat in bed, talking about the hard road their daughter had been through and the hard times to come. They knew that they were Renee's only support group. They would be there to help support and care for their daughter and their grandbaby. Christine wondered if Ted and Nancy Hamilton knew that there was a grandbaby on the way would they accept Renee as part of their family, or was Renee correct in hiding their grandchild from them. She had a feeling that the Hamiltons would make Renee's life unbearable. The baby would have to be kept a secret for now.

Christine kissed her husband good night and turned off the light, as morning would come soon enough.

***

Renee got up bright and early. She took her shower and got dressed, then carried her suitcase downstairs and left it near the entrance door. She walked into a silent kitchen and started making a pot of coffee and the mixture for French toast. She was not hungry, but she knew that she had to eat something, so she put two slices of bread in the toaster to have with her coffee. Her mother was the first to come down; she could smell the aroma of the coffee from upstairs.

"Hi mom! Did you sleep well? I made the mixture for French toast, would you like me to prepare a few for you?"

"That's fine dear. I can make my own. Thank you for starting breakfast, though. How was your night? Did you get any sleep? Renee, don't you think this little trip may be a mistake? It hasn't been that long since our last trip, and here you are, ready to go off again. Don't you think you are wearing yourself thin? You look so tired, and I am worried about you and the baby. What happens if you get sick or something goes wrong with the baby? Did you think of that?"

"Yes, Mother, I have thought of that, and don't forget I am going to visit a family in which three of the members are doctors. I think I will be in good hands. Don't worry, Mother. I will call you every day to let you know how I am doing. Does that make you feel any better?"

Worried, Christine said, "Yes and no, but I guess you have your reasons for going. Please take care of yourself and call us when you have arrived safely in New York."

"Will do, Mom. I think I'm going to let Dad sleep, and I will call for a cab."

"Are you sure, Renee? I know your dad will be upset you didn't wake him up to take you to the airport or to say goodbye."

"You tell him to call me on my cell when he gets up for breakfast." Renee called for a cab, gave her mother a kiss goodbye, and walked out of the house, where her cab was waiting for her.

Chapter 31

Renee was a little afraid to travel on her own. She was getting bigger by the moment. When she arrived at the airport she went directly to get her ticket. Her plane was to leave in an hour and a half; she had lots of time to read some emails and text some of her friends that she hadn't been in touch with for a while. She sent an email to Karen, her teacher's aide, who had sent her a concerned email.

Karen,

I am terribly sorry for not contacting you sooner, but I have been on a roller coaster ride. My life has been turned upside down since Paul's death. I have had many bad days since 9/11. I have had to spend some time in the hospital because of exhaustion. My parents had planned a vacation for the three of us to the Dominican Republic, and we enjoyed ourselves tremendously. There was nothing there to remind me of Paul, which was very nice in a way. Here, at home, everything reminds me of him, and it makes me ache for him. I miss him so much that I cannot breathe at times. So, I am leaving again for a short duration to get away from it all. My parents will be putting my house on the market while I am gone. I need to start fresh, and all these things that make me think of Paul are pulling me down. I promise to stay in touch. Please let everyone at school know that I miss them and that I hopefully will feel better soon so that I can return back to work.

Love, Renee

Renee's plane was boarding, and she was advised by one of the airport staff that she could board with the adults with children. She was in such a hurry that she did not see the Robinsons, close friends of the Hamiltons, waiting to board the same plane. When she was seated in her assigned seat and had put her carry-on bag in the overhead compartment, she was shocked to see the Robinsons coming directly toward her. There was nowhere for her to hide—she was busted. Renee tried to conceal her baby hump and hoped they did not see her boarding the airplane with the families.

Mrs. Robinson had stopped at Renee's seat and bluntly asked her, "Renee, how are you? We haven't seen you at church in ages. I have to ask you a personal question, dear, but do my eyes deceive me or are you pregnant? Don't deny it, for we can see the lump. So, Renee, who is the father of your little bastard child? Do we know him?"

Disgusted, Renee answered, "I'm sorry, but I have no comment. Now, if you both can please go to your assigned seats and let me be."

Renee was so devastated by the Robinsons accusation that she could not stop sobbing. She knew that the gig was up. Now that the Robinsons knew about her predicament, would she be seen on the front page of the local paper? She could see it now: *"That scarlet woman is carrying a bastard child while husband is still warm in the ground."*

What was she to do? She had no control of this situation, so she would have to face the accusations when she returned home—that was, if she returned home. How would she be able to face everyone in her community? She asked the stewardess for a small glass of red wine to relax her nerves. She did not drink usually, but she needed one right about now. She was wondering if Mrs. Robinson was on her cell phone calling Nancy Hamilton with the news of her daughter-in-law's indiscretions.

The stewardess served Renee her drink, and Mrs. Robinson turned to speak to her husband, "Did you see that? The stewardess just handed her a glass of wine and she is with child. She is not fit to be a mother."

Renee was correct, just before the plane left Boston, Claire Robinson called Nancy Hamilton with the news.

"Hi! Nancy, guess who I just bumped into on our flight to New York?"

"Claire, you know darn well I hate guessing games. Now, just tell me who you bumped into," Nancy asked.

"We bumped into Renee, your daughter-in-law, and she is with child," Claire answered.

Confused, Nancy asked, "What do you mean? She is pregnant?"

"Yes! That's exactly what I mean."

"Claire, how many months pregnant would you say she is?"

"I can't really tell, but she can't be that far along because it looks like she is still wearing her normal clothes and she doesn't look that big."

Fuming, Nancy said, "I can't believe that tramp. My son, her husband, has just died and she is already sleeping with some other man. I cannot believe this. I can just see it in the paper: *Renee Hamilton, the widow of the late Paul Hamilton, son of the wealthy Nancy and Ted Hamilton, is pregnant with another man's seed.* We will be outcasts in this town. Now, I have proof that this little gold digger just married Paul for his money. The minute Paul dies, she digs her claws in another victim. I wonder who the new victim is and how much is he worth?"

"Nancy, I have to let you go. The plane is about to leave and the stewardess is telling me to disconnect. I will call you when we get back."

"Okay, Claire! You have a nice trip, and thank you for calling me with the news," Nancy said.

***

Renee could not enjoy her flight knowing that Claire had probably advised Nancy of her condition. She could not do anything about it—what was done was done. She could not wait to land in New York and talk to Jo about everything that had happened on her flight. She was glad when the fasten-the-seat-belt sign came on and the captain advised everyone that they were descending and that he hoped everyone enjoyed their flight.

Renee wished she could say she did, but this was the most nerve-wracking flight she had ever been on. When the plane landed, she asked the stewardess if she could be taken off the plane first since she was not feeling well and did not want to be trampled on getting off the plane. The stewardess accompanied her off the plane before everyone else.

Renee was so pleased to see Jo waiting for her in the terminal. She cried out, "Jo! I am so happy to see you."

"Renee, I am happy to see you too, but I have to say, you look terrible and you cannot conceal your baby bump anymore. You seemed to have just popped right out since the last time I saw you."

"Thank you for noticing, Jo, but that's why I am here in New York, seeking your help." They picked up her luggage and then walked to Jo's car.

"Renee, I think we will go right to the hospital. I think you are dehydrated and that you may need to be hooked up to an IV. You need to replenish your liquids. I also want to hook you up to a baby monitor to see how the baby is doing. What has happened to the girl we met in Dominican? I am worried about you and the baby," Jo said.

"I know, Jo," Renee replied. "If my parent's call, just tell them I am out and that I will call them when I get in."

"Renee, you want me to lie to your parents?"

"Yes! The less they know about what's happening with me, the less they will worry. I want them to think I am being a typical New York tourist who is enjoying herself sightseeing," Renee said.

Chapter 32

When Renee was admitted into the hospital, she was reluctant to stay. She felt trapped and claustrophobic. Renee had a private room, thanks to Jo, who had pulled some strings. Jo came to see her after Renee was settled into her room.

"Jo, I can't stay here in the psych ward. All these people are . . . I'm not crazy, Jo. I don't belong here. I've made an error calling you and asking you for help. I have to get out of here. I cannot breathe; this place is suffocating me." Renee was having a panic attack.

"Renee, calm yourself down. You asked me to help you and that is precisely what I intend to do. You are here because you want to get well for the baby, right? Now take a big cleansing breath and slow down your breathing," Jo advised her.

Renee did as she was told and started breathing somewhat better.

"Good, that is very good, Renee. I am going to give you a little something to calm you down and help you rest," Jo said.

"Jo, this won't hurt the baby, will it?"

"No, this will not hurt the baby. I think if you stay worked up, like you are right now, that's more dangerous for the baby." Jo administered the shot and then stayed with her until she dozed off.

Now that Renee was resting, Jo had to find a way to help her friend out. The woman she had met while on holiday was not the same woman she had just admitted. This girl was nervous, tense, fragile, and frightened—a real mess. She felt sorry for Renee because she knew her to be fun-loving and strong. She thought that perhaps she should give Renee's case to another doctor, but she decided to stick by her friend, who was in need. Renee was in a very fragile state right now and giving her up as a patient may just push her over the edge.

***

Renee awoke from a nightmare. She was panting and her gown was drenched in sweat.

Jo was there to calm her down. "Renee, you are fine. You just had a nightmare, that's all. Calm yourself. I am here with you and you are in no danger."

Renee put her arms around Jo's neck in search of a safe harbor. Jo started rocking her as though she was a baby, feeling safe in her mother's arms. In Jo's arms, Renee felt safe and loved.

"Renee, you were having a nightmare. Would you like to share it with me?" Jo asked.

Now that Renee felt safe, she unlocked her grab on Jo's neck and settled herself quietly down on her bed. "Jo, I had a terrible nightmare. Paul was alive and well, and I was trying to reach for him, but he was pushing me away. He did not want me anymore; he had started a new life and I was not in it. He called me all sorts of terrible names. He did not believe this baby was his, and he called me a whore. He was leaving me for good. He was walking away from me, hand in hand with another. I believe he had loved me so much, but in the dream, he just threw our love away, like it meant nothing at all. I tried to hold on to him, but he pushed me away and spat on me." She started crying again.

Jo-Ann consoled her friend, "Renee, it was just a dream. What is really bothering you?"

"Yesterday, on my flight to New York, there was a couple on the plane who are good friends of my in-laws, and I know that they called them with the news that I am pregnant."

"Renee, you mean that Paul's parents don't know about the baby?" Jo asked.

"That is exactly what I mean; that's why I haven't left the house since coming home from Punta Cana. Paul's parents hate me and think that I am a gold digger. They don't believe that I ever loved Paul. They want nothing to do with the likes of me. I am so afraid that if they know I am carrying their grandchild, they will maybe try to take him or her away from me."

"You can't be serious. There is no way that could ever happen."

"Are you sure about that, Jo?" Renee asked. "Because I'm not."

"Girl, you are safe here with me," Jo answered.

Renee grabbed Jo's hand and thanked her.

A hospital staff member came into her room and laid down a tray of food for her diner.

Jo explained, "Renee, as your doctor, I want you to eat all the food on your tray and then I want you to rest. I will be back to see you in the morning."

"Thank you, Jo!" Renee replied. "I know that I am a basket case. I shouldn't have brought you into my messed up life, but I don't know who else to turn to."

"Don't you fret, girl. You know that we consider you Clarks as part of our family, and we take care of our family."

"Okay, sis, whatever you say. I promise to do as I am told," Renee said.

***

Renee got up early the next day. She did not sleep very well. She had forgotten to call her parents, so she decided to do it then. Her parents were early birds too.

"Hi, Mom! I'm sorry I didn't call you as I promised, but you know how we girls are when we get together; time just flew by."

"I thought as much, and I told your father that you would probably call us today and you did. How are our friends the Reynoldses doing? Tell them that we miss them and will be calling them soon."

"I will, Mom. How are you and Dad doing? Did Dad get in touch with a realtor about selling the house?"

"Yes!" Your dad did as soon as he got up yesterday. He was a little upset that you did not wake him to drive you to the airport, though. He has gone to show the house to the realtor as we speak. He wanted to know if you have a survey of the house?"

"I'm not sure about that, Mom, but he could look in the filing cabinet in Paul's office or contact Peter—he may know something about it."

"Will do, dear. You take care of yourself and call us when you get a chance."

"Okay, Mom! Tell Dad thanks for everything."

Renee hated lying to her parents, but she did not want to worry them more than they already were. She got up and took a shower. When she was done with her shower, she found her breakfast waiting for her on her table. She was happy to see that breakfast included French toast, rice crispy cereal, orange juice, milk, and hot water and a tea bag. She devoured it all, as she was famished.

Jo came to see her as she had promised. She talked to Renee about sending her to get an ultrasound of the baby since she had never had one before.

"Jo, the ultrasound won't harm the baby, will it?"

"No, this is just giving us a picture of the baby to see how it is doing and give us a better due date, that's all."

"Jo, do you think you could come with me when I go get my ultrasound?" Renee asked her friend.

"Sure, Renee, I've just got a few more patients to see on this floor, and then I will meet you down in Ultrasound."

***

Jo kept her word. She arrived just in time for Renee's ultrasound. The technician started rubbing some gel on her stomach and then put a little machine that looked like a vacuum head onto her gel-covered stomach. Renee was amazed to see the picture of her baby on the monitor. The technician came right out and said, "Your babies seem to be doing well."

"Babies! What do you mean 'babies'?" Renee cried out.

"You didn't know you were carrying twins, Renee?" The technician asked.

Renee looked at Jo and then the technician in surprise and said, "Twins! Twins! I had no idea at all that I was carrying twins."

"You can see here is the first one, and there is the second one." The technician pointed two fuzzy images out. Then she started her measurement of the babies while Renee was crying and freaking out all at the same time.

"Jo, do you see this? I am having twins. I cannot believe it!"

"Yes, Renee! I see your two little miracles, and they seem to be doing very well, in there."

"I can't seem to stop crying," Renee sobbed. "I think my body is in shock. I just cannot believe it. Now there will be three of us to take care of. I was scared about not being a good mother to one child, but two, two kids? I don't know if I can handle it."

Jo calmed her friend and said, "Renee, the good Lord only gives us what we can handle."

"I don't know about that because I don't think God has been looking out for me. He has taken Paul away from me when I need him the most."

"You are not alone in this, Renee," reassured Jo. "You have a family that loves and supports you, and then you have us, your extended family, who will help you get through all of this. Don't you fret."

"You're right, Jo, I have all of you as a support system. I want to tell you how much I appreciate you being here for me. I don't know what I would do without you." Jo bent down and gave Renee a well-needed hug.

The technician reassured her that her babies looked well. She told Renee that she estimated that she was about thirty weeks pregnant.

"I did not think that I was so far along. This is really happening," Renee acknowledged.

***

Renee was doing well in Jo's care. She had been invited to participate in group bereavement counselling, which Renee had her doubts would help her but decided to give it a go anyway. To her amazement, the counselling did help her, and after a while, she even took part in the discussions. Hearing other people's stories seemed to help her convey her own feelings of loss and betrayal.

Renee began to feel much better now, and Jo told her that she was ready to be discharged. Renee pleaded with Jo to let her stay awhile longer.

"Jo, I don't think I'm ready to leave just yet." Renee started to cry because she was afraid of the unknown.

"Okay, Renee! Stop your crying. I can wait a few more days before discharging you, but the hospital is not a place for you to hide from the rest of the world, you know?" Jo stated.

"I know. I know. I just need a little more time. I'm not ready to go back home just yet."

"How about this, Renee: After you leave the hospital, why not come and stay with me for a while, just until you are ready to go back home?"

"You know, Jo, I think I will take you up on your offer."

***

The day Renee was dreading for so long finally came—the day she had to leave the comfort and safety of this institution that had become her home. She packed her things and went looking for Jo. She found her in her office.

"Hi, Jo! I was wondering if the offer to stay with you still stands?" Renee asked.

"Yes, it does. I am so proud of you. I know this is a big step for you to take. Give me half an hour, and I will be ready to take you home."

They arrived at Jo's apartment with Chinese food in hand. The apartment was very modern, but was in need of a house cleaner.

"I know the apartment is a mess and that I should hire someone to clean the place. I don't like strangers touching my stuff, though, and that includes my garbage," Jo said.

Renee had a proposition for Jo. "How about I make you a deal? What if I help out around here? I could clean up, make meals, do laundry, and do the shopping for groceries while I'm here."

Jo liked the idea and said, "You are a great girlfriend. I was wondering, though, when are you going to tell my lovesick brother you are here in New York, living with his sister?"

"I have an idea, how about you invite him over for Chinese food tonight, and we can surprise him by saying I've come for a visit," Renee said.

Jo called her brother to invite him for dinner. He accepted, as he had nothing else planned. Jo's pager vibrated, and she called the hospital to see what was going on. There was an emergency and she was needed.

"Sorry, Renee, but I am needed at the hospital, so you will have to entertain Mat on your own."

"Are you kidding me? Call Mat back and tell him you were called out and will not be able to make dinner," Renee pleaded.

"Can't do it. He will be here in a few minutes, so you will have to surprise him alone. Tell him I'm sorry I could not stay for dinner because I was called out for an emergency."

Jo had left her alone to entertain Mat. Mat rang up, and Renee let him in. When he knocked on the door, she was so nervous, it was like being on her first date. Renee opened the door, and Mat was so happy to see her that he grabbed her and gave her a real hard kiss, right on the mouth. She would be lying if she said she did not enjoy Mat's touch or hunger for her.

Mat let her down softly and said, "What are you doing here? You look beautiful! You are glowing. I am so excited to see you. I have missed you like crazy. Where's Jo?"

"Hi, Mat! It's great to see you too. Jo wanted to be here, but there was an emergency and she had to leave. She sends her regrets."

"Why didn't you call me? I would have dropped everything if I knew you were coming," Mat said.

"I know you would have, Mat. Why don't you come in and let's eat the Chinese food Jo ordered for us before it gets cold."

He took her chair out for her and they both devoured the food.

"I think this is the best Chinese food I have ever tasted," confessed Renee. "You know, Mat, I wanted to call you so often since I have been here, but I felt so ashamed of myself."

"What are you talking about? Renee, how long have you been staying here with Jo?"

Renee sighed and replied, "I arrived here just hours ago, but I have been in New York for about four weeks. I had called Jo from home, and I had asked her for some medical advice. I was getting worse with my depression and was hiding myself in my childhood bedroom at my parents' home. My parents were asking me to go back to work, get on with my life, and sell my house, and I just couldn't breathe. I was suffocating there. Jo asked me to come to New York and be hospitalized under her care. So Mat, this is where I have been for the last four weeks. I wasn't ready to leave the hospital and go back home, so Jo invited me to stay with her for as long as I needed. So, that's my story."

Mat just put his arms around Renee and whispered in her ear, "You are the bravest soul I know and I am so proud of you." He then laid a passionate kiss on her lips, and she didn't push him away, but instead she pulled him in closer.

They sat down on the sofa and talked for the longest time. It was after midnight before Mat decided to leave. He could see Renee was getting tired, so he got up from the sofa and kissed her good night. Before leaving Jo's apartment, he promised her he would call the next afternoon to make plans with her for the weekend.

Renee made up the sofa and got ready for bed. The moment she laid her head on the pillow, she fell fast asleep. She slept so soundly, she did not even stir when Jo came back from the hospital.

***

Morning came, and she made a pot of coffee for Jo and a cup of tea for herself. She was not very hungry but forced herself to eat two pieces of toast with her tea. Jo got up, smelling the freshly made coffee.

"Hi, Jo! What time did you get in this morning? I made a fresh pot of coffee if you need a caffeine fix," Renee said.

"I know, and it smells heavenly. To answer your question, I got home at three. How did you know it was morning and not late last night when I returned from the hospital? You looked sound asleep when I came in."

"Well, when Mat left here last night, it was after twelve and you were not in yet," Renee divulged. "So, that's what I deduced, dear Watson."

"Well done, Sherlock. So, was Mat surprised when he saw you here in my apartment?" Jo asked.

"He was totally surprised, and I told him everything that has been happening in my life. He was so nice about it all. He even said he would call me to go out on a date this weekend."

"The old charmer still has all the right moves. He always seems to get the girl he has his heart set on," Jo said.

Renee blurted out, "You can say that again."

They both had a good laugh.

Chapter 33

Mat was a man of his word; he had called Renee that afternoon to invite her to go out on Saturday. She had no reason to decline his invitation, so she accepted happily. Mat told her to bring an overnight bag because they were staying at a friend's place on Sunday night. He did not give her any details about where they were going, but she had to admit she was excited to go on this little adventure with Mat.

Renee decided she had to start keeping her end of the bargain; she had to clean up the untidy apartment. When the entire apartment was spick and span, she realized it was almost dinnertime and she had not even stopped for lunch. She wondered why her stomach was gurgling all this time. She had called Jo's cell phone to see if she was coming home for dinner.

Jo advised her that she had a double shift today; one of the doctors on call was home sick with the flu. She told Renee to call in for something to eat for herself and gave her the number of a pizza place that was close by. Renee thanked her and then phoned for a double-cheese deluxe pizza, as she had not yet had any protein or vegetables in her diet today. She was told that her pizza would be delivered in about thirty-five minutes, so she had time to take a shower.

The doorbell rang, so she hurried out of the shower and buzzed the pizza delivery person in. She dashed to get her wallet to pay for her pizza. But when she opened the door, there was Mat, standing outside her door with a dozen red roses in hand. He also held a bag of food that smelled heavenly.

"Mat, what are you doing here?"

"I came bearing gifts. You shouldn't just let anyone in; there is a security door downstairs to protect you from strangers."

"Yes! I am aware of that, but I thought you were the delivery person with the pizza I had ordered for dinner."

"Does that mean you want me to leave or am I to be let inside the apartment?" Mat asked.

"I'm sorry, Mat, yes, please come in. Are those roses for me?"

"Yes, they are and I bought us dinner. On the menu tonight, we have lasagna, garlic bread, and Caesar salad."

"That was so nice of you to think of me. You should know I am starving and I think we should eat right now. We could have the deluxe pizza for dessert or a late night snack."

Mat entered the apartment and said, "Wow, this place looks great. I have never seen it so clean, and it looks so much bigger in size too."

"It just needed a little elbow grease and some organizational skills," Renee replied.

They both sat down to eat when the pizza arrived. Mat let him in and even paid for the pizza. He brought the pizza to the table and opened the box to find a huge pizza covered with veggies and meat.

"I said I was hungry, and I am eating for three now," Renee acknowledged.

Mat shook his head in disbelief and said, "What do you mean, you're eating for three?"

"You are the first to know, other than the ultrasound technician and your sister, that I am carrying twins. Doesn't that just blow your mind? I can't believe it myself."

"That's wonderful news, Renee. Congratulations. I think those babies are the luckiest babies in the world to have you as their mother." Mat grabbed Renee into his strong, masculine arms and kissed her so urgently and forcefully that she knew he was being sincere.

Renee accepted and needed that kiss more than she needed the uneaten food that was on the table. She started to cry, and Mat automatically thought that he must have said something to upset her.

"Renee, did I say something to hurt you? I can be an ox sometimes."

"No, Mat, you didn't hurt me. It's just these hormones of mine. You are one of the kindest men I have ever met. I am crying because you always seem to know exactly the right things to say to me. You telling me that I will be a great mom is the nicest thing you could have said to me. I am so frightened that I will screw up my precious babies' lives."

Mat held her for a few moments, then said, "You will do just right by those babies, you'll see. Now, let's sit down and eat. You did say you were hungry, did you not?"

They sat down and ate the entire meal, other than the pizza. The pizza would have to wait to be eaten on another day because they were both very full. Mat told Renee to sit down and chose one of the many DVDs in Jo's collection for them to watch while he tidied up the table.

Renee found the movie, *Weekend at Bernie's,* that she had not seen in years. She remembered that it was a comedy, and she needed to laugh tonight. She had cried enough for one evening. Mat joined her on the sofa and placed his arm around her shoulders. He wanted to comfort her and reassure her of his amorous affection for her. Renee believed that she was exactly where she was supposed to be and with whom she wanted to be with that night.

The movie she had chosen for them to watch had them both laughing. When the movie was over, Mat had said to her, "That was a perfect selection. I love to see you laugh like that. I think you need to have more laughter and fun in your life."

"You know what, Mat, I agree that it's time to stop crying and moping around and start living. I need to stop living in the past and start living for today, and the future."

Mat yelled, "Hallelujah! That is music to my ears. I have to tell you that I have wanted to hear you say that to me since the Dominican." He grabbed her and kissed her so tenderly and passionately that he began to lose control of his senses. He had to stop, as he did not want Renee to see how aroused he was getting.

Mat decided then that he should leave before he made unwanted advancements toward Renee. "Renee, I think I should leave now before I do something that you may not be ready for."

She thought she would play with him a little and teasingly said, "What do you mean by that, Mat?"

Feeling awkward, Mat answered, "Come on now, Renee, you can't be that clueless? I would love to take you in my arms and carry you to bed."

Renee playfully advised him, "Mat, you wouldn't need to carry me anywhere because we are already sitting on my bed."

He jumped up and said, "Well, isn't that convenient? Now, I will be a gentleman and go home and take a cold shower."

She laughed and walked him to the door, saying, "Thank you, Mat, you are what I needed tonight and I appreciate you waiting for me."

They kissed and then he left.

Renee had to laugh; she had a great evening with this new man in her life. She had honestly thought life would end for her after Paul's death. Paul was her everything—her days, her nights, her ups, her downs, her laughter, her tears, her heart, and her soul. God had sent her Mat to help her live and love again. There was a saying Renee had heard once: "When one door closes, another one opens." Paul's door was closed for good now, with his passing on, but Mat's door was wide open and he was waiting for her to walk through it and join him in a new life. He still wanted her even though she was carrying someone else's children. He was an extraordinary man and would make an excellent husband and father to her two little ones. She sat down and decided she would write a letter to Paul; she needed to say goodbye and she needed some closure.

To my loving husband,

Paul I am sorry you are missing out on knowing and raising your two little ones. I can feel them moving inside me. It's the greatest feeling. I think they may be soccer players one day. I hope you understand that I meant those wedding vows, where we promised to love each other and no other until death do us part. I had hoped you would be here with me forever. I hope you understand that I am not strong enough to do this on my own. I just can't do this alone, and I hope you will forgive me, as I have found another. He could never take your place, but he is helping me live again.

I promise the babies will know that you are their father. I will tell them how much you would have loved and cherished them. They will know the kind of lasting love we shared.

I will never stop loving you, for you will always be with me; these two little ones are proof of that. I vow to you that if we have little boys, I will name one Paul and the other I would like to name James, after my father. I am sorry, but I will never name our children after your parents. They have been most horrendous toward me. They accused me of killing you and marrying you only for your money. They want nothing to do with me. I've decided, if they want nothing to do with me, then they want nothing to do with my children. I wish you could see how awful I have been treated by your parents, so I hope you understand why they will never have anything to do with these precious babies I am carrying.

Be happy for me, my love, for the happiest and safest place I have ever been is in your loving arms. Mat is a good man, and he will take good care of the three of us. Our children will be blessed with loving parents. As you cannot be here for them, I ask that you can look out for them as their guardian angel from up above. Please keep them safe from danger and from those who would harm them. I will see you again one day, but until then, goodbye, my love.

Your loving wife

She kissed the bottom of the letter and put it into an envelope to one day share with her children.

Chapter 34

Renee found the time passed slowly alone in Jo's apartment. She couldn't wait for Saturday to arrive because Mat was taking her out. She had no clue what Mat had planned for them to do, but he did specify to pack an overnight bag.

When Mat arrived on Saturday morning, he grabbed Renee's overnight bag as he kissed her good morning. He looked like a man on a mission. He took her hand and led her down the stairs to his car. She could see how happy he looked this morning and hoped he could see how very happy she was to be with him.

"Where are you taking me?" Renee asked.

"It's a surprise you will figure it out soon enough," Mat said.

They drove to the JFK Airport where they waited to board a plane. They were booked on American Airlines from New York to Las Vegas. They boarded the plane at nine a.m.

Mat asked Renee after they were seated, "Are you ready to go on an adventure with me, Renee?"

She closed her eyes and found the courage to say, "Let's do this before I lose my nerve."

He took hold of her hand, kissed it gently, and said, "That's my girl."

The plane left at nine forty. When she seemed to be comfortable, Mat said, "This weekend, Renee, is all about you and me, kid."

"Now, you are stealing your lines from Humphrey Bogart?" Renee replied. "How very lame, Mat."

They both laughed at her comment.

Then Renee said to him, "This is great. I have never been in Vegas before and I always wanted to walk the Vegas stretch and see the sights."

Renee slept for most of the flight to Las Vegas. They arrived shortly after twelve thirty, and she was thankful that they had landed safely on the runway.

As they embarked the plane, she was pleased to see that a chauffeured limousine was waiting for them. The driver had taken their bags, and Mat held the door open for Renee to take a place in the car. Mat sat next to Renee and bent over and kissed her. She had to remind herself that she was not married anymore and that being with Mat was okay.

Renee asked him, "Can we open the window above our heads? I want to stand up and see the sights of Vegas."

He opened the window and decided to join her.

"Mat, this is fantastic!" Renee exclaimed. "I would have never guessed in a million years you were taking me to Vegas. I didn't bring any fancy clothes to wear."

Mat replied, "Don't you worry. I knew you didn't know what clothes to pack, so I got someone from the casino motel to purchase a few things for you."

"You had someone buy clothes for this whale?" She pointed to herself.

"Yes, I did. Are you angry with me?"

"Not at all. I hate shopping for myself, and I bet she has better taste in clothes than I do. Thank you so much for being so thoughtful."

She put her arms around him and then she initiated a kiss. This excited him to no end, because he was the one always initiating the kissing but not this time. This time, she kissed him, not like a girl kissing her brother or her father, but like a woman kissing a man she cared for. He felt like dancing and screaming out to the world saying, *"She's mine! she is really mine,"* but he didn't want to scare her off.

They entered the Mirage, where there was a beautiful fountain in front of it. The foyer was so beautiful; it had marble flooring and Greek like columns holding up the ceiling. The room held provincial looking chairs and glass tables with beautiful huge floral arrangements. A few smaller floral arrangements sat on the front desk, giving the Mirage a look of elegance.

They walked to the front desk, and Mat asked for the keys of the two adjoining rooms that he had reserved for them. Renee was pleased that he had reserved two rooms because she was not ready to share a room alone with him. The staff at the Mirage were cooperative and pleasant.

When they got into the elevator, Mat gave Renee the key card to her room.

She took the key card and said, "Thank you, Mat, for reserving my own room. That was so considerate of you. Anyone else would have pressured me into sleeping with them since they had paid for the trip and all. That shows me the gentlemen you really are, and I am lucky to have you as a friend."

"You know I see you much more than a friend, Renee."

"I know that, Mat. I care for you much more than a friend as well. I guess we could say you are my boyfriend or is that lame?"

"Boyfriend sounds great, and I know that this is a big step for you to take. You don't know how much I appreciate it." He took her hand and brought it up to his lips, then gently kissed it.

They got off the elevator, and Mat walked her to the door of her room and asked her, "Renee, did you want to rest for a while before I show you some of the sights of Los Vegas?"

"Are you kidding? I can't rest right now; I am too excited. Just give me a few minutes to freshen up and I am ready for anything," Renee replied.

"Okay then, how about we meet up in the lobby in twenty minutes?"

"How should I dress for today's adventure?" Renee asked. "Should I wear something casual or dressy?"

"I think you should wear something comfortable for now, but for tonight, you should wear something a little dressier, as we are going out for dinner and then a surprise," replied Mat.

"I am so excited, Mat. You can't even know how much I needed this and you." Renee reached up on her toes and gently kissed him on his soft lips.

Mat whispered into her ear, "Renee, I can get used to you kissing me like that."

"Me too, Mat." Then she entered her room.

The room was so beautifully decorated with bold colors of red and black. She lay down on the big bed, and it was so comfortable; it had to be one of those Posturepedic pillow mattresses. She would have to get one of those for herself. When she looked out of her window, she was surprised at the beautiful fountain. She could not wait to look at it at night. She was told that through the cascading water of the fountain, you could see the colors of the rainbow.

Renee could not believe she was really there. She knew how blessed she was to have found two wonderful men who wanted to share their lives with her. Life was not over for her; it was just another beginning. She was one of the lucky ones—when door number one closed, she found Mat waiting there for her behind door number two. All she needed to do was find the courage to open the door and let Mat in.

Renee felt guilty that she cared for Mat. She felt like she was cheating on Paul. She believed that Paul would want her to go on with her life and that he would have approved of her choice. She had to think of not just herself now but of those two little innocent babies she was carrying. Mat would be a loving, caring, protective, thoughtful, and attentive father to her children. If someone had to step in and take on the role of father, she could not do any better than Mat. She could already see that he had a bond with her children, even though they were not his biologically. How could she be so blessed?

Renee had decided on a light sundress that flattered her shape at this time of her pregnancy. She couldn't believe that Mat had asked someone to buy all these outfits for her. Mat had even asked his shopper to pick out shoes for her. They got her a pair of sandals to wear, plus a pair of dressy low-heeled shoes to go with those two gowns that she could not wait to try on tonight. Mat had thought of everything.

Renee met up with Mat in the lobby, and he was dressed in a pair of brown shorts and a light cream shirt. He wore a pair of sunglasses on top of his head and handed a pair for her to wear as well.

"You thought of everything Mat, even the sandals and sunglasses. You are too wonderful to be true."

"Stop it! You are going to inflate my ego. Now, Renee, are you ready to have some fun?"

Renee answered joyfully, "I am ready for anything you have planned for us, Mat."

He grabbed hold of her hand and met their driver, who was waiting to take them on an adventure. The driver took them to the airport where they boarded onto a helicopter that took them on a tour of the Grand Canyon. Renee was like a child on Christmas morning; she was so excited that she didn't want to miss anything. Mat was having the best time just watching her. She kept hold of his hand and would give him little pecks now and then throughout the tour.

The tour guide informed them that the Grand Canyon was known for its overwhelming size, colorful landscape, beautiful sunset, and serenity. He was right on all counts. They saw it all, from the top to the bottom, and it was breathtaking. Renee was in awe when she looked down into the canyon. She felt so small, ant size really, when overlooking the canyon. They also enjoyed views of Lake Mead, Hoover Dam, and Boulder City.

The pilot landed the helicopter, and they got off, ready to get into a comfortable luxurious coach bus where they visited Eagle Point, Guano Point, and Hualapai Village, where a cowboy cookout was awaiting for them at Hualapai Ranch. It was so rustic and charming. Renee felt like she was in an old western movie. Everyone on the ranch was so hospitable; they made them feel like they were part of their family. After a big delicious lunch, they boarded the bus to their next destination. The pair boarded a pontoon boat and cruised down the Colorado River.

Once their adventure was over, they were headed to the helicopter, which took them back to their hotel.

"Mat, this was the most amazing day I have ever experienced in my entire life."

"So, you enjoyed yourself?"

"Da! I don't want this day to end."

"Well, for your information, young lady, the day is not over yet. I have another adventure planned for us. Now, you go up, relax, take a shower, and take a rest. Then at seven p.m., I will come and get you for dinner. We will be dining here at the Mirage. I would like to see you in one of those fancy gowns that was picked out for you. After dinner, we start our next adventure."

"Mat, I am so lucky to have found a gem like you."

"Renee, I am the lucky one." He then kissed her, and she kissed him right back.

Renee then realized that she was in love with Mat and it scared her a little. "I will be ready when you come for me," she said.

They kissed again before going into their separate rooms. She felt all tingly inside after his lips left hers.

When she entered her room, she just wanted to soak in that big soaker tub. She had lit the many candles that were placed around the tub and got into the warm bath filled with soft white bubbles. The heat of the water and the aroma of the soap had her in a restful state. She couldn't stop thinking that she wished that Mat was here in this tub right now, touching her all over her entire naked body. She couldn't believe it herself. Here she was seven months pregnant and having sexual thoughts of a man that was not the father of her babies.

She just couldn't stop thinking of Mat, though—how wonderful he was being to her, how he made her feel when he was around her, how he had never pushed her into anything she wasn't ready for, and that he cared for her and her babies. She couldn't believe that he planned this surprise getaway just for her. She got out of the bath and into that snuggly terry cloth robe that was hanging in the wardrobe. She lay down on the bed and dozed off as soon as her head hit the pillow.

***

While Mat was taking a shower, he thought of how pleased he was with how the day was going. He enjoyed every moment he shared with Renee. She was his silver lining at the end of the day. He couldn't get enough of her. He wanted more from this relationship but did not want to push himself on her. He had to be patient because she was worth the wait. He loved her more and more each day. He would wait for her forever if that was how long it would take. One day soon, she would love him, and then they could start making plans for their future.

He could see that she was beginning to have feelings for him. Those kisses that were being initiated by her were driving him crazy. He turned on the cold water to extinguish the fire that was building inside him. He got out of the shower and wrapped himself in the terry cloth robe and called to see if everything was in place for this evening.

The concierge replied, "Yes, Mr. Reynolds, you have a table in view of the waterfall, and the chauffeur will pick you up in the lobby at eight thirty p.m. sharp to take you to the airstrip where you have reserved a helicopter. The pilot will take you both on a sunset helicopter flight of Vegas."

"I want to thank you and the staff at the Mirage for helping me plan this wonderful surprise weekend for my girlfriend."

"You're most welcome, Mr. Reynolds, and if there is anything else that the Mirage staff can do for you, do not hesitate to ask," the concierge said.

"I will and thank you," Mat replied.

Mat decided to take a little rest before the evening's adventure, but before he did, he called down to room service and asked if they could send him up a bottle of their best beer at about six p.m. He thought that if he fell asleep that this would wake him up and he would have something to drink as he got himself ready.

Chapter 35

Renee got up and decided to call down to the front desk to ask about having her hair done. The person at the desk made arrangements for someone to come up to her room and help her get ready since she was pregnant and it would be easier on her. She was pleased that the concierge was thoughtful enough to have arranged for the hair dresser to make a house call.

The hairdresser was a nice woman called Mary. She had decided to straighten Renee's hair and then offered to do her makeup. Renee was being treated like royalty by this stranger. She looked at herself in the mirror and couldn't believe the transformation.

"Mary, you have just performed a miracle. I cannot believe that the girl looking at me through the mirror is truly me. You've made me look like a pregnant supermodel."

"There is no need to thank me. I had a lot of fun. I was wondering if you needed help with dressing before I leave you for the evening."

"If you could, that would be wonderful," Renee said.

Mary helped her dress in a beautiful vibrant-red silk dress that was quite fitting at the bosoms and then fell loosely to the ground.

"Renee, you look beautiful in that gown. You would think it was made for you. The cut of the dress and its color is quite flattering and quite slimming. You can't even tell that you are pregnant," Mary exclaimed.

"You mean, you can't see my baby bump?"

"Exactly! Now let me help you with this strand of pearls and its matching earrings," Mary said.

Renee conveyed her appreciation, "Mary, I cannot thank you enough. You are a true artist. You took a blank canvas and transformed it into an elegant and beautiful painting. Perhaps you are my fairy godmother, like in *Cinderella*."

"It has been my entire pleasure, but unlike *Cinderella,* your makeover will not disappear when the clock strikes twelve."

Renee got her purse and gave Mary a nice big tip for going above and beyond the call of duty in helping her get ready for her night out with Mat.

"Thank you, Renee, but that is not necessary."

Renee pleaded with her, "Please, Mary, I really want you to take this money. You deserve it."

Mary accepted the money, saying, "Thank you again, and you have yourself a wonderful evening, Renee. I hope this man of yours realizes how lucky he is to be taking out my most beautiful masterpiece." Tears began running down Mary's cheeks when she got up to leave.

Not long after, Mat knocked at Renee's door, right on time. When Renee opened her door, Mat was taken aback at the sight of her beauty. When Mat saw the vision that opened the door, he had to whistle at her.

"Hi, beautiful lady, I am here to take Renee Hamilton out about town this evening. Can you tell her that her date is here for her?"

Renee smiled and said, "You're so funny, Mat, and I have to say you look quite dashing in that tuxedo. You put all those best-looking men of the year to shame. I'll have to keep a tight grip on you tonight. I would think that all the single ladies and perhaps many married ones will be trying to snatch you away from me."

"Renee, you look stunning in that gown and your hair straightened like that makes you look like another woman all together. Do not fret; my eyes will never leave your beautiful face tonight. To be honest, since the first time I saw you, my eyes have only been on you. I do hope you will keep a tight grip on me tonight, so that way I won't have to fight off all the eligible men here in Vegas."

"I wouldn't worry, Mat. I am a good poker player and I know when to stick when I have a good hand and you, sir, are a full house."

They both laughed. Then Mat grabbed Renee's shawl, wrapped it around her shoulders, and said, "Renee, I have to say you look hot tonight. You look like a real supermodel."

"I want to thank you, Mat, for purchasing all these beautiful outfits for me, but for the rest of the transformation, I give thanks to my fairy godmother."

Mat didn't ask any more questions; he was so proud to have this stunning woman holding his hand.

***

They ate a delicious meal downstairs in the Mirage's elegant restaurant. Renee was eager to know what Mat had planned for them tonight.

"Would you like to have some dessert now that we have finished our meal Renee?"

"No, I am full. I am curious to know what else you have planned for us this evening."

"You will have to be patient, my love."

He took her hand and kissed it gently. He then got up from his chair and helped her out of her chair, like a true gentleman.

After paying for their meal, they left the Mirage, then entered the limo that was waiting for them to take them to their next destination.

The car stopped at an airstrip where a helicopter was waiting for them, Renee asked, "Mat, we are going on another flight."

"Yes, Renee! But this time, we are going on a sunset helicopter flight."

They both got seated and strapped in ready for their adventure. The helicopter pilot took them on a flight over Hoover Dam and Lake Mead.

The pilot said, "The sunsets are incredible here, and this is the best way to appreciate the scenic view."

"You are so right. I have never seen anything this beautiful in my life and will probably never see anything this beautiful again. It's all thanks to you, Mat, for taking me here with you." She reached over and gave Mat a kiss.

"We are not done with our tour yet, Renee." Mat advised her.

The pilot flew them by the Stratosphere Tower, and they flew them over the lighted Las Vegas strip. Renee was amazed by the dancing waters of the Bellagio fountains, the Eiffel Tower of Paris, the New York–New York Hotel skyline, the Greek Pyramid and the Sphinx of the Luxor. After the tour was over, the pilot took them back to where their limousine awaited to transport them to anywhere they wished to go.

"Renee, what would you like to see before we have to leave Vegas?" Mat asked.

"I would like to see the thousand Fountains of Bellagio; they say it dances to music. Then I would like to return to the Mirage to see the volcano erupt and spew smoke and fire one hundred feet above the water."

Their limo driver took them to the Bellagio, and the fountains danced wistfully to the beat of the song that was playing. Mat asked Renee to dance to a song sung by Pavarotti and one by Sinatra. The evening was enchanting and so magical. Renee felt like she was Cinderella dancing in the arms of her Prince Charming. They then ended their evening at the Mirage looking at its spewing volcano.

Mat and Renee walked hand in hand into an empty elevator. When the doors closed, Mat took the time alone to wrap his arms around his beautiful date and kiss her, as he so wanted to all night. When the doors of the elevator opened, they both stopped kissing and were taking in some well-needed air. Renee understood the saying, "He took my breath away," as that was exactly what Mat did to her.

They took hold of each other's hands and walked slowly to the door of her room.

"Mat, I was wondering if you'd be kind enough to come into my room to help me unzip my gown? You see, I needed help to zip up my dress, and I am sure I will need someone's help to unzip it as well."

Mat swallowed hard. "Sure, I can come in and help you with your zipper." Mat took her card and unlocked the door to her room. They both walked inside and Mat helped her with her wrap.

"Mat, I want to thank you so much for making this weekend one that I will never forget. You know when God made you, he broke the mold. You are a one of a kind gem. I am so lucky to have found you—a real gentleman, a bachelor and a doctor, to boot. I can't understand, Mat, why you would be interested in me, a widow, unemployed teacher, and a mother who is pregnant with another man's children. Why me, Mat?"

"Renee, I have been with my share of women, and not once have I felt a connection like I have with you, for any of them. We have this chemistry that electrifies every nerve cell in my body every time I think of you or I am near you. My heart beats double time when we are together. No one has ever made me feel like this. I cannot see myself without you, and I cannot truly be happy without you in my life."

Renee walked over to Mat and lifted herself onto her toes to reach up to kiss her man. "Now would be a good time to unzip my dress. While you're at it, can you unfasten my necklace and my bra?" She started unbuttoning his shirt one button at a time.

Tongue-tied, Mat asked, "Are you sure that this is what you want? I don't want to rush you in any way."

Flustered, Renee answered, "You're not rushing me into anything. I just feel so connected to you and want to connect with you all night."

Mat kissed her, hungrily taking her in. They both were undressed, and Mat wrapped himself around Renee's naked body. Then he carried her in his arms to the king-sized bed.

"Renee, I have seen thousands of pregnant women in my career, but I have to say, you are hands down the most beautiful Madonna I have ever seen."

She held his gaze with her eyes, and as he laid her down on the bed, he started kissing her all over her body.

She started feeling guilty about being with Mat. She had never been with anyone but Paul, and right now, she felt like she was cheating on him. Why couldn't she let Paul go? She knew that he was gone from her forever; maybe it was because she was carrying Paul's babies.

Suddenly, Renee pushed Mat away from her, hoping he would understand why she couldn't let this go on.

"Why are you pushing me away? Am I hurting you?" Mat asked, confused.

"I'm sorry, Mat, but I can't go through with this. I feel so guilty. I know that sounds stupid because Paul's dead, but I feel so connected with him still. I feel terrible leading you on like this."

"Renee, I understand you are carrying his babies, and those two little ones will always be a reminder of the love you shared with Paul. I understand why you can't let yourself love me right now, so let's just snuggle and hold each other tonight," Mat suggested.

"I really did want to make love to you tonight. You are the most under-standing, patient, and caring man I have ever met."

She placed her head on his chest and silently listened to the beat of his heart. Before falling asleep, she mumbled, "I love you so much, Mat. You're my other half." Then she kissed his chest and she was out.

Mat never felt more love for anyone in his entire life than he did for this crazy female sleeping on his chest. He was a little disappointed that they did not make love, but he would wait until she was ready. He kissed the top of her head and fell asleep, content with just holding her.

***

Early next morning, Mat decided to order them some breakfast before they started their busy day. He looked at the menu and wasn't sure what Renee would be hungry for this morning, so he ordered the entire breakfast menu. He ordered buttermilk pancakes, fresh fruit platter with banana, organic yogurt parfait with granola, croissants, scrambled eggs, bacon, potatoes, and toast, with a pot of coffee, some freshly squeezed orange juice, and one glass of milk for Renee. He then called down to the spa to see if their reservations were still on for ten a.m. Everything was set for their day. He was sad to see their little weekend getaway coming to an end.

There was a knock on the door that awoke Renee from a restful sleep. Mat went and opened it, and the Mirage employee brought in their breakfast. Mat thanked the young man and gave him a nice tip for his service.

"Get up, you sleepyhead. I ordered us a little breakfast."

Renee looked at the feast and replied, "This is what you call a little break-fast? At my house, this is a breakfast banquet. For heaven's sake, Mat, did you order us the entire menu?"

"Well, I didn't know what you would be hungry for this morning. So, yes! I ordered the entire breakfast menu. I hope you are hungry."

"I know I'm supposed to eat for three, but you have enough food here for ten pregnant women. Everything you ordered looks and smells so good, though. I think I can take down a good portion of this food on my own. I am famished," Renee said.

"I too am hungry this morning. After we finish eating, we have a date at the spa downstairs. I thought a little pampering before we go back to our real lives would be a great ending to our little vacation."

"That sounds like a heavenly day to me. I feel like I'm one of the rich and famous. I may never want to go back to my ordinary life again," Renee replied.

"After you have eaten, you should get dressed because our spa reservations are in fifteen minutes. I scheduled us for the Quintessential Pre-Wedding Bliss." He started reading the description of their spa to Renee. "We are going to get the Swedish massage, which is a full body massage that will soothe our aches and pains and relieve all our stresses and tensions. I booked us a one hundred-minute massage for each of us. Then we are going to get a deep cleansing facial for about an hour, and then we finish off our spa day with a manicure and pedicure treatment."

"That all sounds wonderful. You are the most caring man I have ever met." She reached up and gave him a tender kiss. "I will only be a minute. I am so excited; I've never gotten a spa day in my entire life. You know something, Mat, I think I am mostly looking forward to this Swedish massage. I could use a little stress and tension release before going back home."

Mat wondered to himself if she meant going back to his home or going back to her home in Boston.

Renee got ready quickly, and they both left the room in a hurry to make their appointments at the spa on time.

***

After her spa treatment, Renee felt like she had no cares in the world.

"Renee, did you enjoy the massage?"

"Hell yes, I loved every minute of it. I've even decided to treat myself to a spa day once a month if I can afford it when I get back home. The entire experience was therapeutic for the body and the soul."

"I'm glad you enjoyed it."

"You are a good man, Mat. You planned every part of this vacation just for me. I am so happy to have met you. I was so lost and alone before you came into my life. I lived in darkness for what seemed to be a lifetime. Then

I met you, Mat, and you brought light back into my miserable life. I am so thankful for you and our families for helping me live again."

"You give me too much credit. All I did was fall in love with you, and Jo did the rest. All you needed was some looking after and some tender loving care. You know that your parents and my family just want to help you through this difficult time," Mat replied.

"Can you just accept my thanks and my undying gratitude for being a true friend when I truly needed one." She then jumped into his arms, and he enveloped her with his as they kissed for what seemed to be forever. Time had stood still, and they felt like the only two living souls on this entire earth.

When they got back into their rooms, they showered, got dressed for dinner, and packed for their trip home. They were leaving right after dinner. Their wonderful vacation was over. Renee had to go back to reality and go back home and prepare her nest for her two little ones. These babies were growing so much that the clothes that she had brought with her already felt snug. She had to prepare for their arrival in about two months. The time would go by quickly because she needed to get a new place for the three of them to live. She was done with her old life. There were too many memories standing in her way. She needed a new start in life, a new beginning for her and her two small ones. She hoped that with time, maybe Mat would consider joining their little family. Her babies would be very lucky indeed to have Mat as their father.

Mat called for Renee to meet him in the lobby where they would have a quiet dinner before taking a car to the airport. Renee arrived promptly after being called. Mat took her hand, and they walked into the Mirage restaurant together for their last meal in Vegas. They were seated and each ordered an ice tea to start.

"Do you know what you want to order or do you want me to order for you?" Mat asked.

"I'm not very hungry tonight, Mat."

"You know you must eat something, Renee. What if I order us some appetizers and we share?"

"That sounds great to me," Renee replied.

When the waitress arrived to take their order, Mat ordered them nachos, mozzarella sticks, and a large garden salad, with light balsamic vinaigrette dressing.

He took Renee's hand and asked her, "What's the matter, Renee? You are so quiet."

"I think I'm just a little tired, that's all."

"You sure that's all?"

Renee divulged, "Mat, I don't want to leave here because I am afraid of going back to our routine lives. How will this work? I'm in Boston, and you are in New York. How do you see this relationship working for us after today?"

Mat took hold of her hand and replied, "I know; I have been wondering that myself, but I know that we have to try because I cannot lose you. I love you so much, it hurts to think of you away from me."

"Mat, I need to go back to Boston to sell my house and to see my parents. I promise that when my affairs are in order, I will be on the next bus back to you. I will not be allowed on a plane when I am almost ready to deliver these two little ones."

"You call me when you are ready and I will come for you," Mat said.

Renee smiled and stated, "That sounds like a very good plan."

The waitress brought over their meal, and it looked delicious. The nacho platter was huge and so was the salad, but they both nibbled on the meal.

"You haven't even eaten enough to sustain a mouse. Do you not like the choices I made? I can order something else for you," Mat said.

"No, Mat! Everything is very good, but I told you before ordering that I was not very hungry."

"Okay, I will stop being a mother hen then," Mat replied.

"Mat, I love that you are always looking out for me."

After paying the waitress, they both walked to the lobby where their bags were waiting for them.

"I settled everything at the front desk before you joined me for dinner, and I think this is our transportation to the airport."

They both got into the car and took one last look at Vegas, the city of lights. Renee thought to herself that this getaway was one of those great memories that you never want to forget.

Chapter 36

At home in Boston, Renee's parents received an offer on Renee's home but from the Hamiltons. They were willing to pay the full price of the house and purchase all of the furnishings. The offer was great but would their daughter want to sell it to them? The Clarks had tried to get Renee on the phone, but she hadn't been returning their calls. They knew their daughter had a lot on her plate but this was her house to sell, not theirs.

Christine and James went over to their daughter's house to start packing up Renee's personal belongings when they were joined by Ted and Nancy.

"What are you both doing here?" James asked. "If you want to look at the house, go through our realtor."

"James, we were just passing by when we saw your car parked in the driveway. We wondered if we could just come in for a few minutes just to talk," Ted answered,

Nancy could not hold her tongue. "We heard from a friend that Renee was with child, and we wanted to console you both because of the shame you must feel, having a daughter carrying a bastard child."

Christine blew a gasket and flew to defend her daughter's good name. "What kind of people are you to spread these malicious and terrible lies? I can see now why Renee did not want to tell you about her having your grandchild. You are not fit to be grandparents."

Nancy just gasped at the news. "You are telling us that Renee is having Paul's baby? This has to be more lies. What does she want from us now? Does she want to blackmail us for more money? She has the audacity to call this bastard child our grandchild just to save face in this community."

James had had enough of all this bad mouthing of his daughter. "I will show you to the door, and I never want to have words with you both again. Also, this house is not for sale to the likes of you. I feel sorry for you both because you had a great daughter-in-law in my daughter and now a grandchild, and you are going to miss out on both of their lives. Now, if you both don't mind, we want you out of here."

Ted spoke up before exiting the premises, "James, are you telling us the truth about the baby being Paul's?"

Renee's parents both responded, "YES!"

Ted and Nancy left with all kinds of questions rolling in their heads that they wanted answered, but they knew that they would not get them answered by the Clarks. The pair drove home in silence.

When they entered their home, Nancy told Ted, "Ted, you know that Renee won't want us to see the child after the way we treated her. We have to do something. Ted, do you think we could legally get guardianship of the child, being that Renee is not mentally or physically fit to take care of a child?"

Ted answered, "You know, Nancy, with my connections, we could probably win custody of our grandchild. I will get in touch with our lawyer first thing in the morning, and then I will call Judge Preston to see if he would meet me at the country club for lunch."

Nancy, all excited, said, "Oh! To think, Ted, we could be this child's new parents! I know that Paul would want this for his flesh and blood, and if this child is a boy, we could name him Paul in his memory. This has to work for us, Ted. I want Renee to know how it feels to have one's child taken away. I hate her with all my being, and I want her to never see this child after she gives birth to it. She will regret having taken our only son from us. That bitch will get what she deserves in the end. She can rot in hell while we are raising Paul's little one—our little one."

Ted went into his den and started making some calls to some influential people in the legal field to infer what steps to take to legally adopt Paul's child. He was told that the only way a judge would legally give them custody would be if the mother was totally unfit to raise the child on her own.

Ted had to find evidence. He would have to find some medical professionals to testify that Renee was mentally unfit to care for herself and a child.

They would have to find influential witnesses that would collaborate with their finding, witnesses that could be bribed to testify that the child would be in danger by staying with their mother. They would also need testimonials indicating that they were the best candidates to raise this child. They had to show everyone that the child would be living in a safe and nurturing environment. The Hamiltons wanted sole custody of the child so that they could raise the child in a stable home and with parents that could give him or her a rich and fruitful life.

***

Nancy was in Paul's old room. The room was still decorated the way her son left it when he moved out for college. She did not want to get rid of Paul's belongings, but they had to make room for the new arrival. She thought she would store some things in the attic but keep some in the room so that the child will be surrounded by Paul's things and it will give the child comfort. She wanted the child to know who his or her father was and that Paul would have loved being there for all the moments in his child's life. Nancy knew that Paul would have been a great dad, as he had a great capacity to love and would have been a great role model. Even now, she believes that Paul would never forsake his child not in life, and surely not in death.

Ted and Nancy were thrilled to be proud parents again, and Renee had no say about it.

Ted joined Nancy in Paul's room, and Nancy said, "Ted, that evil woman will never see her child again after we get full custody. We know that she is mentally unbalanced and unfit to be a parent to this child. We can only hope that something terrible will happen to her while giving birth to our grandchild. We could not be so lucky, but after she loses everything she has ever cared for, she will wish she had died while giving birth. Renee will regret the day she messed with the Hamilton family."

They had so much to do before the baby arrived. Ted had to find a private detective to find Renee's whereabouts and to see what she had been doing since she left town.

He proposed, "Nancy, you start working on the nursery, and I will get all the information I need to get Renee out of our lives and her baby's life for good."

Chapter 37

Rachel and Darren were home with Philip enjoying the beautiful sunny day. They had decided to go to a matinee movie and order pizza from home afterwards. Since the moment Darren proposed to Rachel, she had become a bridezilla. She spent most of her free time looking through the pages of bridal magazines, looking for the perfect gown. She loved reading all the "dos" and "don'ts" of preparing for the special day. She had always dreamed of having her wedding in a small chapel.

They had decided to have a small wedding and reception with only their closest friends. Rachel had decided that she wanted to marry Darren as soon as possible. She could not wait to be called Mrs. Darren Michaels. She had already planned to be married in the little chapel they had attended Christmas Eve. It was so quaint and its basement could hold their little reception. Rachel wanted everything to be perfect because she had no intentions of ever getting married again, as Darren was the man of her dreams.

Philip was so excited to be going out with his parents, as they had not been out together as a family for what seemed like forever. Darren and Rachel had been working full time since Christmas because they wanted to pay off their Christmas purchases—the sacrifices one makes to have a happy jolly Christmas. Darren knew that the extra hours Rachel and he worked were hardest on their son.

Philip would be dropped off early in the morning at his daycare and picked up late, usually at the daycare's closing time. It was hard for a child to understand money problems, but both Darren and Rachel hoped that it did not affect him, but it had. Now that all their Christmas purchases were all paid for they had decided to go out as a family and have a little fun.

Rachel and Darren decided that he would try to work more hours at the pub, while she would go back to her regular scheduled hours at the grocery store. They hoped that this would help Philip's life get back to some normalcy.

The family outing was enjoyed by all. Darren did not realize that Philip was not the only one missing out on their family time. After going out to the movies, they had all decided to go home, play some board games and order out for pizza. Philip was so thankful for having his parents all to himself. He and Rachel started a pillow fight in the living room, and Darren was happy just watching his bride-to-be and their son laughing away. After a full day of fun, Philip fell asleep quite early.

Darren carried his son up to bed, then went and filled the tub with water for a bubble bath. An early night for Philip meant that Rachel and he could get in some alone time. He called Rachel up from the kitchen, and she found him in the tub with candles burning on the floor next to it.

"Well, I see you have taken advantage of Philip's exhaustion to have a little fun in the tub," Rachel acknowledged.

"Well, Rachel, I haven't started having any fun yet because. you're not in here with me. Now, take off your clothes and come and join me."

"What are the magic words?" Rachel asked.

Darren smiled. "PLEASE take off your clothes and come join me. My body is aching for you, woman."

She undressed so fast that she was in the tub in a flash. They made love in the tub for hours. When they got out of the tub, the water was fringed. They fell asleep in each other's arms as soon as they hit their pillows.

***

Their daily lives started to get back on track. Darren wanted to be able to give his family everything they desired. He worked full time at the pub to save some money for the wedding Rachel always dreamed of. His memories of his past were getting more frequent, but figuring them out was like working on a million-piece jigsaw puzzle. He could not fit the pieces together. He was sure of one thing: the woman in his dreams, who popped up now and then in his daily life, had to be someone who was important in his life, but who? Who was she? Where was she? How did she fit into his life? All he had was questions, but no answers.

He had realized that perhaps he would never know her identity and he would have to be content not knowing. He made up his mind to look forward to his future and that included Rachel and Philip and to stop trying to put all the jigsaw pieces together.

Darren said aloud to himself, "Darren, look forward to your future because your past has been forgotten."

Everything was falling into place. He loved Rachel and her son and would do everything in his power to make them both happy. Rachel was not the only one excited about getting hitched—Darren was also anxiously waiting for the big day.

Chapter 38

The Hamiltons had gotten a judge to give them temporary custody of Renee's unborn child. This was not something that was usually done in Boston. Usually the child always stays with the parent unless the child is in danger from that parent, but the Hamiltons had a compelling story to tell the judge. It also didn't help Renee's case that the Hamiltons were friends with the judge. Now, all they had to do was find her and bring her home so that the moment she gave birth, they would take the child from her and hopefully rip her heart out in the process, just as she did to them.

Mr. Hamilton had been given the name of a good private detective, Robert Blackheart, to look into the whereabouts of Renee. He had been called and arrived at their door to get the ins and outs of the case. He had decided that the best way to pinpoint where she could be found would be to put a tap on her parents' phone, which would not be too hard to do. Mr. Hamilton said he could ask the Clarks to meet them at Renee's home to see about purchasing it once again. They would try to persuade them to let them buy their son's home if they offered an outrageous amount above the asking price.

Once the Clarks had been contacted, they had agreed to meet the Hamiltons at their daughter's home within the next half hour. That would give Robert, the PI, time to do his work. He assured the Hamiltons that the moment Renee called her parents, he would know where she was located. This pleased the Hamiltons immensely.

After the Hamiltons discussed the purchase of the house again, James Clark told them that they would contact Renee and would give them an answer as soon as possible. James had decided to stop playing cat and mouse with the Hamiltons and get the best buck for their daughter's home.

Not a couple hours later, the Hamiltons returned home after wasting time with the Clarks. They hoped it gave their PI enough time to do what was needed in the Clarks' home. Robert Blackheart was waiting for them. He had told them that all was in order and that he would contact them as soon as he located Renee. They had given him a down payment for his services and would give him the rest as soon as Renee was located.

***

When James and Christine got home, they made a call to Renee. They were happy to talk to her and see how she was doing.

"Hi! Mom, Dad, how are you both doing? I was just about to call you," Renee said.

"Hello, darling, I have you on speaker. How are you feeling, sweetheart, and when are you coming home? We miss you," Christine said.

"I'm doing fine, Mom, and I miss you too. I'm not coming home any time soon. Why don't you both come up and visit. I am sure that the Reynoldses would love to see you too."

James came out and said, "Sweetheart ,your mom and I would love to come see you and the Reynoldses, but we have an offer from the Hamiltons for your house again, and I think you should take it."

"Dad, if they want it so badly, sell it to them. I don't think I am ever going back to Boston to live. I like it here in New York. I have no reminders of Paul everywhere I go. I think I will be moving here, making a new start for me and the baby."

Christine, upset at the news, asked, "When did this all come about, Renee? We thought you would be raising your baby here so that we could help you and be part of your baby's life."

"Mom, let's talk about it when you come to New York, and we will discuss it in length."

"Give us a few days, and we will contact the Reynoldses to let them know we will be in town."

"I know they would love to see you, and so would I. I miss you both so much."

"See you soon, sweetheart," and hung up. Then she turned to James and said, "I cannot believe Renee is not coming home. She has no one there to look after her."

"You don't know that, maybe she is staying there for the young Dr. Reynolds, who has been smitten by her from the moment he met her in the Dominican Republic," James answered.

"Do you think that's why she is thinking of moving to New York, James?"

"I do, and I am going to call the Reynoldses right now and see if they wouldn't mind some company sometime next week."

James called the Reynoldses' number, and Steve Reynolds was delighted to hear from his good friend.

"Hi, Steve! How are you and Sue doing? We just talked to Renee and she invited us to come to New York and see you all. I was wondering if you would like to get together when we get into town?"

"We would love to have you stay with us. We can have the kids come stay for the weekend, and we can all be together again. How does that sound to you and Christine?" Steve asked.

"That sounds great, but are you sure it won't be an inconvenience having us stay over?" James replied.

Steve assured him, "No, we would really love to have you to stay with us. Now you call us when you arrive at the airport, and we will come pick you up. Is that alright with you?"

"That sounds great and we will call you when we have the date and flight information. Thanks again, Steve, and we cannot wait to see you and Sue as well."

***

When both were offline, Robert, the private investigator, had all the information he needed; he just had to wait and follow Renee's parents right to her whereabouts. This was going to be easy money.

***

James called the realtor and told him that his daughter agreed on the new offer that the Hamiltons put on the table and that he would like the closing date to be by the end of the week. That would give them ample time to get Renee's personal items out of the house before the Hamiltons took over the house.

By the end of the week, the money was in Renee's bank account and her things were put into storage.

The Clarks had reserved a flight to New York for Monday morning, and they had contacted the Reynoldses and their daughter with all the information. They were anxious to see their daughter and see how she was progressing. Christine was hoping to go shopping for baby things with Renee when she was in New York. This might be her only grandchild, and she wanted to be there for all the big moments in her life.

Christine had to make a few errands before leaving for New York. She had to stop at the jewelers to get a new battery for her watch and pick up her laundry at the dry cleaners. When she got to the jewelers, she was handed a little box that contained Renee's and Paul's wedding bands.

The jeweler said, "Mrs. Clark, I am so glad to see you. I have had Renee's and Paul's wedding bands here for quite some time. They wanted them engraved, but with Paul's death, I didn't know how to bring the subject up. There is no cost; it was my wedding gift to the newlyweds."

Christine opened the velvety box that contained the matching pair of wedding bands. She picked up Renee's band and read the inscription: "*Till Death Do Us Part.*" A tear rolled down her cheek.

"Mrs. Clark, I am so sorry, perhaps I should have just kept them buried in the back, but they did not belong to me." He handed her a tissue, and she thanked him.

"I am the one who is sorry. I am pleased with the engraving. I am sure Renee will be very happy to get the rings back."

She left the jewelers, forgetting to purchase a battery for her watch. She got into her car and started crying for the life and love that had been lost. How things would have been different if only Paul would have lived.

She then looked up and started speaking to the air. "Paul, I don't know if you can hear me from up there, but if you can, please look out for Renee and your baby. Yes, you heard me right, you are going to be a daddy and I know you would have been a great dad to this little person who is growing inside your wife. Help her, Paul, for she needs your strength to help her get through the pregnancy, the labor, and the raising of this innocent child. I have to say that I am not proud of your parents' behavior toward my baby girl. They have been quite horrendous to Renee, and she has taken it very hard; she even left town to get away from them. Please, Paul, if you can hear me, take care of Renee and that precious package she is holding close to her heart. Know that we all miss you and Renee has been lost without you."

Christine drove off in the direction of the dry cleaners, and there she had heard the most outrageous news.

Mrs. Craven, the dry cleaner's wife, said, "I heard that Mr. Hamilton had contacted a private detective to find Renee's whereabouts. The Hamiltons have started legal proceedings to take the baby from Renee as soon as she gives birth to their grandchild. Mrs. Clark, is Renee expecting?"

Upset and flustered by the information she was given, Christine answered, "Yes! Mrs. Craven, she is, and we are so happy about becoming grandparents. Um . . . can I have my laundry? I am sort of in a hurry. Mr. Clark is waiting for me in the car."

Seeing how upset Mrs. Clark had become, Mrs. Craven answered, "Yes! Yes! I'll just go and get them for you."

After claiming her laundry, Christine ran out of the shop to her car. She drove quickly home to tell her husband about Hamilton's plan.

James couldn't believe his ears. "How could the Hamiltons be thinking about doing this to Renee? Christine, what makes them think they have the right to take her baby from her? They must have lost their minds!"

"I don't know, but I am afraid that they will make things harder for Renee."

"Christine, I think that we should cancel our trip to New York so that we don't lead the private detective and the Hamiltons directly to where Renee is staying. I think we should get in touch with Renee to tell her the Hamiltons are looking for her and they plan on taking the baby away from her."

***

They called Renee and told her what was happening at home. Renee was frightened that if the Hamiltons wanted her baby, they would find a way to make it happen. As she hung up the phone, she started having terrible pain in her lower back.

Upset, Renee said aloud, "This can't be happening! It's too early." She started yelling, as the pain was getting stronger and more frequent. She got to her phone and called Mat.

"Mat, it's Renee. I think . . . The babies are coming. You know . . . it's too early. Oh no! My water just broke and I am in so much pain! Mat, I am so scared."

Mat advised Renee, "Don't worry, I have an ambulance coming for you right now and you have to just stay calm. I'll be waiting for you at the hospital. Everything is going to be alright."

Renee replied in agony, "Oh, Mat, I think I hear the sirens of an ambulance."

"All right, Renee, I'll see you soon. Don't worry, the first pregnancy always takes more time," Mat said.

"Okay, Mat! The ambulance is here."

The phone went dead and Mat was honestly frightened for Renee.

***

Mat had prepared everything at the hospital for Renee's arrival. As she entered the emergency room, Mat collected her and brought her directly to the maternity ward. She grabbed on to Mat's hand and squeezed it very hard with every contraction. Mat took her into the delivery room and told her, "Renee, I know these babies are early but thirty-seven weeks for twins is quite common. I am just going to check how dilated you are, okay?"

Renee just nodded her head and grabbed hold of the railings from the bed that they had just transferred her to.

Mat looked up and told her, "These babies are coming out now. Sweetheart, I want you to push when you get your next contraction, okay?"

"Okay, Mat! I'll try."

"Okay, Renee, now push," Mat said. That's good . . . now you have to push again. Yes, just like that."

"Mat, I am so tired. I need to take a break."

"There is no taking a break right now. I can see the baby's head. The head is out, stop pushing." He cleaned the baby's mouth and nose and then he told her to push again. "Renee, he's out and he looks fine."

She felt better when she heard her baby cry. He brought the baby to her, and she cradled him in her arms and gave him a kiss on his head, then returned him to the nurse before the next contractions started.

The second baby came out very quickly, but this baby was very premature. She was very small and needed to be taken by the neonatal team.

Frightened, Renee asked, "Mat, what is it? Is he okay? Why is he not crying?" Renee was getting anxious and started yelling, "Mat! What's going on? Where did they take my baby?"

Mat took her hand and tried to calm her down. "Renee, your son is fine. He is six pounds three ounces, but your daughter is very small and needs to be looked after by the neonatal team. She is in good hands."

Renee started crying and asked, "Mat, she will make it right? I need her to make it."

"Renee, I am sure she will be fine."

"Can I please hold my son?" Renee asked.

"Let me finish up with you first. The nurses will get you washed up and I will physically get your son for you," Mat replied.

Renee voiced, "Mat, let the nurses bring me my baby boy. I need you to go see my little girl. I need you to look after her because she is probably so frightened being alone with these strange nurses surrounding her right now, but she knows you. Mat, she knows your voice; she has heard it so often, so please go comfort her for me?"

He saw how worried she was for her daughter's well-being that he agreed and let the nurses finish up. Before leaving her, he gave her a kiss and told her, "I am so proud of you. You did great today. Renee, I love you so much."

"I love you too, Mat. Now, go see my daughter and tell her I love her. I need to know how she is making out."

Mat agreed and said, "Okay! Okay! I'm out of here." He left her alone to be washed up by the nurses.

After she was all cleaned up, they wheeled her to her room where her son was waiting for her. The moment she saw him, she asked the nurse to bring him to her. She put him to her breast and he latched on and suckled. She started to cry, seeing her son so content and feeding. She couldn't believe how emotional she was after delivering these two miracles.

Chapter 39

Robert, the private investigator, got off the plane in New York, and took a cab straight to where Mat worked at North Shore University Hospital in hopes to find out more information on Dr. Mat Reynolds. Arriving at the hospital Robert inquired about Mat at the information counter, he was told that the doctor was on duty today and that he was in Delivery at the moment. Robert felt lucky and went right up to the maternity ward and asked the nurses for Mat's whereabouts. The nurse at the desk asked him what his business was on this floor and he had told her that he was a college friend of Mat's and was just looking him up.

The nurse advised him that Mat was just out of Delivery and was checking up on a patient. She asked him to wait in the waiting room and told him she would let the doctor know he had a visitor. Robert did not need to wait for Mat, as he saw him walk into a patient's room. Robert sneaked in and saw Renee there holding what appeared to be a baby boy. He was wearing a blue hat and wrapped up in a blue blanket. He had to let Ted Hamilton know of this event.

Robert called his clients, and they had said that they would be right there with their lawyer.

"Robert, do you know the sex of the baby off hand?" Nancy asked.

"Mrs. Hamilton, Renee had a baby boy."

"Ted, we have a little grandson."

They called their lawyer and told him to meet them at the airport, where they had chartered a private jet to take them right to the airport in New York.

The flight took them just over an hour. They took a car right from the airport to the hospital.

The Hamiltons arrived at the hospital and marched right into Renee's room, demanding the child.

Nancy declared, "Renee, we are here to take our grandson."

Renee was surprised to see her in-laws. "Nancy, what do you mean coming here and asking for my son? There is no way in hell that I am handing my son over to you."

The Hamiltons' legal representative showed Renee the legal papers that gave the Hamiltons the legal right to take her child.

Renee exclaimed, "This is not right! He is my son! I don't care what these papers say! You are not taking him away from me!"

Mat could hear her yelling at them, so he ran into her room and asked, "What business do you have in this room? You're upsetting my patient and her son."

"We have the right to be here since we are taking our grandson with us right now back home to Boston," Nancy acknowledged.

Upset, Renee showed Mat the legal papers she was given, and in shock, Mat told her, "Renee, this gives them the legal right to take him."

Renee became furious and yelled, "You have to be joking? I will not give him up to them! Please, Mat, help me! I can't lose him. He is my son, not theirs."

Mrs. Hamilton snatched the child right out of his mother's loving arms and left her there screaming and sobbing alone in her room.

Mat tried but there was no comforting her. He could not believe that this was happening. He could honestly say that in all his years as a doctor he had never seen or experienced anything like this. When Renee talked about her in-laws, he had thought that she had been embellishing her stories a little, but he was wrong—they were as bad as she described.

Mat needed to call Renee's parents because she needed them right now. "Hi, James! It's Mat."

"Hi, Mat! What's going on with you? You sound frantic? Is Renee all right?"

"No! Renee is not all right. The Hamiltons were just here with their lawyer and they took Renee's son right from her arms. They had legal papers that made them the boy's temporary guardians."

"You gotta be kidding?" James said, confused.

"No! I am not," Mat answered. "Renee is frantic and I am worried about her, so I was wondering if you could come here as soon as possible. She needs you."

"Mat, we will be on the next flight out, and please tell her we are coming."

"I will, and I will have Jo-Ann pick you up at the airport. Just let me know when you will be landing."

"Will do," and hung up.

***

"What's going on, James? Is Renee all right?" Christine asked.

"Christine, I will give you the particulates on the ride to the airport. Just hurry and pack yourself a suitcase. We have to be on the next plane to New York!"

Christine obeyed her husband, and on their drive to the airport, he explained what was going on.

"You are telling me that the Hamiltons took the baby from her shortly after conceiving our grandson? Who the hell gave them custody of the baby?" Christine asked.

"Didn't Mrs. Craven from the laundromat tell you just the other day that this was what the Hamiltons were planning?"

"Yes! But I didn't think there was a judge in this whole country that would give them custody of Renee's baby. I haven't had a chance to even hold my grandson, and now I may never get to."

"Christine, we will get the boy back in Renee's arms. We just have to because what they have done is criminal."

Christine started crying and James consoled her.

***

The flight seemed to take forever, but when they landed, Jo was there waiting for them. She welcomed them but saw how concerned they looked, so she drove them straight to the hospital to see their daughter.

They looked for Renee in her room, but she was not there. Mat had noticed them and guided them to their daughter. They saw Renee holding a little baby in the neonatal unit.

"Mat, who's the little baby Renee is rocking?" Christine asked.

"That is your granddaughter."

"I thought you said she had a boy and that the Hamiltons took him," Christine said confused.

"Renee had twins, a little girl and a little boy," he replied. "The Hamiltons did not know that Renee was expecting twins, so they only snatched the one that Renee was nursing at that moment."

"I cannot believe that this is happening, and why is Renee dressed in a mask and gown? Is our granddaughter all right?" asked Christine.

"She's perfect, just a little small. The boy was bigger and that is why Renee had the baby in her room with her."

Renee saw her parent's and got up. She brought her daughter to the observation window so they could see her little one close up. Christine started crying to see how beautiful her granddaughter was. Renee gave her daughter back to the nurse and walked right into her father's arms. He held her, not knowing how to console her.

Sobbing, Renee said, "Daddy, they took him away. Why would they do such a thing? And who gave them the right to do it?"

"Renee, we had suspicions that they were working on a plan to take your baby from you, but we didn't think that they would be able to do it," James said.

"Their legal papers said I was an unfit mother. How do they know what kind of mother I would be when they didn't even give me a chance to be one?" Renee started crying again.

"Renee, you need to eat something and try to get a little rest to keep your strength up. Listen to me, your daughter needs you to be strong and healthy and so does your son when you get him back," Mat stated.

She listened to him and started eating what looked like lasagna and promised to rest a little after eating her dinner. Christine stayed with her daughter to help her during this most trying time.

***

Mat took James out in the hallway to speak privately. "James, I had to sedate Renee because she was having an emotional breakdown. I think if she does not calm down, the Hamiltons will have more ammunition to use against her. The legal documents that they had with them said that she had been put into the psych ward at the hospital in Boston and that she was to be seen by a psychiatrist but did not follow up with her appointments."

James confirmed, "Yes, that is all true, but I thought that Jo might have been seeing her here?"

"Yes, she was, and that will help Renee when she goes to court to try and get her son back. She needs to stay healthy, physically and mentally, if she has a chance to get custody of her son. We also have to keep your granddaughter a secret, or they will take her away as well. I believe that if Renee can show to the court how well she is doing with her daughter, it may help her win her case."

"I see what you are saying. I think that Renee should come back home with us, and perhaps she can get the court to let her visit her son," James agreed.

"I think you are right," Mat replied. "She needs to go home and maybe she will even get to nurse her son if her physician believes that nursing her baby is important for the child's health and well-being. They may say that she can pump her milk in a bottle to give to her son, but it is a proven fact that the child needs that physical attachment, that bonding with his mother, to help him become a healthy, happy individual."

"Mat, when do you think that our granddaughter will be well enough to go home?" James asked.

"If she keeps on gaining weight, I think that she can probably go home in a few days. That's if she keeps on gaining weight."

"I think that I will rent a car to go back home. This way, no one will know that Renee had a second child. We have to stay under the radar," James said.

"I think that is a great plan, and you don't need to rent a car. I am sure my father will let you borrow one of his, and I can pick it up when I come to visit. I will be coming down to see how my patients are doing if we are to keep that little one a secret."

"Mat, you are invited to stay with us any time you are in Boston. Now, I am going to visit with my daughter and let her in on our plan. Thank you, Mat! You have been a true friend to my entire family, and we do appreciate it. I don't know what Renee would have done without you and your sister's help while she has been here in New York."

"James, I want you to know that I love Renee and those babies of hers, and I would do anything for them."

James wrapped his arms around Mat and said, "I know son, and she is very lucky to have you on her side."

"I think you are mistaken, James. I am the lucky one."

Mat left James so that he could join his wife in consoling his daughter. Mat had other patients to visit before his shift was over and then he would be able to spend the night with Renee while her parents visited with his parents. Her parents were invited to stay with the Reynoldses until Renee and the baby were ready to be discharged from the hospital. The Clarks were pleased to see their good friends, even under these terrible circumstances.

Chapter 40

In Boston, the Hamiltons were just arriving at their home when they saw all the reporters on their front lawn.

Mrs. Hamilton asked her husband, "Ted, how do they know what's going on?"

Ted answered, "I don't know, but they always seem to have their sources." Ted took the car seat with the baby into the house. He was pleased that the baby did not fuss too much on the flight home. The nurse they had hired had taken care of all the baby's needs. This baby will never want for anything, just as Paul would have wished for his only son.

The staff were all briefed on the situation and asked not to talk to the press. Nurse Rose was shown to her room adjacent to the baby's nursery. The nurse put the baby into its new crib, and he never awoke from his slumber. Rose then was introduced to the staff and was given a tour of the home. She would probably only get to use the kitchen to heat up a bottle for the little one when hungry. She was told that she could eat in the kitchen with the staff or she could have her food sent to her in the nursery, which she preferred. She was also to give the cook her dietary requests if she did not like what they were serving that day. Rose told the cook that she was fine to eat whatever she was served, as she was not fussy.

After the introductions and her meals planned out for her, Nurse Rose went up to check on the infant; then she unpacked her suitcases in her room. She was pleased that the baby seemed to be made of hardy stock, as he only fussed when his diaper needed changing and when he was hungry. She was also pleased with her employment here at the Hamiltons, as it was going to be easy money. If truth be told, she felt bad for this little tyke's mother tonight. Nurse Rose knew she was probably crying non-stop after losing her little bundle of joy. The child's mother did not deserve what the Hamiltons were doing. Rose promised the boy that she would take good care of him until he was back with his mother.

The story on the front page of the newspaper stated how the Hamiltons had snatched the baby from its mother's loving arms. The picture showed the Hamiltons leaving the hospital in New York with the baby in tow. The paper read:

"The Hamiltons employed a private detective to hunt down their daughter-in-law, Renee Hamilton, just like a hound hunting down a fox. She had just given birth to a healthy baby boy when Mr. and Mrs. Ted Hamilton got the news and chartered a private jet to take them to New York. The Hamiltons were accompanied by their lawyer and a nanny they hired to take care of the little Hamilton heir. The Hamiltons used their influence to get temporary guardianship of the newborn. A source tells us that Renee was nursing her infant son when Nancy Hamilton snatched him out from the warmth of his mother's loving arms. Renee had been so frantic and beside herself when her in-laws took away her son that she needed to be sedated.

"The source's comments were, 'It must be nice to be wealthy enough to be able to pay off legal figures to get you the guardianship of someone else's baby. The Hamiltons have always used their status to get them whatever they wanted. When does the madness end? There is a mother, one of our own, crying for her son back. As a person who knows Renee to be a good and caring person, a loving daughter and wife, and someone who has taught many of our youngsters in this community, I am appalled at the lengths the Hamiltons have gone to just to hurt that poor girl. Is there no end to what the rich think they can get away with? When this poor girl goes to court to reclaim her son, I hope she will get full support from this community as

*well. I would like to say to the Hamiltons for shame for stoop-
ing so low as to kidnap your own grandson from his loving
mother's arms.'"*

Ted and Nancy could not believe what they had read. They appeared to
be the villains once again. The phone started ringing nonstop. Everyone was
complaining and appalled at what they had done to poor Renee. The community could not understand how these two upstanding individuals from their
community could be so cold and heartless toward their own daughter-in-law.

The story got picked up in New York because it had taken place in their
city. The reporter got pictures of the Hamiltons leaving the hospital with
Renee's son. Somehow, they had gotten pictures and video footage of Renee
frantically crying and calling out for her son. She looked beside herself with
sorrow and agony for losing her newborn son. This story was going viral. It
was picked up in all the papers and even broadcasted on the television. This
was a big human interest story that would interest anyone who had a heart.

Chapter 41

Renee's little girl, whom she had decided to name Hope, was ready to be discharged from the hospital that had been her home for the last twelve days. Renee was so happy to get to go home in search of her son. She and little Hope had time to get their strengths up to face what came next in their lives. She had every intention of getting her son back to where he belonged, with her and his sister.

Mat was both happy and unhappy to see both of his girls go. He wanted them to stay where he could protect them, but Renee's son was in Boston, and that is where she had to be—he understood that. James had brought the car close to the entrance to pick up his daughter. Knowing that reporters were waiting to talk to her and to take pictures, Mat had come up with a plan where Hope would be picked up next to his car in the doctors' parking lot, where no one would see Renee's little secret.

Renee was so sad to say goodbye to Mat; she was going to miss him terribly.

"You call me when you arrive home, and I'll see you soon," Mat said.

Renee held his hand. "Promise me, Mat, that you will come and visit us in Boston as soon as your schedule clears?"

Mat kissed her hand and said, "Pretty lady, I promise to come and see you as soon as I can." He gave Hope a kiss on the head and gave her to James.

James fastened Hope's car seat in the back seat next to where Renee would be sitting. Mat kissed Renee goodbye. It broke both their hearts to part. As they drove off, Renee looked back at Mat, feeling as though she was leaving part of her heart in New York.

***

The ride home seemed long because Hope wanted to be fed every couple of hours. They made certain no one saw the baby in the back seat of the car when they drove through town. Hope needed to stay a secret if Renee wanted to keep her. She knew if the Hamiltons knew of Hope's existence, they would take her away too. Renee had decided to breastfeed and use cloth diapers so that she would not have to purchase any of these things in town and Hope would stay incognito.

The next day, she hired Peter, her husband's partner, to take on her case. She wanted to petition the court for legal guardianship of her son. She knew this would take time, so she had asked to have visiting rights to her son so that she can bond with him and nurse him during the day. To her surprise, the court agreed to her demands but only during the day. She would pump milk for him for his night feedings.

The Hamiltons did not like this plan at all; they wanted to exclude the mother from the child's existence. Peter made time to go with Renee to the Hamiltons to make sure that she was able to see her son without any problems.

When Renee saw her son, tears flowed down her eyes. She was so happy to see him. "Peter, look at him. He is so beautiful, and he has put on some weight. He is a little butter ball." She could not stop kissing his round cheeks.

The baby's nurse came in and said, "Hello, Renee! I am Rose, your son's nanny, and I have to say, he is the best baby to look after."

"Hi, Rose, when does baby Paul have his next feeding?"

"You came just in time for his feeding," Rose advised her.

"Oh, wonderful! Just so you know, I am going to come nurse him every day, and I will pump milk so that you can feed him at night."

Peter and Rose left her alone for a moment to get her and her son ready to breastfeed. When they came back into the room, Renee was rocking and feeding her little baby boy. She looked like a Madonna there holding her son. Peter could see how wonderful a mother Renee was and that her son needed to be back home with her. Baby Paul needed to be raised by his mother and not raised by his grandparents and their nanny. Peter was going to make this his mission to get this little family back together. He needed to do this for

Paul, as he knew that Paul would be so disappointed with his parents for what they were doing to his family.

After feeding baby Paul, Renee changed him and put him down in his crib, as he was fast asleep. She hated leaving him there, but she had no choice. Renee asked the boy's nanny, "Rose, promise me you will take good care of my baby since I cannot be here with him?"

"Renee, don't fret. I will take good care of him until the day you get him back."

"Thank you, Rose! You don't know how much that means to me."

Peter took hold of Renee's shoulder, and they both walked out of the Hamiltons' front door. Renee could not wait for her son's next feeding.

"Renee, I think we should try and get an early date for your legal proceedings. It would be in the best interest of your son," Peter suggested.

"The faster I get my son back, the better. I want to thank you for taking me on as a client; I know you and your family are close to the Hamiltons."

"I have to say that I think what the Hamiltons are doing to you is appalling, and my family backs me up on this one. I know that Paul would be ashamed of his parents' actions. He would hate that they are keeping little Paul from his mother," Peter said.

Renee hugged him and said, "Thank you, Peter! You are a good friend."

Peter drove her back home to her parents' and told her that he would come for her in about three and a half hours for baby Paul's next feeding. Renee thanked him again, and she went into her parent's home, knowing that it was close to Hope's feeding time.

Christine asked her, "Renee, do you think that your father could go with you for baby Paul's next feeding, so that he can meet his grandson, and then we can take turns that way I get to meet him too?"

"Mom, I think that's a great idea."

Her parents left her alone to nurse her little secret.

Not long after, Peter came back to pick her and her father up for baby Paul's next feeding. The Hamiltons were fuming; they had to do something to get this woman out of all their lives. They had been calling favors all day, but no one wanted to get involved in their insanity.

Peter had good news for Renee: the judge was willing to bring this matter to court two weeks from now. That would give him time to get Renee checked over by a psychiatrist, a psychologist, and as many doctors as possible who would be willing to check her over and vouch for her health, mental and physical state, and ability to care for her son.

***

In the week prior to her court date, Renee had been tested and probed by all types of medical professionals. She was pleased that these influential people had all accepted to speak on her mental and physical being. Peter had also asked Mat and Jo-Ann Reynolds to come and give their professional testimony on Renee's state of mind and character.

The news of this case became a big story not only in Boston but also in New York, as the people wanted to know more about this abduction that had happened in their city, on their watch.

Mat and Jo came to Boston to retrieve their father's car and be interviewed by Renee's lawyer, Peter. Mat was so happy to see Renee; he had kept in touch with her every day, but getting to see her and hold her was something that he missed. He gave Hope a good bill of health and her mother as well.

Mat and Jo-Ann said that they would come back to Boston whenever they were needed to testify on Renee's behalf. Peter thought that he had a lot of good witnesses who were ready to testify that Renee was a mentally and physically healthy woman who was able to care for her son on her own. He was hopeful that she would get sole custody of her son in the next few weeks.

Chapter 42

As the wedding was getting closer, Rachel was getting all the last minute preparations done. Darren was working at the pub when he saw someone he recognized on the television. There was the woman from his dreams getting interviewed on the television! A sudden jolt ran through him, and he knew she was—his wife, Renee.

"Oh my God! I have a wife and that's her. Yes! My name is Paul Hamilton and she is my wife, Renee Hamilton. My parents are Ted and Nancy Hamilton, and we all live in Boston. I remember it all now!"

He did not get everything that was said on the television broadcast, so he asked his boss if he could use his computer, as it was important.

His boss told him, "Sure, Darren, take a break and use the computer in my office."

Darren ran to his boss's office and typed out his name and he read that he had died on 9/11—so everyone had thought. That was why no one was searching for him. Then he typed out Renee's name and read that his wife had had a baby—their baby—and his name was Paul Jr., in memory of his late father. He had a son. He kept on reading and could not believe what his parents were putting Renee through. They had taken their son from her arms after just giving birth. What the hell were they thinking? He needed to help her. He could not let his parents take their son away from his mother. He could not let that happen.

Then he came back to his life as Darren—he was engaged to be married and he had a son here and a new life in New York. He could not marry Rachel, as he now knew he was already married to Renee and he had a son in

Boston who needed a father just as much as Philip did. Suddenly, he ached for Renee now that he thought of her. He loved her and had promised her "till death do us part."

He had to talk to Rachel and get her to understand that he had to get back to his first family and make things right. He talked to his boss and told him he couldn't work the rest of his shift because he had urgent business to take care of at home. His boss told him to go; he would make do without him.

Paul caught a cab home, knowing that Rachel was there with Philip. He was trying to figure out how he would break the news to Rachel. There was no easy way of telling her that he had another family that he had forgotten about. Before getting out of the cab, Paul paid for his fare and then he walked right into his and Rachel's love nest. Rachel was surprised to see him home so early.

"Darren, I thought you said you would be working late tonight. What's up? Rachel asked.

Before he could explain, Paul asked, "Rachel, has Philip gone to bed?"

"Yes, he has been in bed for a while now."

"Good, I have some news that I want to talk to you about in private."

"Darren! You are scaring me, what's going on?"

"You better sit down for what I have to tell you. Tonight. I was watching the news . . . and I saw someone I knew from my past on the television."

"That's great news, Darren, you are starting to get your memory back, or is it?"

"The person that I saw that I remember from my past is Renee Hamilton."

"Who is she to you, Darren?"

"My real name is Paul Hamilton . . . and she is my wife."

Rachel asked hesitantly, "You mean, your ex-wife don't you, Darren?"

"No, Rachel! She is my one and only wife. I have a home in Boston, and I have just learned that I have a new born son."

"How do you know he's your son and not someone else's child?" Rachel asked anxiously.

"She named him after me, his father. Renee and I have a love that was made in heaven. We were made for each other. I am so sorry, Rachel. I know that this is not what we had planned for our future, but legally my future is with my family in Boston."

Rachel started crying frantically. She had just lost her whole world. She had just lost her husband-to-be, and Philip lost his father. Paul tried to console her, but there was no way that he could make this better. Rachel was furious about losing Paul. She had to think fast and she blurted out, "What about your child that I am carrying inside me? I was going to tell you about the baby on our wedding day, as my wedding gift to you."

Surprised, Paul said, "Are you serious? You are with child?"

"Yes! I am carrying your child inside me right now, one that we conceived with our love making." Rachel felt badly about lying to him about being pregnant, but what else could she do? She was desperate; he was a big part of her family and she would fight to keep her family intact.

"Rachel . . . I can't believe this has happened, but I will not forsake you."

"I'm so glad Paul because I don't know how I could get through this alone. You made a promise to me and Philip that we would be a family. You wanted to marry me, be my husband and be Philip's dad."

"Rachel, I am already his dad," Paul replied, then wondered how he would live there with Rachel, knowing that he had a family in Boston, who needed him just as well. He knew that Renee had her parents and friends to help her with the baby, but how could he abandon them? He knew they believed he was deceased, but not being in his son's life was not right. His son was his flesh and blood and conceived in pure love, and the love Paul still felt for Renee was a one-in-a-lifetime kind of love. Paul loved Rachel, but Renee owned his heart and she always would. He knew Rachel needed him; she had no one to help her. Knowing that, Paul decided he must stay with her and forsake his heart's one desire. In his thoughts, he prayed, *Please God, help me. I don't want to abandon Renee, but Rachel needs me.*

Paul and Rachel went to bed in silence, both thinking of their futures. Rachel realized that she had to get pregnant and fast so that her lie would become truthful. Renee reached over toward Paul to get things started between them. She began kissing him and hoped that love making would begin, like it had most every night. Paul tried, but he could not let himself love her knowing that he was married.

After all, he had made a promise to Renee on their wedding day to love her and be faithful to her till death do them part. He knew that he had already broken his marital vows, but he did not know that he was married at the time. Now, making love to Rachel would be wrong. Paul said, "Rachel, I can't. I'm just too tired."

She was afraid she had lost him now that he knew he was married. How was she to get pregnant if he wouldn't touch her? She should never have lied to him. What was she to do?

Rachel could not sleep because she was thinking about how to get herself out of this predicament. During the night, she thought of a plan that could work. She would lose the baby—that could work—and maybe he would stay with her because she was so distraught from losing their baby. She was not pleased about all the lies, but she had no other way out.

Chapter 43

In Boston, Renee was getting ready for her day in court. She hoped to God that Peter would be able to win this one for her because she needed to get her son back. She was afraid that even if all the medical professionals deemed her sane and capable of caring for her son, the Hamiltons would do everything and anything in their power to keep her away from Paul Jr.

Renee's father was waiting for her in the kitchen while she finished nursing Hope. Her mother would stay home today and care for the little one. Renee came down, had a bite of her toast, and then followed her father to the car. She did not want to be late. Peter advised her to arrive early, as he wanted to talk to her before they entered the courtroom.

Peter had every intention of winning this case today. When she arrived, Renee sat down with Peter and he drilled her with questions that she may be asked when on stand.

Terrified, Renee said, "Peter, I am so scared about saying all the wrong things today. I need to get this right. My son's life depends on it, but so does mine. I cannot live without my son in my life."

"I know, Renee. I think that Paul's parents have wronged you, and I know that Paul would be so furious if he could see what they were putting you and your son through."

Renee started crying. "Peter, I have to get him back. Please don't let them keep him away from me. You are my only hope."

***

The court room was filled mostly with Boston's wealthiest and a few of Renee's closest friends. Renee was so pleased to see Mat and his entire family sitting in the courtroom. She sat next to Peter, waiting for the judge to make his entrance into the courtroom.

Renee was asked to sit next to the judge and to solemnly swear to tell the truth and nothing but the truth. She said, "I do."

The prosecutor asked Renee about Paul's death and how she tried to kill herself while being pregnant. Renee replied, "I did not take Paul's death well because I loved him. He was my entire world. I did not try and kill myself. I was overwrought with grief and I could not keep any food down. I didn't know at the time that I was pregnant and that what I was feeling every moment of the day was morning sickness. I would never endanger myself or my unborn child."

The prosecutor asked, "Renee, did you not get admitted into the hospital and seen by a psychiatrist after your father found you out cold in the basement of your home?"

"Yes! That is true. They had thought that I needed professional help with my grieving process," Renee answered.

The Hamiltons' lawyer asked, "When your father called for an ambulance after finding you in the basement, did he not believe you had harmed yourself by taking an overdose of prescription meds?"

"Yes! I think that he did, but he was incorrect, as I had fallen down the stairs because I was weak from fatigue and dehydration."

The lawyer again asked, "The doctor who had seen you was Dr. Ross, and he is the one who told you that you were pregnant. He also suggested you see Dr. Chamberlain, who is a psychiatrist, correct?"

"Yes! Dr. Ross did give my case to Dr. Chamberlain. I had told her about my story and how I was not managing my life very well since Paul's death. I told her everything that I had been going through."

The lawyer disclosed, "Dr. Chamberlain had diagnosed you with depression. She had prescribed anti-depression medication for you to take and you were also asked to follow up with her after your discharge from the hospital, but you never kept any of the appointments, nor did you get your prescription filled. Am I correct, Renee?"

"Yes! I did not get the prescription filled because I did not want to harm my unborn baby, and I did not keep my appointments with Dr. Chamberlain because I couldn't leave the house due to my morning sickness."

"Your parents took you on a trip because they saw that your depression was taking over your life again, so they thought that a change of scenery would do you good, right?" the lawyer asked,

"My parents did take us to Dominican Republic for a mini vacation. We all had a great time and met some great people. The vacation did us all a world of good."

The opposing counsel asked, "Is it on this vacation you met with Matthew Reynolds? Did you not have an affair with him during your family vacation? It did not take you long to forget about your late husband, that you say you loved and missed."

"My family did meet the Reynolds family on our trip and we became good friends. I spent most of my time with Matthew and Jo-Ann because they were fun and I needed a little fun in my life, and they were a good distraction. I did not have an affair with Mat in Dominican. We enjoyed each other's company, but we did not have any sexual relations."

The opposing counsel indicated, "You kept your pregnancy a secret, did you not? You didn't want the Hamilton family to know you were pregnant. You left town and went to see Mat Reynolds in New York because you were in love with him, correct?"

"Yes, I did not want the Hamiltons to know that I was pregnant because they have always been so cruel to me. They have made my life a nightmare. So, yes! I did want to keep my baby a secret from my in-laws. They didn't deserve to know my son because they never showed me an ounce of kindness. Why would I want all that hatred in my child's life? The reason I left Boston, to tell you the truth, was I wanted to see Jo-Ann for her medical advice. I needed help for my depression, and Jo-Ann admitted me to the hospital and she took care of me as my doctor. You see, I knew I needed help and I went out and got it."

The lawyer remarked, "I commend you on finding help, but did you not get closer to Matthew during your long stay in New York? Did you not take a little vacation for two to Las Vegas? I was informed that you both had a very romantic vacation in Vegas. Did you not stay in the same room at some time during your little vacation? Did you not take a chance with your pregnancy by flying to Vegas? They say that you shouldn't fly when you are just about to have the baby. So, you thought that having your little affair was worth the health of your child. You do not care about this child because if you did, you would have stayed close to home during your last trimester, instead of flying away to have your secret fling with your Dr. Reynolds. You cared more for this man's affection than you did your unborn child. I say, shame on you!"

Renee was crying frantically. She was ashamed of herself. She had gone to Vegas not thinking of her unborn child's well-being. She had just needed to get away and have a little fun before going back to her life in Boston. "I did go to New York to get Jo-Ann's help. She is a psychiatrist, and knowing her made it easier to talk to her and to ask for her help. She is a good friend and doctor to me when I need her. I did go to Vegas with Mat, and we had a great time. He has been a good friend to me too. We did stay in the same room, even slept in the same bed, but he never made any sexual advancement toward me. He only showed me kindness as a friend. I did not think I was endangering my unborn child since I was on vacation with a doctor. If he thought that I was in any danger, he would never have asked me to go with him. I trust Mat completely with my well-being and my unborn child's well-being. He is the one who delivered my son. I am grateful to him and his family for taking me in when I was lost and showed me the way out. They have been more like family to me than Paul's family ever were."

Peter asked the judge if they could have a little recess so that Renee could have a moment to compose herself. The judge decided to adjourn for the day and that they were to return tomorrow morning at nine a.m. to continue the trial of Hamilton versus Hamilton.

***

Renee's father came over to console his daughter as soon as the judge left the courtroom.

"Renee, you did great," James said.

"You think so, Dad, because I didn't think I helped my case much. Everyone will think I am a trollop." All Renee wanted to do was go nurse her son, but she was asked to stay away from the Hamiltons' home until the trial was over. "Dad, I want so much to hold one of my babies, so can we just go home right now? I need to hold Hope."

"Sure, sweetheart, but do you mind if I invite the Reynoldses to dinner?"

"That sounds great, Dad."

Before she left, Mat came over to her and asked, "How are you holding up, Renee?"

"I can't wait until the trial is all over, but I don't think that the outcome is going to be in my favor, Mat."

He wrapped his arms around her to comfort her, but he could feel her tensing up as though she didn't want anyone seeing her in his arms. He let her go, feeling like she didn't really want him here. He thought perhaps she was wondering what the papers would say about seeing her in her lover's arms: *"Unfit Mother Found in Lover's Arms."*

Coming out of the courthouse, Renee was harassed by reporters. She was told to say, "No comment," to them by her lawyer, and she did. Peter advised Renee that he would speak to the news reporters instead. Peter did not want Renee saying anything that would be damaging to her court case.

When Renee arrived home, she ran up to the nursery to hold her baby girl. Her father told his wife of all she had missed and that he had invited the Reynoldses for dinner. He told her they would order takeout from that Chinese restaurant they love. She got out the phone book and called with an order for eight people. They wanted a little extra, as they knew how much Mat could eat.

Christine went up to check on her daughter and tell her that Hope did well with the bottle of breast milk she had given her during her absence, but she found Renee asleep in her bed, with her little one nursing beside her. Christine went over and placed a kiss on her little girl's forehead.

Christine whispered, "Renee, I know you can't hear me right now, but everything will be alright, I know it. Renee, you have had a year of hell. You deserve a little happiness, so I believe all will end well."

She took the baby away from her, burped Hope, and put her back next to her sleeping mother. Looking at her daughter and granddaughter sleeping made her think of her grandson, who must be missing his mother. She hoped that soon he would be here, next to his mother and sister, making this little family complete.

***

When the Reynoldses arrived for dinner, they were happy to see their good friends, even under these circumstances.

"Where are Renee and Hope?" Mat asked.

Christine advised Mat that Renee and the baby were both asleep upstairs in her bedroom.

"Christine, do you think it would be all right if I went upstairs and had a peek at the sleeping beauties? I just want to make sure they are doing well."

"Sure, I'll go up with you and check on them again."

Mat was so happy that Renee had Hope to keep her sane, as he knew that she was keeping it all together for her children. He gave them each a kiss good night and left them there sleeping soundly.

"Christine, if it wasn't for little Hope, I think Renee would be a basket case about now."

"She needs all of us to help her get on with her life, especially in the event she loses her son to the Hamiltons," Christine replied.

"I think that I may be the one hindering the case. I don't want to be the reason she loses Paul Jr. I know she would blame me if she loses her son and then she would never let herself love me. Christine, I love her and those babies. I would do everything in my power to make them all happy.';'

Christine took hold of Mat and said, "I know, Mat, but right now, she needs to know we are here for her. She needs all her strength to get her son back. Right now, she can live a life without any one of us but not her children. She needs them in her life, even more than they need her."

The Clarks had enjoyed having the Reynolds's over for dinner. The Reynolds family had been very hospitable to both of them when they waited for Renee and Hope to be strong enough to come home from the hospital. Christine would have loved having them stay with them, but with Renee and Hope living there as well, there was no room for anyone else. Their friends understood and did not mind staying in a motel for a few days. The Reynoldses insisted that they all go out for dinner tomorrow night. The Clarks accepted the invitation, as they loved the Reynoldses' company and had thought of them as their honorary family.

***

Renee awoke when Hope started to fuss. She looked at the time; she had slept for hours. She must have been more tired than she had thought. She had missed the dinner with the Reynoldses; what must they think of her? She then thought about whom she was talking about; she knew the Reynoldses would understand that she was tired after her trying day.

Renee got up and changed her little one's diaper, then nursed her and put her back into her crib. She was getting hungry herself, so she went down to see if there were any leftovers in the fridge. She had found a plate with Chinese food wrapped in plastic wrap left for her, so she microwaved her plate of Chinese food and enjoyed every bite. After washing her plate, she returned to her bed and fell fast asleep.

During the night, Renee got up to her daughter's cry and went to see her. She said to her, "Hello, Miss Hope, what is all this crying about? Stop all this fussing. I am here to change your bottom and feed Your Royal Highness."

Hope stopped the fussing the moment her mother picked her up. When Renee nursed Hope, her thoughts were of Paul Jr. She wished that she was greeting him and nursing him right now too. She had to pump milk for both babies before leaving for the court house. She wondered if today was the day she would bring her son home or was this the day she had dreaded—the day she would not bring her son home at all?

Chapter 44

Paul went to work very early the next day because he couldn't face Rachel. He knew how disappointed she was in him. He also went to work early today because he had left early the day before. He wanted to stock up the bar with more alcohol that would be needed for today's crowd. He looked on the television to see if there was anything on the news about his wife. He was shocked to hear that Renee was on trial in Boston, trying to win custody of her son. He saw footage of his wife crying and his parents watching her and enjoying seeing her in pure misery.

He thought to himself that Renee was right—his parents never liked her. It was all just a show for his behalf. He regretted not believing his wife when she told him that his parents were cruel toward her when he was not around. He now believed her, but could not help her, as he was dead to all who knew him as Paul Hamilton. He had a new life in New York with Rachel and Philip. He wanted so much to be there for Renee, to go back to the life he had before his amnesia, but he had made a promise to Rachel.

However, he made a promise to Renee too, and so he decided to drive down to Boston and tell everyone that he was alive and that their son should be with his mother.

Paul asked his boss if he could borrow his car for the day because he had some business to look after in Boston. His boss threw him his keys, and Paul was off to hopefully save the day. He wondered how everyone would take his resurrection from the dead. He drove as fast as he could. He wanted to get to the courthouse before the judge decided who should get his son. He had a feeling that his family would not play fair when it came to Renee. He saw the hatred they had for his wife, and he did not want them to poison his son against his own mother. He just had to get to Boston before a judgement was rendered, Renee's happiness and sanity depended on it. He wished he could have taken a plane to Boston; he would have gotten there sooner, but with no identification, he had no other choice but to drive.

Chapter 45

Renee had made it on time for her court case and wanted to speak to Peter before her second day in court.

"Peter, what do you think my chances are of getting my son back?"

"Renee, we shouldn't even be in court. Your son belongs with you, and everyone knows that, but Nancy and Ted have a lot of clout in Boston. So, my answer is that I don't know how this will turn out. You may want to say a little prayer for all this to turn out well. I know I did," Peter said.

The custody case began, and Renee was not hopeful. After listening to the many doctors, police, friends, family, and the Hamiltons, the judge decided to take a lunch break before rendering his decision.

"Peter, after listening to all the depositions, I think we are doomed. The judge will never give Paul Jr. back to me. I see the scale of justice leaning more toward their side," Renee said.

"Renee, please don't lose hope. The judge has not decided yet."

Defeated, Renee said, "I think this trial has been a farce. You don't see the Hamiltons perspiring or even worried about losing Paul. I think they have the judge's decision in the bag and we are just wasting our time." Renee began crying again.

Her mother was devastated to see her daughter so distraught. Christine just wanted to go up to Nancy and Ted and give them a good shake and ask them, what the hell they were doing. Knowing Paul, she believed he would have been ashamed of them both for putting Renee and her son through so much anguish. Christine composed herself before doing anything rash.

Everyone waited patiently for the judge to come out and declare his verdict. When the judge finally returned, he sat in his chair and looked at the people sitting in his courtroom. He had made his decision, and it was a simple one: he had a deal made with the Hamiltons and he would stick by it.

Just before the judge announced his verdict, Paul barged into the courtroom and yelled, "I want to be put on the stand before you make your final decision, Your Honor."

Everyone turned around and saw the son and husband they had thought to be dead. Nancy Hamilton fainted in her chair, and Renee was weak in the knees to see Paul alive and well.

"Peter, tell me if what I see is true. Is that Paul who just barged into the courtroom or am I hallucinating?" Renee asked.

"Renee, it's me, Paul, your husband," Paul tried to reassure her.

She could not speak; she was flabbergasted to see her presumed-to-be-dead husband alive and well.

After Nancy came to again, the judge asked Paul to the bench so that he could tell everyone where he had been all this time. Paul sat down looking at his beautiful wife that he had forgotten but who had visited him every night in his dreams. He wanted so much to take her into his arms and tell her that all was right in the world, but how could he?

"You are Paul Hamilton, son of Nancy and Ted Hamilton, and husband to Renee Clark, is that correct?" the judge asked him.

"Yes, Your Honor! I am Paul Hamilton and Renee's maiden name was Clark, but her married name is Renee Hamilton. I am also father to Paul Jr."

Peter got up and wanted to ask him a few questions, and the judge allowed it.

"Good to see you, Paul. We have all missed you since your death in the Twin Towers on September Eleventh, 2001. We all assumed you died when you didn't come home. Where the hell have you been all this time, Paul? I think we would all love to know what kept you away from your loving wife and parents? Did you not care what we were all going through here at home? We buried an empty casket, we all mourned you, and we had to live without you. Renee has had to cope with losing a husband and being pregnant. She had to give birth to your son alone without you. She had a terrible time, and you were alive and well somewhere else. What was more important out there than being here with your loved ones? I think all of us here need these questions answered."

"Hi, Peter! You're right, I need to give you all the answers of my whereabouts, but before we get to that, I want to ask my parents to please give Paul Jr. back to Renee, where he really does belong. I am ashamed of both of you for putting Renee through all this pain and agony. I can't believe that you hate her so much that you've stooped this low, that you took her child away from her. I always believed that if anything ever happened to me, you would be there to support and love her. But, instead of helping her through these hard times, you have been tormenting her. I love you both, but your actions here have made me realize that you are terrible in-laws and would be terrible role models for Paul Jr. So, from this day on, you will no longer have any contact with my family. I am sorry, Mother, Father, but you have let Renee and me down, and I cannot forgive that," Paul acknowledged.

Ted Hamilton whispered to his lawyer, "Tell the judge we do not want custody of the boy. He will be given back to his mother as soon as we finish up here."

The Hamiltons' lawyer asked to speak to the judge. Both attorneys from both sides advanced toward the judge.

The opposing counsel divulged, "Your Honor, because of their son's return, my clients wish to give the boy back to his mother. Now that their son is back, the Hamiltons believe that Paul Jr. will be well raised."

"Paul Jr. is to be placed into Renee's custody from this day forward and this case is now closed" the judge declared.

Renee was in tears. She was finally getting her son back for good. Paul came to her side and wrapped his arms around her. She was happy to have her son back, but unsure of how she felt about her husband.

"Paul, where have you been all this time? I needed you and you were not here. What do you have to say for yourself?" Renee asked, desperate for answers.

"I know I have so much to answer for, but right now, I want to go meet my son," Paul said.

She understood the yearning of wanting to see his son, as she yearned to see him as well. Christine hugged Paul, welcoming him back home and congratulated Renee for getting her son back.

"Can you drive us to the Hamiltons to collect our son back and take him home, where he belongs?" Renee asked her mother.

"You got it, kiddo. Let's go get us a baby boy."

Christine drove them to the Hamiltons and waited in the car for them. She thought it was best to let them collect their son on their own. While they did so, she called James to let him know of what happened.

When they entered the house, the baby was all packed up and ready to go, as the Hamiltons had called the nanny in advance with those instructions. Renee ran to her son and coddled him in her arms, kissing his little face. Renee held Paul Jr. toward his father and introduced him to his son.

Renee made the introductions, "Paul, this is our son, Paul Jr. He is named after you."

Paul's eyes were tearing. He could not believe this bundle of joy was theirs; he was so small and so beautiful. "I'm sorry, Renee," Paul stressed. "I was not here to help you. You were put through hell by my parents, and I will never forgive myself for not being here for you both."

"Let's get this little one home. There is someone waiting to meet him there," Renee replied.

Paul agreed, "Renee, where is your father? I didn't see him in the court-house today. Is he ill? I know your dad, and he would never let you go through this alone."

"Let's just get this little guy home where he belongs, and you will see who is waiting for all of us there," Renee said.

When they arrived at the Clarks, Paul asked why they were not going home. "Paul, this is where I have been living. I sold the house to your parents. I couldn't live there anymore. That empty house reminded me of you and that you were not coming back, so I sold it and I have been living here with my parents. Now, can you take the baby out of the car seat and let's go inside," Renee said.

Paul was happy to oblige.

When they entered the house, waiting for them was James holding a baby in his arms. Paul looked confused.

Renee made the introductions. "Paul, I would like you to meet your little girl, Hope. She is Paul Jr. 's twin sister."

Paul walked toward her and gave their son to Renee. Then he reached out to take his little girl. She was smaller than Paul Jr. but she was beautiful. Teary eyed, Paul said, "Renee, she is beautiful. She looks just like you. How is it that my parents did not take Hope too?"

"You see, when I gave birth to Hope, she was so little that they had to keep her in an incubator in the neonatal unit, so your parents did not know about her. I was nursing Paul Jr. in my room when your parents took him away from me. I am thankful they did not know about Hope. It broke my heart when they took Paul Jr., but I had to stay back for Hope. The moment she was healthy enough to leave the hospital, I came back home to fight for my son."

"I can't believe you had to go through so much alone. I am so sorry."

"I was never alone. My parents and the good Lord have been by my side through it all. My parents have helped me get through the tough times, and I had some good friends that helped me as well," Renee declared. Thinking of good friends, she wondered what Mat must be thinking right now. He must be so confused and heartbroken. Renee had to speak to Mat before he left for New York. She turned to her parents. "Mom, Dad, did you make plans to have dinner with the Reynoldses tonight?"

"Yes! We should cancel, right?" Christine said.

"No, I think you should go out to dinner. Paul and I need to talk privately," Renee said.

"All right, sweetheart, but did you want me to say anything to the Reynoldses before they go back home?" Chrisitine asked.

"Just tell them I will call tonight and say my goodbyes."

When her parent's left for their dinner, Renee nursed her two little ones while Paul began to tell her his story of his whereabouts for the past several months.

"Renee, I have been in New York this whole time. On September Eleventh, I was in a Twin Tower when it was hit. I was just about out the door when I saw this old older woman being trampled on by the herd exiting the burning building. I turned around to help her, and when we left the building, shrapnel from the plane or building above hit me on the head and I fell down. A first responder helped me up. I started walking and found myself resting in someone's front yard. The woman and her son who lived there helped me inside and she nursed me to health. I could not call you or anyone else I knew because I did not know who I was. I had amnesia. Rachel, the woman who looked after me, was very kind to me," Paul said.

"So, you're telling me you were living with a woman and her son for almost a year now? Did you fall in love with her, Paul?"

"Yes, I did. I fell in love with Rachel and her son. We became a family. I am engaged to be married to her in a few weeks," Paul answered truthfully.

Renee started crying because she had lost Paul again—this time, to another woman. "So, when did you get your memory back then?" Renee asked.

"Believe it or not, I got my memory back yesterday, when I saw you on the television. All of a sudden, there you were, the girl that I was dreaming of every night. I just suddenly remembered who you were and who I was, so I looked us up on the computer and understood why no one was searching for me. You had all thought I died. I rushed home to Rachel and told her that I finally knew who I was and that I had a wife, whom I loved very much, and that I could not marry her. She took it hard and then she told me that she was pregnant. So, she asked me to forget about you and my life in Boston. Rachel wanted me to keep my promise to her."

"Your promise to her? What about your promise to me? Till death do us part—do you remember that?"

"I know Renee, but Rachel is alone; she has no one, no family, no real friends to help her out. But you, you have family and friends that care about you and will be there to help you. You even endured the year from hell and are still standing here as strong as ever. You have always been a fighter, and that's one of the things I love about you."

His words angered Renee, and she said, "Is that what you think? That I am strong? Then you should have been here to see how strong I really was when I was admitted in the hospital because my father found me out cold on the floor of our basement, or when I checked myself into a psych ward in New York because I was falling apart at the seams. Is that what you call strong? You should have seen me on the day of your funeral, when I made a spectacle of myself over your empty casket. Paul, is that your definition of a strong person? I think not.

"Can't you see? I needed you then and I need you even more now that we have these two precious babies to care for. Don't you think that our children need their father in their lives for all the important moments like their first words, their first steps, and their first day at school? You are going to miss out on so much of their lives. Are you ready for that? Where is the man that I married, who loved me and who hated to be away from me for even a few hours? Where is he? I want him back. Paul, I thought we had that special forever kind of love, a union of two bodies that made a whole." She was really crying now.

"Renee, I am still that man. I want to be here with you—I do—but like I said, I am needed somewhere else."

Frustrated, Renee asked flatly, "Paul, do you love this woman and her son more than you love me and our two little ones? If you do, then go. If you aren't willing to fight to be with us, then go. I will manage to be a mother and father to our children. But let me tell you, that you are not the man I married because no one—nothing—would keep that man away from me or his children. You are a stranger to me, and I wish you would have stayed dead." Renee ran upstairs crying.

Paul ran after her and called, "Renee, my love, I could never love anyone more than I do you. And for our children, you know, that I will help support them. I will come and visit you and the children as much as I can. I want to be a father to them, and I want to be in their lives as much as possible. I hate to leave you and the babies, but I will come and visit as much as possible. Renee, I love you and will never love another as much as I do you, but I have to go back to Rachel. She needs me more. I have to go, but I will contact you soon I promise."

"I guess this means that you will be filing for a divorce then?" Renee asked,

"I don't know." Before leaving, Paul gave Renee and his twins a kiss goodbye and then he was gone.

Renee spoke softly to her twins, "I cannot believe this: your daddy doesn't want us. I was better off believing he was dead than knowing he is alive and not wanting us." She put her babies down, as they were both sleeping, and she cried herself to sleep.

***

Renee was awoken by a phone call.

"Hi, Renee! It's Mat. I didn't know if I should call you, but I'm leaving in the morning with my family and I just wanted to say goodbye."

" Hi Mat! Would you be able to come over? I need to talk to someone."

"Sure, I'll be right over."

When Mat arrived, Renee was waiting for him at the door. She led him to the kitchen, where she had made a pot of coffee.

Though happy to see her, Mat could sense something was wrong. "Renee, what's going on? I didn't know what to think when your husband, Paul, showed up. Where has he been all this time? Where is he now? I would have thought you would be catching up and making decisions for your future."

Renee answered with difficulty, "Well, Mat, he has left us again. He told me that he had amnesia and that he has another family that needs him in New York. He has gone to be with them."

Flabbergasted, Mat said, "Wait a minute, did you say that he has another family? How is that possible?"

"He had forgotten about me and hooked up with a single mother, who is now carrying his child. You would have thought that now that he remembers me and that I have had his children, he would want to stay here with us. But no. He said he is sorry but he has to go back to New York to be with his other family. He is on his way back now. But before he left, he promised to help me support our kids financially. Paul is to marry this woman from New York in two weeks, but being already married, that would make the union bigamy. I think he wants to divorce me so that he can marry her and start a new life with her," acknowledged Renee.

Mat came close to her, wrapped her in his loving arms, and declared, "Renee, if your husband doesn't see how lucky he is to have you and those adorable babies, then he is a fool. I can only dream of having all that he has, and he throws it away, just like that. He is throwing away what most men only dream of having. Renee, stop crying; your children need you. You don't want them to see you fall apart like this, do you?"

"You're right, Mat. I have to stay strong for my two sleeping angels, who need me. I will show everyone that I can be both mother and father to my children. I don't need Paul to help me raise my children." Then she started singing, "For I am strong, I am invincible, I am woman" from Helen Reddy's "I Am Woman."

Mat started to laugh and said, "Yes, you are, Renee, and don't you ever forget it."

Chapter 46

Paul arrived at Rachel's very late. When he entered the house, Rachel was there waiting for him. She was worried that he had decided to stay in Boston with his wife and child.

Relieved, Rachel said, "Darren, you're back. I wasn't sure if you would come back. I called the pub to see why you were late, and I was told you borrowed a car and were on your way to Boston."

"I'm sorry. I did not want to upset you, but I could not let my parents keep my son from his mother."

"Did you succeed in doing that?" Rachel asked.

"Yes! Luckily I did," Paul replied. "I even got to meet my children."

"Children?! You have more than one baby?" Rachel asked, confused.

" We had twins: a boy named Paul after me, and a little girl named Hope, and they are the most precious babies I've ever seen."

"You're talking like a proud father," Rachel said.

"I am a proud father. When I held them in my arms and when Renee nursed them, I was in awe. When you meet them, you will understand what I mean. They are two blessings from God; they make me believe in miracles, and that's exactly what they are—little miracles given to us from God," Paul reported.

" What do you mean? You want me to meet them?" Rachel asked.

"I thought since they will be part of our family, you being their step-mom and Philip their big brother that you should meet them."

Rachel ran into his arms and hugged and kissed him. He had picked her and Philip over his wife and two children.

She then wondered why. Why would he choose them over his real family? She realized it was because of the baby that she was not carrying. How could she keep him from his real children? She felt horrible but needed to keep up the farce, as she knew she and Philip needed him more, and that was the excuse she was sticking with.

Rachel suggested, "Darren—I mean Paul—let's go up to bed. Morning will soon be upon us. Philip will be so happy to see you; he missed not seeing you today."

When they were together in bed, Rachel felt that he was far away, as he was not as affectionate as he normally was toward her. He did not want to cuddle or even sleep facing her; he was distant. She decided not to lose the baby until they were close again. She needed him to stay, and if she lost the baby now, he may be tempted to go back to his wife and kids.

***

The next morning, Philip was overjoyed to see his father back home. He began jumping on his father, yelling, "Daddy, wake up! I need to talk to you."

Paul, happy to see his son, said, "Hi, Philip! What can I do for you?"

"I want to know if you are going to work today because if you have the day off, I want to stay home with you."

"Well, this is your lucky day, Philip, for I am free to play with you all day."

"Yippee! Mommy, Daddy said I can stay home with him today because he doesn't need to work and we are going to play all day!"

"Well, that sounds great! I wish I could play hooky from work today, but I can't, so I guess you'll have fun without me."

Paul lay in bed, missing his family in Boston. How he wished he was getting up next to Renee and watching her nurse his little ones.

Philip was calling for him, "Dad, are you getting up? I want us to play with my blocks. I want you to help me build a big castle with a bridge. Will you help me make a fort with the kitchen chairs and blankets? Get up, Dad, I know you are pretending to sleep because you don't snore that loud when you are really sleeping."

Paul laughed. "Okay! I'm getting up! Just let me put my track pants on and a sweatshirt and I'm all yours."

"Mom left you some coffee in the kitchen. I know you need your coffee in the morning just like Mom." When Paul came down, Philip said, "Why do you like coffee? I sneaked a sip from Mommy's cup once. It's so yucky."

Paul answered, "I know but you have to be an adult to love it. That's why you should never drink coffee until you are very big."

"I don't think I will ever love the taste of it, Dad. I prefer chocolate milk or juice," Philip stated.

"Philip, milk and juice are a better choice of beverage. They make you big and strong."

"Did you drink milk and juice when you were little because you are big and strong now?" Philip asked his father.

"I sure did. I loved to drink chocolate milk and orange juice all the time; they were my favorite beverages when I was a kid."

"Then when I get big like you, maybe I'll drink coffee too," Philip said.

"That sounds like a plan there slugger," Paul replied. "Now, let's build us some castles and bridges."

Philip was so happy to have his dad back home; he missed him. Paul thought to himself that he would miss doing this day-to-day stuff with his own children. He had to find the time to be with his own children; it was imperative. His body was here in New York, but his heart and soul were in Boston. He really did not want to miss out on his children's lives, and he realized he was more in love with Renee than he thought possible.

Paul never saw Renee so vulnerable and so strong at the same time. She was like a mother bear looking out for her cubs, and when she nursed her little ones, she looked like a Madonna. He had to find a way to change things around, but he did not know how. He loved Rachel, but not the way he loved Renee. How could he marry her and say the vows "till death do us part" when he had already promised himself to Renee. He couldn't marry Rachel—Renee was still his wife and she owned his heart. That was why he had been seeing her in his dreams because she was part of him. He had to find a way to get back to her.

Chapter 47

Renee was enjoying having her twins together again. She decided to take them out for their first outing: she would take them to church and introduce them to the congregation. If the Hamiltons were there, they would be shocked to see that they had both a granddaughter and a grandson.

Renee's parents waited for her in their vehicle. Her father had placed both car seats in the car ready for the twins. Renee looked tired, but she was happy to get out with her babies. When Renee walked into the church carrying a bundle in pink and her father carrying a bundle in blue, everyone was in awe to see that there were two babies, and not just one.

The minister asked Renee and her family to come up and introduce the new members of their church to the congregation. Renee got up, like the proud mother that she was, and introduced her son, Paul Jr., and her daughter, Hope, to everyone.

Nancy got up and walked toward Renee and her family. "Is this true? You had twins all this time and you didn't tell anyone?"

"Nancy, did you really think I would tell you about Hope so that you could take her from me as well?"

"Where is Paul? He should be here with you," Nancy said.

"Maybe you should ask him," Renee replied.

Getting testy, Nancy said. "No! I am asking you, Renee."

"Paul has gone back to his family in New York," Renee replied flatly.

Ted shouted, "What does that mean? What family in New York?"

"Paul is divorcing me to marry a single mother that he has been playing house with for the last year, and they are expecting a child."

Nancy insisted, "You are lying. He would never abandon his children. I know my son; we raised him right."

"Well, I thought I knew him too but he left us," Renee said.

Nancy replied hesitantly, "I'm so sorry, Renee. I have been such a fool. I have been a true monster-in-law, and I know it's too late to ask for your forgiveness, but I am truly sorry."

"Nancy, you come to church every Sunday, you want people to think you are a good Christian woman, but the woman that I know is far from Christian. You have never shown me an ounce of tenderness since I have known you. You took away my son right after giving birth to him, and now, you want me to forgive you? Well, I'm sorry, but I am not as Christian as you. I cannot forgive you for the hell you have put me through. Nancy, if I do forgive you, it will be because I want my children to know their grandparents, but for right now, the only grandparents I want my children to know are my parents. I am sorry if this hurts you, but I don't give a damn if it does." Renee apologized to all those attending mass and then walked out of the church, never looking back.

"Renee, I think that maybe you could have waited to humiliate the Hamiltons somewhere less public?"

"I know, Mother, I realize that, but I was like a volcano erupting and could not stop the lava from flowing. I'm sorry if I embarrassed you."

"Don't apologize, sweetheart. Nancy deserved everything you gave her, but from now on, let's do our outbursts in private."

Renee agreed, "It's a deal, Mom."

***

When Renee got home, she had a message on her phone from Mat, asking her to call him when she had a moment. After nursing her little ones and putting them down for their nap, she called Mat.

"Hi, Mat! You called?"

"Hi, there, how is motherhood?"

"Motherhood is great. I love knowing that my children are together and I love taking care of them."

"You were meant to be a mother; you are a true caregiver."

"Thanks! But you didn't just call me to tell me that, did you?"

"No! I just wanted to hear your voice and to stay in touch. I just needed my Renee fix. When you were here in New York, I got to see you all the time, and now, I don't. I miss you and want to know when I get to see you again?"

"To tell you the truth, I can't just leave whenever I feel like it. I have precious cargo, and traveling is not something I intend to do any time soon. You are more than welcome to come here to see us."

Mat joyfully said, "Do you mean that? I would like to continue where we left off when you were in New York."

"Mat, right now, I don't know what to do about you and me."

"Fine, let's take this slowly and see where this goes."

"I don't want to rush things. I am still legally married to Paul."

"Yes! But you said he wants to file for divorce so that he can marry this single mother he met in New York, right?" Mat asked.

"Yes, that's exactly what he said to me, but I am still married to Paul. Mat, until the divorce is final, I think we should just be friends."

Crushed, Mat said, "Renee, you know I want much more than that and I thought that we were getting closer."

"We are close, Mat, but like I said, I am still Paul's wife and he is still my husband in the eyes of the church and the law."

"Okay! I won't push the matter, but I would like to see you again. How is next weekend?"

Renee felt for him. "Sure, that sounds great. Have to go; Paul Jr. is crying, so I will see you soon."

"Yes soon," Mat replied.

Chapter 48

All was well in New York. Paul and Rachel were both at work, and Philip was in daycare. It was a normal day for the three of them. However, Rachel and Paul had not really been physical since he got his memory back. She missed him, and she wanted things to go back to normal.

Rachel was at the grocery store alone when two men wearing ski masks came into the store and locked the front doors, demanding cash and lottery tickets. The few customers in the store were asked to lay on the floor while Rachel was fumbling with the money. Rachel gave them the little money she had in her cash drawer, but they were not happy with the amount given.

One of the masked men said, "Lady, we know you have more cash in the back."

"I don't know where the store owner keeps the money, but if I did, I would give it to you," Rachel answered, terrified.

The man replied furiously, "You are lying. You have worked here for years. I know, I have seen you, and you know where the money is. If you don't get it, I'll have to shoot you and you don't want that, do you?"

"Please, mister, I am a single mother and I don't want to die."

"Then maybe you should cooperate with us and get me the money."

Rachel got out from her cash register and walked to the back of the store where the stock room was located. The masked man who followed her, tripped, and his gun fired. The bullet penetrated her chest. Rachel fell to the ground. The two masked men panicked, grabbed the money and the tickets, and rushed out of the store.

One customer ran to Rachel and tried to stop the gushing blood that flowed from her chest. She yelled, "Someone call 911. Rachel's been shot and needs medical assistance. Rachel, stay with me. Help is on its way."

The paramedics arrived and lifted her into the ambulance, but they lost her on their way to the hospital.

Rachel's boss, who had just been out at the time of the robbery, followed the ambulance to the hospital and was shocked about hearing the news that she had died. He was distraught and could not think straight. A doctor came to see him, asking if he was her next of kin. He said no, but advised the doctor, "I brought her purse, and I think her fiancé's number is in her cell phone. His name is Darren Michaels." He handed the doctor Rachel's phone.

The doctor called Darren's number.

"Rachel, what's up?" Paul asked.

The doctor reported, "Mr. Darren Michaels, this is Dr. Johnston, here at New York- Presbyterian Hospital, and I am sorry to say that Rachel was shot in a robbery earlier today. We need you to come down as soon as possible."

"Is she all right?" Paul asked.

The doctor declared, "I'm sorry to say she has passed away. The medics tried to save her, but she was shot in the chest and lost so much blood. There was just too much damage for them to save her. I am so sorry."

Paul lost hold of his phone. He asked his boss for his car again and told him, "That was the hospital. Rachel was shot during a robbery . . . and she's dead."

"I'll drive you to the hospital Darren. You are in no condition to drive," Darren's boss advised.

"Thanks." Paul answered.

***

When they arrived at the hospital, Paul was guided to where they had Rachel's body. Rachel looked like she was sleeping soundly. He grabbed hold of her and rocked her in his arms, kissing her forehead. She was gone and so was his unborn child. What was he to do now? What about Philip? How would he take the news of his mother's death? He would be devastated.

"Mr. Michaels, do you have a preference for a funeral home that you want us to send her body to?" the nurse asked.

"I don't know. We never talked about that. Is there one close by?" Paul asked.

The nurse replied, "Yes, there is one. We will arrange for them to collect her, and you should call them as soon as possible. In the meantime, we will bring her to the hospital's mortuary until they pick her up."

"Thank you. I just need a few more minutes with Rachel before you come and take her away, if that's okay?" Paul asked.

"Yes, take your time. There is no rush."

He was left alone with Rachel again and started weeping. He then started talking to her as though she was still alive. "Rachel, I promise that I will take good care of our son and that he will never forget you. I love you and miss you already. Goodbye, my love, I'll be seeing you again one day."

Paul left looking like a zombie. His boss drove him to Philip's daycare and waited for him to come out with his son to drive them home. Philip was so happy to see his father; he had no clue that his life was about to change. Paul's boss drove them home and, before letting him go, advised him, "Darren, I mean Paul, if there is anything you need, just ask."

"Thanks, Ron, all we need is some time alone right now."

His boss left, and he and his son entered their house.

"Philip, I need to talk to you about your mother. Your mommy was hurt at work today, and they called for the doctor, but they could not take the hurt away, so she had to go where there is no more hurt. She has gone to heaven with the angels."

Philip innocently asked, "Daddy, is mommy coming back home? I can make her feel better."

"I know you would try, but this hurt was so bad that she couldn't take it anymore and she died," Paul replied.

"Died, like when my friend Tim's grandpa died? He never came back; he was gone forever. Mommy would never leave me forever; she loves me and I need her to make me my snacks and to read to me before bed and to make me chicken noodle soup when I am sick. I want her to come home right now. Daddy, where is she?" Philip started crying and ran to his room.

Paul ran after him and consoled him, and he cried himself to sleep.

***

Paul called the number of the funeral home and made arrangements to have Rachel cremated and to have a little showing for the few friends they had to pay their respects and say their goodbyes. Paul had decided to cremate Rachel's body. He thought it would be easier on Philip to not see his mother in a casket. The funeral director said that Rachel would be ready for her showing in about three days.

The phone kept ringing, but Paul let the machine pick up the messages. He did not want to talk to anyone. He had a son to take care of and a fiancé to bury.

During the funeral, everyone paid their respects to Paul and Philip. Paul had put Rachel's remains into a gold urn. Philip was too young to understand all that was happening. Paul had told him that his mother had already gone to heaven.

One of the daycare providers came up to Philip and told him, "Philip, you know your mommy didn't want to leave you right? Your mommy loved you more than anyone else in this world. Now that she is in heaven with God, she is one of his angels. Your mommy is probably your guardian angel, and she is looking out for you here on earth."

"Do I get to see her again?" Philip asked.

The daycare provider answered, "One day, hopefully when you are an old man, you will get to see her again, but you will always carry your mommy in here." She pointed to his heart.

He started crying and she took him into her arms and rocked him until he calmed down.

Paul thanked her and stated, "I heard what you said to Philip. You explained all this better than I did."

The daycare worker replied, "Don't worry about it. You know, if you need us we are just a phone call away."

"Thanks." Paul said.

All was over, and Paul, Philip, and Rachel's urn were back home after a long day at the funeral. Now, he and his son had to grieve and heal before deciding what to do next.

Chapter 49

In Boston, Mat arrived to spend the weekend with Renee and the children. Renee was happy to see him. She missed him and had a lot of time to think about their relationship and where she saw it going. Mat wanted to take her and the children out for dinner, but instead, she asked her parents if they would sit with the twins. She needed some time alone with Mat to talk about their future.

Mat was pleased to have Renee all to himself. He had thought this would be the perfect moment to ask her to marry him. As they both were seated, Mat ordered a bottle of champagne for them to drink.

"Champagne, what is the occasion?" Renee asked.

He then got down on one knee and took out a little red velvet box that he had been carrying with him since their time in Vegas. "Renee Hamilton, will you make me the happiest man on earth and agree to be my wife?"

"Mat, please get up. I can't." She quickly got up and ran out of the restaurant.

Mat threw money on the table and rushed to catch up with her.

When he caught up with her, she was sitting on a bench in a little park just across the restaurant.

"Mat, I cannot marry you. It wouldn't be fair to you. You deserve to have your own family with a woman who does not love another."

Hearing her declare her love for Paul devastated him and he fell to the ground crying. Sobbing, Mat said, "You and the babies are my family, the only family that I want. Renee, you are the love of my life. I love Paul Jr. and Hope as if they were my own."

Renee coddled him in her arms. She did love him, but she could not be the wife that he deserved. He pleaded with her, but she could not deny the love she had for Paul.

"Mat, Paul had stolen my heart a long time ago, and now knowing that he is still alive, I cannot in good conscience give my heart to another. I love you, Mat, but you deserve more. You deserve a woman who is free to give her entire heart to you. I want you to find someone who loves only you, and you should want that too."

"I thought that's what I had. I was hoping that Paul would just vanish from our lives, but I guess that's just wishful thinking. I cannot see my life without you and the twins, but I guess dreams don't always come true. I thought that I could be enough for you, but I guess I was wrong."

Renee felt tormented. "Mat, it's not that you are not enough because you are; you are more than enough for the right woman. The woman that gets you gets the whole package: you are a true romantic, your loving, caring, spontaneous, and a gorgeous hunk of a man. You and I had a love affair. But the love I have for Paul is a one-of-kind, never-ending love. That is why, Mat, I cannot marry you. There is someone out there for you; it's just not me. I will never forget the friendship you showed me all these months. I am truly sorry."

She kissed him on his damp cheek and said her goodbyes. Then she grabbed a taxi and left him there sitting on the park bench.

Chapter 50

Paul had put Rachel's house up for sale. He had decided to go back home to Boston where he had family and had his job waiting for him. He hated leaving New York, but he and Philip needed a new beginning. The house sold very quickly. A caregiver at the daycare viewed the house and wanted to purchase it. Paul sold the house with all the furnishing, except for Philip's things. He thought that the transition would be less difficult if Philip had his own things for his new room.

They drove to Boston in a moving truck. He had planned to move back into Renee's and his house. His parents were very pleased that he was returning home, but they did not know that he was coming home with a son.

When Paul arrived home, his parents were there waiting for him. Paul introduced his son to his parents and then showed his son his room. Philip was shy and stayed behind Paul.

"Paul, how is this boy your son?" Nancy asked.

"Mom, Dad, I lived in New York with a woman and her son, both of whom I cared for very much. She died over a month ago, and I took Philip as my own. We are true father and son, and now he is your grandson."

Nancy stressed, "So, when Renee told us that you were getting married to another woman, she was telling us the truth? You were living with another woman in New York, leaving your wife and children alone to fend for themselves?"

"Yes and no," Paul replied. "I had every intention of helping Renee and my children financially. I had asked Philip's mother to marry me before I remembered who I really was. Mom, I love Renee. I realized after leaving her here with our children that I couldn't marry Rachel. My love for Renee is too strong. I couldn't get her out of my mind and my heart. I hope that she can forgive me for being a damn fool."

Nancy informed him, "Paul, we had heard that Renee's doctor friend from New York came here to see her and he asked her to marry him. I don't know if she accepted his proposal, though."

"I can't believe she would marry someone else," Paul replied, confused and disappointed.

"Why shouldn't she marry another? You left your wife and twins to marry someone else, right?" Ted said.

"Okay! I get it. I have been a big jackass, but I love Renee and want to share my life with her."

"Perhaps you should be telling this to Renee and not us," Ted suggested.

"Dad, can I borrow your car? Philip and I need to put our family together again."

His father threw Paul his keys and he and Philip rushed off.

***

Paul stood in front of the Clarks' front door, holding his son's hand. Paul rang the bell, and James opened the door, surprised to see who was standing there.

"Hi, James, is Renee here?" Paul asked.

"Yes, she is. She is resting; the twins keep her very busy. Why are you here, Paul, and who is this boy with you?" James asked.

Paul made the introductions, "James, I would like you to meet my son, Philip. We moved back here to be close to the family and work."

"I see, and where is this boy's mother?"

"My mommy is in heaven with God and the angels," Philip informed him.

"Yes! She is Philip, and she is looking down on us right now," Paul reassured his son.

"Renee is in her old room. How about I take Philip into the kitchen to have a piece of chocolate cake and some milk?"

Philip took James's hand and followed him to the kitchen, while Paul went upstairs.

"Christine, we have a guest who would love a piece of your famous chocolate cake. He came here with Paul."

"Paul is here right now? What does he want?" Christine asked.

"I think he wants his life back," James replied.

***

Upstairs, Paul looked in on his twins, and they were sucking on their soothers quiet and content. He went into Renee's room and found her sound asleep. He lay next to her and kissed her on the lips. He startled her.

"Paul? What are you doing here?" she asked.

"I live here."

Renee asked confused, "What do you mean you live here? Last I heard you lived in New York with your other family."

"I did, but I couldn't stay away from you any longer. You see, Renee, you're in my blood and I can't stop missing you and loving you. I gave my heart away once and you still own it."

"What does that mean? You chose them over us, or did you forget that?" Renee said.

Paul replied, ashamed, "No, I know what I did and said, but the moment I left, I knew I made a big mistake. I was going to leave Rachel. I could not be the man she wanted me to be because the moment I remembered you, she had lost me forever. I was ready to tell her that when she was killed in a robbery. I would have been here sooner, but I had to organize her funeral and sell her home before returning."

Renee shouted, "Rachel died? Is that why you've come back? She dies so you come back to me, your second choice?"

"Are you not hearing me? I had decided to come back to you and the twins before she died. This is where my heart is and always has been, Renee. But I hear that you got engaged to your doctor friend, is that true?" Paul asked.

"Yes, I was proposed to but had to decline the man's offer because I am a married woman. Even knowing you were going to divorce me, I could not be with another. I meant those vows we declared to each other the day we married. I only ever loved one man, and he is here next to me. Being with another man was just not written in the cards," Renee replied.

"Renee, are you telling me you still love me?" Paul asked, hopefully.

"Yes!"

Paul stood up, then went down on one knee and asked her, "Renee Hamilton will you marry me?"

"Paul, we are married."

"I know, but I want us to be husband and wife again."

Renee got down on her knees and wrapped her arms around him and kissed him saying, "Welcome home, Paul."

They did not come out of her room for some time. Renee's mother had to interrupt them so Renee could feed her hungry babies. Renee and Paul were back together, but Paul forgot to tell her about Philip. When she entered the twins' room, she was surprised to see a young boy there.

"Hello there, and who might you be?" Renee asked.

"Renee, I would like to introduce to you my son, Philip. We've just moved back into our old house. Philip and I want to come home if you'll have us?"

"Philip, I want you to meet your little brother, Paul Jr., but we call him Pauly, and your little sister, Hope. I think you will be a great big brother to these two little ones. Hey, Philip, would you like to hold your little brother when I feed Hope?" Renee asked.

Philip looked at his father and asked, "Daddy, can I?"

"If you want to, but be very careful; he is still very little."

Renee placed Pauly into the little boy's loving arms, and tears began flowing down her cheeks.

"What's wrong? Why are you crying, Renee?"

Renee confessed, "These tears are tears of joy, Paul. I am so happy that we are together as a family." She then whispered softly, "Welcome home. boys."

Printed in Canada